A PLUME BOOK

THE PERFECTLY TRUE TALES OF A PERFECT SIZE 12

Robin Gold lives in New York City without her husband, because she hasn't met him yet. She has spent the past eight years working in independent film production as a development executive and associate producer. She is usually a perfect size 10 and is working on her second novel.

The Perfectly True Tales of a Perfect Size 12

Robin Gold

PLUME
Published by Penguin Group
Penguin Group (USA) Inc., 375 Hudson Street, New York, New York 10014, U.S.A.
Penguin Group (Canada), 90 Eglinton Avenue East, Suite 700, Toronto, Ontario, Canada M4P 2Y3 (a division of Pearson Penguin Canada Inc.)
Penguin Books Ltd., 80 Strand, London WC2R 0RL, England
Penguin Ireland, 25 St. Stephen's Green, Dublin 2, Ireland (a division of Penguin Books Ltd.)
Penguin Group (Australia), 250 Camberwell Road, Camberwell, Victoria 3124, Australia (a division of Pearson Australia Group Pty. Ltd.)
Penguin Books India Pvt. Ltd., 11 Community Centre, Panchsheel Park, New Delhi – 110 017, India
Penguin Books (NZ), cnr Airborne and Rosedale Roads, Albany, Auckland 1310, New Zealand (a division of Pearson New Zealand Ltd.)
Penguin Books (South Africa) (Pty.) Ltd., 24 Sturdee Avenue, Rosebank, Johannesburg 2196, South Africa

Penguin Books Ltd., Registered Offices: 80 Strand, London WC2R 0RL, England

First published by Plume, a member of Penguin Group (USA) Inc.

First Printing, February 2007
10 9 8 7 6 5 4 3 2 1

Library of Congress Cataloging-in-Publication Data
Gold, Robin.
The perfectly true tales of a perfect size 12 / Robin Gold.
p. cm.
ISBN 978-0-452-28812-6
1. Women television producers and directors—Fiction. 2. Promotions—Fiction. 3. Office politics—Fiction. 4. Fourth of July celebrations—Fiction. I. Title.
PS3607.O437P47 2007
813'.6—dc22
2006015094

Printed in the United States of America
Set in Bembo and Fling
Designed by Eve L. Kirch

PUBLISHER'S NOTE
This is a work of fiction. Names, characters, places, and incidents are either the product of the author's imagination or are used fictitiously, and any resemblance to actual persons, living or dead, business establishments, events, or locales is entirely coincidental.

For Sister, my hero

Acknowledgments

It sounds like a load of crap, but the truth is the words "thank you" hardly seem adequate in expressing my most sincere gratitude to the following people, without whom writing this book would have been impossible.

I owe a huge debt to Trena Keating for giving me a chance.

It is a privilege to thank Eleanore Bella for your inspired input on every single draft, and for believing in me, and Delilah, from the very start.

Mimsy and Big G, my most loyal champions, I am incredibly grateful for your amazing support and love. Thank you for always encouraging me to follow my dream, and for not selling me to that family down the street. Yet.

Finally, I thank my lucky stars for my perfectly brilliant editor, Emily Haynes, whose patience, inspiration, and wise counsel I would be lost without. Thank you for keeping me in safe hands and leading the way, but most of all, thank you for being a phenomenal teacher.

The Perfectly True Tales of a Perfect Size 12

Prologue

"The studio lights are too hot; they're melting the fucking meringue! And the Forefather's Flourless Chocolate Cake is beginning to fall flat! We need cameras rolling now, people! Not in five minutes, not in thirty seconds, right *now*! Let's do it! Let's do it!" Nick, the director, barks at the frenzied production crew as he paces back and forth in front of the television monitor, punctuating his words with a wooden rolling pin. "We need this last segment in the can. The holiday episode airs *tomorrow*, people—July *second*. We've got to get it over to Network!"

"Alright, quiet on set, please. Everyone settle," Carl, the assistant director, commands, indicating to the crew and studio audience that after waiting patiently for over an hour (and enduring the "riotous comedy" of an "up-and-coming" comedian who was about as funny as one of those "Save the Children" commercials), it's *finally* time to shoot the scene. "Ladies and gentlemen, after we're done with this shot, *it's a wrap*, and everyone can go home and get on with your July Fourth celebrations!" he announces.

Suddenly, out of nowhere, the horrible . . . the unspeakable . . . the worst thing that could possibly happen at this particular moment actually happens: the cake deflates like a sad, neglected blow-up pool toy.

For a moment, time stands still.

Some members of the studio audience say that right before the cake tragically collapsed, it emitted a faint but desperate high-pitched squeal. Others say the sound came from the director.

"Why? Why? Alright, minor setback. Not a problem," he insists. "Nothing we can't handle. We're professionals here. We'll just use the backup cake; that's what it's there for after all."

"Um, actually, that *was* the backup cake," Carl sighs, bracing himself for the temper tantrum he knows is coming.

"Motherfucker bloody hell! *Domestic Bliss*, my ass! We're in hell! We're gonna be here till two in the morning," Nick huffs, waving the rolling pin in the air like a lunatic.

"Make that *four.* It takes three hours to bake one of those cakes, and it's already after midnight," Eleanore, the chief of Pastry Production, states drily, removing her chef's hat. "I say we ax this idea and do something else for the segment."

"Have anything in mind?" Nick asks, eyes bugging out, face and neck turning an alarming shade of raspberry.

"Arsenic pie, perhaps? It's blissfully delicious."

The clever quip is lost on Nick, who has now slumped into his director's chair. "We need Delilah. Somebody get Delilah White on this set! STAT!!!"

Delilah White

Delilah White, producer of *Domestic Bliss*, network television's highest-rated lifestyle how-to program and originator of the popular catchphrase "Now *that's* bliss," checks her watch—2:20 p.m.—and makes one final bathroom break. Pulling her loose ebony waves into a ponytail to avoid a messy tangle during the upcoming convertible ride, she notes her pale complexion and thinks she bears a striking resemblance to Casper the Friendly Ghost. *Dear God! Look at those dark circles under my eyes . . . I look like a linebacker . . . Or a drug addict. Not cute . . .* Delilah sighs and crosses her fingers that she will return home well-rested and with a tan. Her sister, Francesca, has always said Delilah looks her best with a "healthy glow." Miraculously, the holiday weekend weather forecast calls for warm temperatures, clear skies, and low humidity—which is great news for Delilah, who battles a much-dreaded frizz factor. She's fairly certain she's tried every hair gel/mousse/glaze/pomade/leave-in–leave-out–shake-it-all-about product available in America. Due to recent changes at the television show, however, she has spent a majority of her time cooped up inside the studio, working *much* too hard and *way* too late. If it weren't for her sky-high air-conditioning bill, swollen fingers (damn heat!), and daily walk to and from the subway, she'd hardly even know it's summer.

She has been looking forward to this holiday, albeit mini, for longer than she cares to admit and is determined to relax and have some serious fun. Delilah promises herself that she won't take any work with her on the trip or even so much as *think* about her job while she's away. *This is a VACATION, dammit! V-A-C-A-T-I-O-N! Time to drink martinis and laze on the beach in that sassy new bikini scoping out men!* Then again, one never knows when inspiration will hit, and Delilah could use some inspired segment ideas for *Domestic Bliss*, now more than ever. Her career depends on it. On second thought . . . Her laptop contains all her thoughts and ideas for the show. From completed transcripts for future episodes, to potential segment concepts that are still in the incubation stage, to single mysterious words that once inspired her—though now she struggles to recall what the devil "twirsty lizard," "wicked," and "Burkina Faso" were referring to. It's all there on her trusty laptop. She makes a last-minute decision to bring it along. *Just in case.*

Delilah knows it will be next to impossible to make it through the weekend without somebody instigating a conversation about *Domestic Bliss* or requesting an autograph. While she's been making guest appearances on the show since she began producing it five years ago—demonstrating how to fold a well-starched cloth napkin into an elegant swan, or how to bake an irresistible cobbler, or how to make a charming yet durable luggage tag using recycled cardboard and used plastic wrap—it never ceases to amaze her that strangers actually know her name. And she can't fathom why anyone in their right mind would want her silly signature. Of course, at thirty-three she still has David Hasselhoff's autographed picture, which he kindly signed for her when she was sixteen (twenty-four in reality, but she thinks sixteen sounds less demented), tucked away in a very private, very safe spot. But that's different. David's a real celebrity. Delilah's not even one of the four highly adored rotating cohosts of *Domestic Bliss* who are hounded by paparazzi and often seen gracing the glossy pages of celebrity gossip magazines. But still, she is often recognized. How marvelous and refreshing it would be to have three *Domestic Bliss*–free days to clear her head and relax! To stop thinking and thinking and thinking and thinking about work and where her fate lies at the show, which she truly loves, but knows will soon be forever changed. The more Delilah considers it, the more she looks forward to leaning back in a deck chair with a viciously strong beverage—preferably something frosty, tropical, and sporting a festive little umbrella—and not talking about *D.B.* (as the show is known in the industry). *Hmmm . . . I could always pretend to be an endocrinologist. Or a Radio City Rockette. Oh! How about a chimpanzee trainer? Or, better yet? Editor of* Crossbow Enthusiast*!* Delilah eventually resolves to tell anyone who asks that pesky question, "What do you do?" that she's a taxidermist to the stars.

After watering the bright red geraniums on her kitchen windowsill, Delilah collects her suitcase, two thermoses of her famous homemade strawberry lemonade, and makes her way outside. In her breezy crimson sundress and vintage oversize sunglasses, for which she paid a pretty penny, she feels sophisticated and chic. She wishes that the handsome tenant who lives down the hall in apartment 21 would walk out at the same time, but he hardly knows she's alive and calls her Kumiko (the previous owner of Delilah's apartment). Maybe he'd finally stop and notice her. At least long enough to realize she's not an Asian paleontologist who moved to China three years ago.

Delilah stops to say a quick hello to Rodrigo, the doorman,

who immediately perks up at the sight of her. "D.W.! Leaving us, I see. Taking off for the holiday?"

"Yep," she says, beaming. "Delighted to say I am, my friend."

"Well, it's about time you took a break! Have a great trip. You deserve it."

"You deserve a vacation yourself," Delilah says and smiles, glancing at her watch. "I better get going. Sofia'll be here any second." She switches her luggage, which suddenly feels like it's stuffed with Grandmother Violet's lasagna (translation: ten-ton bricks), to the opposite hand and trundles toward the revolving glass door. "Happy Fourth! See ya when I get back!"

"Hey!" Rodrigo hollers. "Think she'll be late?"

Pivoting around, Delilah smirks. "You kidding? *Of course.*"

Call her old-fashioned, but Delilah's big on proper manners and punctuality. Not in a hoity-toity snobbish sort of way, but rather in a kind and genuine fashion you just don't see much nowadays. *Please* and *thank you* are a natural part of her vernacular, and she finds it plain rude to keep people waiting without a damn good excuse, even if it's totally made up (in her mind, nobody wants to hear that their date is late because she accidentally spilled scalding wax all over the Venetian marble floor while tending to her not-so-cute upper lip, thank you very much).

Her best friend, Sofia, is always late. By now Delilah knows better than to pay this any mind and simply factors in an automatic ten- to fifteen-minute delay (ten if they're already on the same side of Manhattan, fifteen if one's on the east side and the other's on the west). Over the years, this basic equation has come to be known as Sofia Time Conversion. When Sofia first began working as marketing director of *Domestic Bliss*, Delilah took offense at the new girl's seeming disregard for rules and her fellow production staff. In a rash snap judgment, she decided they would never get along. Delilah was so positive Sofia's constant tardiness would get her fired, she even placed a bet on it in an unofficial and somewhat mean-spirited F.N.G. (Fucking New Girl) office pool.

Thanks to her killer marketing skills and shrewd negotiating power, Sofia shows no signs of going anywhere, and Delilah's out fifty bucks.

Sofia

Sofia's 1962 classic cherry-red Ford Thunderbird convertible pulls up in front of Delilah's Central Park West high-rise at two thirty—right on time according to Sofia Time Conversion. Predictable as ever.

"Hey, D!" Sofia cheerfully shouts and waves. "Toss your suitcase in the backseat."

She notices Delilah's not carrying her ratty old LeSportsac, circa 1989. "Why hello, Mr. Vuitton. New bag?"

"Guilty," Delilah cringes. "I know I shouldn't have, but it was thirty-five percent off at Bendel's a couple weeks ago. Quite a steal if I do say so myself."

"I'll second that. It's beautiful." Sofia lifts up her sunglasses to get a better look. "Hop in, lady!"

"We're on VACATION!" Delilah belts out, shooting her arms in the air as they speed down the street. "Glory hallelujah!"

At thirty-four, Sofia is one year older and considers Delilah the younger sister and best friend she never had growing up as an only child. Sofia's last name, Trawler, might go unrecognized by a majority of the population, but to those who are knowledgeable about great inventors, Trawler is synonymous with patent royalty. Back in the 1950s, when Sofia's father, Stanley, was a temperamental teen, he once unhappily discovered a large portion of his delicious cheese pizza stuck to the top of the pizza box. Irrationally irked, he set out on a noble quest to solve this problem once and for all and make the world a better place. Several years of research later, he developed a nifty little plastic device resembling a quarter with three inch-long prongs attached to it. When placed in the center of a pizza pie, this ingenious device, known as the Pizza Protector, serves as an effective barrier between hot melted cheese (plus any tasty toppings) and a hostile cardboard lid. Thanks to this two-cent piece of plastic and a few other inventions he's developed along the way, today the Trawler family fortune amounts well into the millions. They live in the proverbial lap of luxury and enjoy the finest of everything without having to work a minute in their lives if they don't want to. Importantly, Sofia wants to. Working gives her a sense of purpose, which she especially needs. The Trawlers own yachts and stables and beautiful homes all over the world—Manhattan, Paris, Napa, and Aspen, to name a few. Right now, Sofia and Delilah are heading to her family's sprawling beachside estate, known as Cherry Pond (so named in the spirit of a grand old Southern plantation for its many cherry blossom trees), in the scenic Catskill Mountains, where Sofia and her family have invited their closest friends to attend their annual Fourth of July celebration. According to the society page of the *Catskill Gazette*, the Trawlers' Independence Day soiree is *the* party of the summer.

There's a dark side to this phenomenal tale of patents and invention. Sofia's father is a cynical man, and he taught his impressionable daughter that not everyone can be trusted, that most people are more interested in the family's massive wealth than in her companionship, or her love. Growing up under his watchful, often disapproving eye, Sofia became a bit of a loner. Delilah relates to this all too well. As a fat child, friends were always hard to come by. "Delilah Doughnut," they used to tease her in the school yard.

Sofia is a natural beauty, like the Noxzema Girl. Her striking green eyes and honey-blonde mane create an appealing and wholesome look, yet she has the figure of a petite vixen with shapely legs, full breasts, and a tiny waist. She's five foot two inches tall and appears even more diminutive next to Delilah, who stands five foot eight barefoot. On a recent shopping spree at Barneys, a sleek black skirt caught the eye of both women. Delilah searched the display rack to find the garment in their sizes. As always, a size 2 for Sofia hung at the front of the rack among a bevy of other size 2s. In the way back of the display, behind at least fifteen other skirts and a misplaced Prada blouse, hung one lone size 12 for Delilah. Someone else had clearly tried on the skirt, as it was replaced backward on the hanger with the zipper down.

While it sometimes seems that most women roaming the streets of New York, and the country's other major metropolises, are stick-thin model types with freakishly plump lips who could survive on six raisins and a small wedge of lettuce a day, Delilah's well aware that the average female in America remains a size 12 or larger. As a result, apparel in this size tends to fly like hotcakes, which, unlike the stick-thin model types, Delilah allows herself to eat. With butter, no less. (Mrs. Butterworth, who always served as a sweet and attentive listener at the breakfast table during Delilah's formative years, is also a dear friend.)

Delilah isn't skinny, but she's not fat either. She's somewhere happily in between. One might describe her as full figured, or big boned, or possibly even plus sized, although this would be a bit of a stretch. One eloquent yet mildly offensive blind date recently inquired if she had always been a "lady of generous body mass." Delilah admitted that, indeed, one could say that. One could also say that this eloquent yet mildly offensive man had a small lump of crab rangoon stuck to his nose, but Delilah kept this information to herself, as it was the most entertaining part of their evening. Years ago she would have been hurt by her date's tactless comment, but now it takes an insult with a lot more venom than that to rattle Delilah.

Resembling a Botticelli beauty with voluptuous curves, Delilah White likes herself just the way she is: a perfect size 12.

While their work at *D.B.* brought Delilah and Sofia together, it was Sofia's fiancé, Brad "the Evil Bastard," who helped them forge a true friendship. When the Evil Bastard left her for a younger model/actress with no last name, Sofia's universe came crashing down. Not knowing what else to do, she threw herself into her job, directing all her energy toward marketing the show. Delilah noticed that Sofia seemed gloomy and curiously punctual. She knew something must be very wrong and decided to try to cheer her up. Before long, the two women realized they shared a lot in common. Besides being smart, independent women with a thirst for adventure, they ran in similar social circles, sported a passion for cheeseburgers, and refused to take themselves too seriously.

Delilah was there to pick up the pieces when the Selfish Prick left Sofia shattered. She listened to her cry, helped her get rid of the mushy CD mixes the Cheap Schmuck had filled with "meaningful" songs symbolizing their eternal love, and dragged her out for champagne against her will to celebrate the Repugnant Fool doing her a favor by heading for the hills sooner rather than later. When Sofia hit rock bottom, Delilah gently reminded her that any man who would choose Phoenix—JUST Phoenix—a girl with poorly streaked hair and a teensy Chihuahua named Mon Ami that she carried around town in a rhinestone-studded BabyBjörn, was not worthy of her tears. This did the trick, and Sofia thanked Delilah profusely for helping her finally see that she was better off without Satan's Burp, and it was time to get on with life.

As they drive toward the Catskills, heading north out of the bustling cement island of Manhattan, Delilah breathes a sigh of relief. "Ditto," Sofia agrees and turns up the radio.

Free Samples Friday

"Can you believe we taped until two in the morning last night?" Sofia marvels as they wind their way up the New York State Thruway. "If you hadn't saved the day with that Berry Patriotic Breakfast Pudding idea, we'd probably still be shooting. Where do you come up with this stuff?"

"Oh please! I thought the pudding bit was *berry boring* if you ask me. I was just trying to save Nick from having a coronary and dying on the spot. I thought the poor guy's head was gonna pop off! Did you see that little vein thingy sticking out of his neck? I almost called for a medic on set."

"That's one director who desperately needs to relax."

"No kidding," laughs Delilah. "It's a *television show*, not brain surgery. Lives are not supposed to be at stake here. A little perspective please . . ."

"I think he needs some lovin'," Sofia rationalizes. "A good, quality romp would do that man well."

"Welcome to my world." Delilah sighs dramatically, stretching her legs out in front of her. "Otto doesn't like me. Talk about a waste of time . . ." She recounts the latest Otto installment, which involved an intimate dinner at a hot new restaurant in the Meatpacking District the week before, tango dancing, and too many tequila shots. Not to mention several doses of extra-strength Tylenol and an extra coat of mascara the following day.

"He didn't call?"

Delilah rolls her ice-blue eyes. "Didn't call. Didn't respond to my e-mail. *And*, to add insult to injury, he hid his stupid little face in his menu when I spotted him having dinner with some leggy redhead on Tuesday night. Pig . . ."

"No . . ."

"Oh yes. He may be interested in sleeping with me—when it's convenient for *him*, mind you—but he clearly has no desire to have a relationship. Don't ask me why I didn't see it sooner. I should really speak to a doctor about this. I might need medication. It could be serious." Delilah remembers the best part. "Oh my gosh! Did I tell you that he refers to sex as 'playing hide the sausage'?"

"That's just wrong on so many levels." Sofia shakes her head and assures her that Otto, a high-profile divorce lawyer at Hirsch, McLean, and Homma, is a complete moron fuckwad who's too jaded to believe in the possibility of a successful union or to realize what an amazing catch she is. "No more lawyers. You need somebody more laid-back and positive, somebody who actually believes in love."

"Yeah, don't we all?" Delilah grins. "Feel free to send Mr. Phenomenal my way. *After* I get my promotion, of course. Anyway, who cares about dumb Odd-O? He has crap taste in music and only tips ten percent."

"That's the worst. Don't you hate when men do that? So embarrassing . . ."

"Can I tell you something? I mean this too. Focusing strictly on my career right now is refreshing. It honestly feels good," Delilah declares.

"Speaking of which, I forgot to tell you: I *love* your idea about doing a segment on how to make the most of an itsy-bitsy city apartment. The part in your e-mail about turning that five-by-five-foot closet into a fabulous guest room was hilarious. I was laughing out loud in my office."

"I'm glad somebody liked it. The whole idea got nixed at the segment pitch meeting yesterday."

"No . . ." Sofia frowns. "Wait. Let me guess . . . Too urban?"

"Ding ding ding! You win! I'm telling you, it was brutal inside that conference room. I got slaughtered."

"I'm sorry, sweetie."

"Yeah, me too." Delilah sighs, gazing out the window at the passing cars with a dreamy, faraway look. "I was really hoping I'd be able to do that segment. I had it all planned out on my computer." She shakes her head. "Blech! Let's change the subject."

"Well, I still think it's a great idea," Sofia reassures her.

When they reach the halfway point to the Catskill Mountains, Delilah requests a bathroom break. She figures her bladder must be the size of a walnut. It drives her batty! God forbid she should be able to sit through an entire feature film without having to stand up, shimmy her way into the aisle, race to the bathroom, and then zoom back to her seat without hyperventilating or missing an important part of the movie. She makes a mental note to remember to speak to Sofia's father about her idea for a new invention called Theater Pants. Sofia, whose bladder is the size of a watermelon, says she wants to stop at Penny London's Candy Shoppe to pick up some fudge for her mom and suggests they use the bathroom there.

As the convertible turns off the exit, the intoxicating aroma of sweet chocolate begins to permeate the air.

The best part of Penny London's Candy Shoppe is the free samples, which Delilah loves. Really now, what's not to like about cute little bites of food stuck to a toothpick? She's even on occasion made a meal out of the vast array of samples offered at the supermarket—all in the name of "quality control." Delilah's also fond of free refills. Yet she doesn't particularly care for the Olive Garden. The irony! She samples several creative variations of fudge before accepting that she's a traditionalist and settles on classic chocolate.

It happens that Penny London, the shop's proprietor, is behind the counter this quiet Friday afternoon. Delilah compliments her scrumptious fare and inquires if she uses condensed sweetened milk or fresh milk in her recipes. Furrowing her brow, Penny hesitates to reveal her baking secrets—that is, until she discovers that the woman savoring her candy is none other than Delilah White from *Domestic Bliss*! "Oh my gosh! Nuh-uh! I *adore* your ideas, Ms. White!" she gushes. "I followed your instructions for making those wonderful little origami stacking boxes and gave 'em away as Christmas gifts last year! Everyone loved 'em! Now *that's* bliss!"

"I'm tickled to hear it," says Delilah, charmed by the woman's exuberance.

"Well, *Domestic Bliss* is just my favorite TV show. I've watched it for ages! Same with my daughter! Even my brother tunes in! He's gay as taffy!" she whispers, hiding her mouth with her hand.

"It's a pleasure to meet you." Delilah smiles, extending her hand. "Your fudge is outstanding, some of the best I've had. I could eat a whole box!"

"Stop it. You're too kind! I can't believe you're in my shop! Wait till the girls hear about this. Here, let me write down the recipe and you can try it out for yourself. See what ya think." Penny London reaches for a peppermint stick–shaped pen and starts scribbling feverishly on a pad of paper.

"Thank you. I'm honored you're willing to share it with me." Delilah grins as Penny hands her the recipe.

"Listen to you! Honey, *I'm* the one who's honored, believe you me. I'm about to wet my pants!"

Delilah wonders if the confection might make an interesting segment on *D.B.* Perhaps she could highlight a few gooey and rich recipes for fudge and explore its even richer historic significance, although she has no idea what the heck that might be. Nobody could possibly suggest this idea is "too metropolitan," something she's been accused of time and time again during her tenure at the show. She tries not to let it bother her, but lately it's been easier said than done.

Delilah insists that Sofia let her purchase the fudge as a thank-you gift for Mrs. Trawler for inviting her to spend the weekend.

No use arguing about this one. "I'm not gonna put up a fight because I *know* it'll be a futile effort, but for the record, giving my parents a gift is completely unnecessary. They think of you as family at this point; they're just happy you're coming. My dad's been talking about it for weeks. He can't wait to see you!"

While Delilah's in the bathroom, Sofia's cell phone rings. She puts down the giant twenty-four-inch-tall cherry gummy bear she's been examining, glances at the display window, and winces. It's Margo.

When Delilah returns, all smiles and much relieved, Sofia shoots her a look that requires no words. "What?" Delilah asks. "What's going on?"

As Sofia fills her in, Delilah's grin fades in less than a second. Margo Hart has had a change of plans.

On their way out of the confectionery, Delilah poses for a quick picture with Penny London, and they exchange e-mail addresses. Delilah promises to let her know how the fudge recipe works out, and Penny beams. "You made my whole week, honey. Take good care! You girls come back soon now! Happy Fourth of July!" She stands in the doorway, her body leaning halfway out of the shop, grinning and waving good-bye.

As Delilah and Sofia hit the road again, the smell of chocolate is quickly replaced with the smell of trouble.

One Month Earlier

The announcement came just after Memorial Day weekend. Nobody anticipated it. After a decade of superior leadership and outstanding service—which had won her three Emmy Awards, a Golden Globe, and a Helpful Homemaker trophy—Agnes Deville was stepping down from her esteemed position as executive producer of *Domestic Bliss*. The industry trade papers and evening celebrity news programs were going to have a field day with this one.

When Delilah joined the television show, Agnes was the first person to take her under her wing and show her the ropes, recognizing that Delilah had the natural talent and, what's more, the personality to go far in the domestic arts. Over the years, Agnes had served as a great mentor and an even greater inspiration. She became a role model and a dear friend, opening many doors of opportunity for Delilah, who can't imagine what it will be like to work at *Domestic Bliss* without her beloved boss.

Of course, someone is going to take Agnes's place, thereby assuming the highest-ranking position on the show and earning a coveted place in the television industry's elite. Perhaps this individual will choose to take the program in a new direction, or make staff adjustments and fire personnel, or even rethink the show's content and format. Perhaps this new leader will be Delilah.

Or maybe it will be Margo Hart.

One thing's for certain: it will be one of these two capable and talented women, and this weighs heavily on Delilah's mind.

When Agnes delivered the surprising news of her pending resignation to an uncomfortably warm conference room packed with the entire *Domestic Bliss* staff and crew, she explained, "Over the course of the summer, between now and Labor Day, I assure you, I will carefully consider who is best suited for the job, and I will elect the person who will ultimately be empowered to run the show however they see fit, leading *Domestic Bliss* into its next phase."

Everyone knew that she was talking about Delilah White and Margo Hart, the two most senior producers in the room.

Delilah didn't know whether to laugh or cry (or drown her sorrows in the extra-creamy "emergency" key lime pie she had stashed in the freezer). She's not particularly graceful when it comes to accepting change. Years ago, when her parents announced they were moving the family into a nicer, bigger home with a swimming pool and a colossal yard with apple trees, Delilah sobbed for days and threatened to run away to Bora Bora. Although she hadn't seen the new house (and didn't own a passport), she declared that she despised it and would never get over the hideous trauma of being forced to move. "Never ever ever! So help me Christ!" Her mother, familiar with Delilah's ongoing struggle with change, instructed her to buck up and try, hard as it may be, to behave like a normal twenty-year-old.

Needless to say, at first the thought of Agnes leaving *Domestic Bliss* was difficult and sad for Delilah to wrap her brain around. But now, the more she considers the idea of running the show, the more she likes it.

The thought of being executive producer thrills and electrifies her. Everything she's worked hard for and accomplished up to this point has paved the way to this opportunity, and she knows she'd be a fool not to take advantage of it. Regrettably, if Delilah considers her predicament for too long, she sometimes unconsciously sings the theme song from *Rocky III*, "Eye of the Tiger." As she recently discovered, this phenomenon is less than desirable when trying to impress a hot date. Her suitor for the evening, an investment banker named Daniel, had excused himself to visit the men's room. Thanks to the pre-dinner martinis and the lovely bottle of cabernet they drained during their meal, Delilah had no idea she was softly humming "Eye of the Tiger" out loud (oops!) until Daniel tiptoed up behind her and valiantly joined in with a booming, *It's the eye of the tiger, it's the thrill of the fight!* Daniel's singing was terribly off-key and loud enough that some of the high-profile patrons seated nearby craned their necks to see where the dying moose might be located. Delilah's cheeks flushed a deeper shade of crimson than the cabernet, and she hasn't heard from Daniel since. Nor has she gathered the courage to return to the trendy scene of the crime.

But then, at times when Delilah's alone at night, lying between her fine Egyptian cotton 650-thread-count sheets (which she totally splurged on), with only her thoughts to keep her company, her mind races in all directions, and worry sets in. During these haunting moments, she secretly wonders if she's deluding herself into believing that she's capable of executive producing a major television show seen by approximately seventeen million viewers per week. It would be easy and safe to remain in the position she's in now. No risk, no challenge, no disappointment.

Margo Hart would love to see Delilah in these times of doubt.

Margo

Margo resembles one of those mannequins at Neiman Marcus: statuesque and flawless, perfectly proportioned, clad in the finest designer wear, yet, upon closer examination, somewhat hollow and hardened, pieced together part by purchased part. Her mother, a former beauty queen, holds several distinguished pageant titles from back in the day, including Miss Baltimore Crab Cake and Miss Maryland. Perhaps this has something to do with it.

Margo's body is a constant work in progress, and it hasn't come cheap. She has a Malibu Barbie haircut with tresses the color of a brand-new penny, thanks to Clairol Nice 'n Easy #108 Natural Reddish Blonde. Thick and gleaming from careful washing and brushing, it requires tedious monthly maintenance to avoid tacky roots. Jodi at New York City's posh Frédéric Fekkai salon chemically straightens Margo's curls once every six months as well. The solution burns her scalp, but razor-straight hair is worth the pain. She has undergone a laundry list of surgical procedures to enhance her exterior, including a brow lift, nose job, lip augmentation, cheek fat removal, chin refinement, breast augmentation, liposuction on the inner thighs, LASIK eye surgery, and porcelain veneers for her pearly whites. Despite all of these painful and costly procedures, when

Margo studies her reflection, the face that looks back at her seems extremely ordinary and unremarkable.

To most people, however, she is a drop-dead stunning work of art. Men want to sleep with her, and women either want to kick her in the shins or be her (some wish to sleep with her too). Delilah swears that if she looked like Margo, she'd walk around naked all day long with a mirror in her hand singing "I Feel Pretty" and signing autographs. Lately, however, Margo reminds her more of a peacock feather with thorns.

Margo had seniority at *Domestic Bliss* when Agnes decided to hire a second producer, hoping fresh blood would help boost the show's sagging ratings. Agnes enlisted Margo to help recruit the best person for the job since they would be working in tandem. Ultimately, Margo was faced with the choice of Delilah White or Gwyneth Halmer, a blonde former runway model whose astounding beauty took everyone's breath away, including Margo's. The only thing Margo Hart detests more than white flour and carbohydrates is not being the prettiest woman in the room. There was no way in hell she was going to help hire gorgeous Gwyneth Halmer. So Margo picked Delilah, whom she viewed as a talented but roly-poly non-threat.

Delilah has never forgotten that she has Margo to thank for the best thing that's ever happened to her. Despite obvious personality differences, they manage to maintain a cordial relationship inside and outside the television studio, as work often transpires beyond *Domestic Bliss* headquarters on Madison Avenue. Sometimes, after putting in unusually long hours, Delilah, Margo, and Sofia will end their day at the bar at the Four Seasons Hotel located conveniently down the street on Fifty-seventh. Underlings at the show often refer to the three of them as the Holy Trio. On the rare occasion that Agnes Deville joins them, they become the Holy Trio plus God. Truth be known, Delilah would rather go home and cozy up with a celebrity gossip magazine and a box of Red Hots (truth *really truly* be known, she'd prefer to go home and snuggle up with Brad Pitt and a dozen Krispy Kremes), but she's familiar with "industry politics," and it's in her best interest to join the girls for at least one round of shoptalk and drinks.

Margo and Sofia, on the other hand, lived in the same dormitory during their freshman year at NYU. From their first meeting years ago, brushing their teeth in the shared bathroom on their floor, Margo took an instant liking to Sofia and has since become fascinated with the Trawlers. Sofia tolerates Margo, even sometimes admires her spicy sarcasm and cleverness, but she's also seen Margo's darker side. She witnessed an ugly glimpse of it just the day before their trip, unbeknownst to Margo.

Margo and Amelia "I'll sleep my way to the top" Miller from Accounts Payable were in the ladies' room at *D.B.* touching up their makeup after a power lunch at the "it" restaurant on the Upper East Side and thought they were alone. Sofia was in the last stall just zipping up when they started gabbing. "I'll destroy her if I have to. Happily. In fact, I plan on it. I have every intention of wearing her down," Margo hissed. "Eventually, the goody two-shoes will cave. Trust me, she has *no idea* who she's up against or how badly I want this. I've worked way too hard for way too long for her to get in the way now. I'm sorry, but there's only room for *one* domestic diva around here, and it ain't her."

Afraid she might be spotted, Sofia climbed up onto the toilet seat, balancing precariously in her black kitten-heeled slingbacks.

"Delilah White, Executive Producer," Amelia contemplated. "I don't know . . . It *does* have a nice ring to it."

"Pfff! Please . . . Over my dead body. That woman doesn't stand a chance."

"I wouldn't want to be pitted against you," Amelia marveled.

"No, doll, you wouldn't," Margo agreed. Sofia heard her close her purse with a sharp, "Hell, *I* wouldn't want to be pitted against me!"

A flourish of female laughter floated through the bathroom and into Sofia's stall. She waited for both women to exit before returning to her office, disgusted, wishing she had used the men's room and avoided the nasty scene.

⊰ ⊱

Margo and Delilah are under intense scrutiny and extraordinary pressure to come up with the most impressive segment ideas for the show that they're capable of. It's time for them to slow-roast, chiffonade, steam, garden, paint, and glue-gun their way to the top. Understandably, both producers remain cautiously guarded and unwilling to reveal what they have simmering under their lids, but the festering tension between them—stemming primarily from Margo—is increasing by the day, making an already difficult situation even worse.

Last Monday, after an unusually tedious and stressful technical rehearsal for that week's show, Delilah knocked on Margo's office door. "Hey, got a sec?" She poked her head in.

"For you?" Margo grinned. "Of course. Come on in." She quickly angled her computer screen away from Delilah and closed the document she was working on.

"Thanks," Delilah smiled, stepping through the archway into Margo's impeccably organized office.

"What's up?"

"Look, I'm not gonna beat around the bush. Something's obviously going on between us here. I just wanted to ask you directly: Have I done something to upset you?"

Placing her hand over her heart, Margo appeared shocked. "No, not at all!" She stood up to give Delilah a huge hug. "I'm insanely preoccupied, please don't take it personally. You know how much I love you! I've just got so much going on at the moment. I feel like I don't have time to blink. *You* of all people know how it is," she smiled, appearing just as sugary sweet as she sounded, though Delilah had seen her use the same puppy-dog eyes on her gullible boyfriend, Preston.

"Are you sure nothing's wrong? I've noticed you've seemed a bit"—Delilah searched for a polite way to say it—"*hostile* lately. It feels like you've been avoiding me like the plague."

"The plague?!" Margo echoed. "Delilah, you are such a riot. I swear! Don't be so sensitive, hun." She straightened the stapler and tape dispenser on her desk so that they were both positioned perfectly parallel to her computer.

"Well, things have been pretty tense. I just wanted to check in and be sure we're okay," Delilah probed, narrowing her eyes.

"*Yes.* Girl Scout's honor! It's just typical television pressure—that's all. Honestly, I'd never want to offend you." She bit her bottom lip. "Think you can forgive me?"

I don't know, Delilah thought. *You've been such a nasty ice princess lately. I'd really like to. But* . . . "If you say so. I just . . . I don't want this promotion to cause a rift between us. It's crazy enough as it is around here, you know?"

"I absolutely agree. I do. Now get out of here and let me get back to planning my segment on the wonders of beeswax. I'm trying to figure out the best way to remove residual wax from a votive," she elaborated while motioning toward the door with her impeccably made-up face. Delilah couldn't help but admire her lip gloss. Clinique Juicy Apple?

"Oh! Try sticking it in the freezer for ten minutes and lightly tap the bottom of the votive. Voilà!"

"Really? Isn't that clever? I'll have to try that." Margo tucked her fiery red hair behind her ear.

"I actually just learned another amazing trick. If you put about a quarter of an inch of water in the votive before you drop the candle in, you avoid the problem all together. The water prevents the wax from sticking. Works every time."

"That *is* amazing. I'll have to try that as well," Margo replied with a stiff smile, though the tiny hint of resentment in her tone did not go undetected by Delilah.

Giving Margo a long, hard look, Delilah wished her good luck with the beeswax and quietly closed the door behind her.

Perplexed, she stood motionless outside Margo's office for a full minute replaying their conversation in her mind, debating whether to pop back inside and let Margo know she's not some naive Betty Crocker from Pleasantville, and she's not sure she bought a single word of what she just heard. But, in the end, like usual, Delilah played it safe—not wanting to create any problems—meandering back to her office with an unsettling feeling in the pit of her stomach.

This same unnerving sensation came rushing back to her inside Penny London's Candy Shoppe when Sofia announced Margo would be joining them at Cherry Pond after all.

Violent Vegetable

"Tell me one more time *exactly* what Margo said," Delilah instructs Sofia. They're back in the convertible making great time on the highway. Traffic is light, and if it continues this way, they'll arrive at Cherry Pond just in time for dinner.

"She told me this morning that Preston unexpectedly got assigned to a big critical case, and now he needs to spend the whole weekend working. I think he has a brief due on Monday. Or maybe a deposition. I don't know, some lawyer jargon. Point being, their plans were canceled and she's on her way to my parents' house. Margo said she feels badly she's been so consumed with this whole executive producer thing lately, and she wants to forget all about it for a few days and let loose. Have some fun with us. Like old times."

"Have some fun with us? Like old times?"

"This is not a listen-and-repeat exercise," Sofia jokes.

"After the way she's been acting lately, it just strikes me as unusual that she'd want to spend the holiday with us, that's all." Delilah unravels a long cherry licorice wheel, pondering it. "Don't you think it's weird?"

"You're preaching to the choir, D. You're the one who told me to invite her in the first place."

For the past several years, Sofia has invited both Delilah and

Margo to Cherry Pond for her family's fabulous Fourth of July fete, and their yearly summer getaway had become something of a tradition. Due to recent circumstances at *D.B.*, however, this year Sofia debated whether it was wise to include both producers. Unhappy with the prospect of being placed in the middle of a tense situation, she briefly entertained the idea of not inviting either of them. But she wanted to introduce Delilah to her cousin Jack, who will hopefully be there this weekend, and she'd hate to offend Margo by demonstrating her obvious allegiance to Delilah. When she consulted Delilah on the issue, they agreed it was safe to welcome Margo as usual, wagering the odds of her agreeing to come along as very low. Sure enough, just as they suspected, Margo sorrowfully explained that she and Preston hadn't spent much time together recently and were going to share a nice romantic weekend on Martha's Vineyard.

As the convertible zooms along the highway, Delilah can't help but wonder if she's being too rough on Margo. *She may be a bit prickly around the edges, but it's not as if the woman is Satan. It's not like she walks up to children with leukemia and punches them in the stomach for no good reason. She just happens to want the same thing I do, and she's putting up the proper fight. Consequently, it's making her act like a wretched beast. But maybe, considering the circumstances, her behavior really isn't all that out of the ordinary. Maybe it makes perfect sense, and I'm the one reading too far into this. I am very gifted at overanalyzing. Perhaps I should put all this competition on the back burner for a couple of days. Back burner? Shit! Did I leave the stove on?*

"Earth to Delilah. Are you self-conversating?"

"Is it that obvious?" She frowns, snapping back to reality.

"Oh yeah. I can see the wheels turning in your head. Electric sparks are about to shoot out of your brain. You have to stop thinking so much! Seriously, it's not good for you. You're on vacation."

"I know, I know. I was just thinking, though. We're all under a lot of pressure. It might not be the worst idea to give Margo the benefit of the doubt here and try to have an enjoyable, peaceful weekend. Maybe she really does just want to spend some time with us."

Keeping both hands on the steering wheel, Sofia faces Delilah and cocks an eyebrow.

"What? Is that so hard to believe?"

Well acquainted with Delilah's endearing but dangerous penchant for believing in the goodness of people, Sofia just smiles and shakes her head. "It's a generous gesture, but I wouldn't recommend getting *too* comfortable with her. Let's not forget that Margo can be a tricky one," she cautions. "Know what I mean? Think about last month's spaghetti squash fiasco."

Delilah grimaces. "I'd rather not. I'm surprised I don't have a white streak in my hair because of it."

Margo had stopped by Agnes's office to show off her latest creation: a standard plastic toothbrush holder with four holes on top, which she had painted silver with black stripes, filled with water, dropped a brightly colored gerbera daisy inside each hole, and presto! She'd transformed a dull, ordinary bathroom object into a fun and quirky vase—all for under four dollars. She hoped Agnes would agree that this would make for an excellent *D.B.* segment. Margo grew excited when she first discovered Delilah was inside Agnes's office, behind closed doors. After all, Agnes rarely, if ever, shuts her door. When she does, it usually indicates someone's in big fat trouble. "How long's Delilah been in there?" Margo—trying not to seem *too* interested—asked Julian, Agnes's trusty executive assistant, also known as the "eyes and ears of *D.B.*"

"About twenty minutes or so."

"That bow tie you're wearing is fantastic, by the way," Margo said, smiling. "Deliciously dapper! Would you happen to have any idea what they're talking about?"

"Your guess is as good as mine," Julian replied, straightening his tie. "Agnes closed the door right after Delilah went in. I wasn't sure if a pink bow tie would make me look a touch feminine—if you catch my drift—but I've received loads of compliments today, so apparently I'm macho enough to pull it off. Don't get me wrong, I'm comfortable with my masculinity." He observed Margo's eyebrows crinkle into an unhappy knot and her shoulders slump. "Are you okay?"

Peering through the vertical glass window next to Agnes's closed door, Margo watched Delilah and Agnes simultaneously erupt into a fit of laughter. Delilah—clearly not in any big fat trouble—threw her head back, giggling, and Agnes doubled over, slapping her hand against her desk as if she'd just heard the funniest joke in the universe.

"You okay, babe?" Julian repeated.

"I'm sorry." Margo forced a tight grin, focusing on Julian once again. "I was just thinking of a way I can improve my vase. Know what? I think I better go work on it some more before I show Agnes . . . You know how it is with vases."

Having no clue, Julian just smiled politely. "Um, okay."

And with that, Margo sped down the hall. When she reached the elevator bank on the forty-fourth floor, she came upon several visibly upset members of the crew.

"What's going on?" Margo asked as she approached the gaggle, her curiosity roused.

"You just missed a fucking disaster in the studio," Nick, the director, replied.

"Disaster!" parroted Darcy, the script supervisor, placing her clipboard over her face.

"What happened?" Margo noticed that Darcy seemed to be on the verge of tears.

"Well, let's just say the set is destroyed and Rodney the cameraman is on his way to the hospital," Nick said, shaking his head ruefully. "Hopefully, he'll be able to walk again."

"What?" Margo gasped. "Someone tell me what you're talking about!"

"We were doing a run-through of Delilah's spaghetti squash Florentine recipe," Darcy explained, her brown eyes welling with worry. "Something went terribly wrong. Right in the middle of the rehearsal, there was a massive explosion and the squash just *burst* out of the microwave." She gestures a huge explosion with her hands.

"It sounded like Vietnam!" Nick interrupted, leaning against the wall. "I'm gonna have night terrors."

Darcy nodded. "Out of nowhere the microwave door *blasted* open by itself and the squash went flying through the air! It was like it had a motor! No exaggeration, there was gloppy squash goo dripping off the ceiling, stuck to the lights, blanketing the whole set."

"It's a squashtastrophe," Nick declared, defeated, his eyes glazing over.

"It'll take a full day to get it cleaned and shootable," sighed Carl, the assistant director. "The Set Decoration Department's gonna need sedatives when they see this one."

"I need sedatives!" Nick shouted, pounding his fist against his chest like Tarzan.

Margo's head reeled. "Well, what happened to Rodney? You said he was hurt?"

"He slipped on a big chunk of squash and thinks he broke his knee!" Darcy moaned. "It was so scary, Margo. He couldn't even stand. We had to call an ambulance. I still don't get what went wrong. We followed Delilah's recipe *exactly*! I'm holding it right here in my hands." She pointed emphatically at her clipboard.

"Let me see that." Margo pried the clipboard away and scanned the orange squash-stained pages. Suddenly, her eyes lit up. "Here, take this!" She quickly shoved her vase at Darcy. "I'll be right back!" She took off like a bandit toward Agnes's office.

Darcy looked at the vase and smiled, amused. "Hey, check it out, guys. It's a toothbrush holder!" She held it up for Nick and Carl to see.

"No shit. Look at that." Nick grinned, impressed.

⁂

Sauntering directly past Julian without saying a word, Margo knocked three times on Agnes's closed door and, without waiting for a response, bombarded inside. "Hi, please excuse me," she said calmly, remaining near the entryway. "I'm sorry to interrupt. I wouldn't disturb you if it weren't an emergency, but, Delilah, I thought you'd want to know."

"Come in," Agnes gestured.

"Thought I'd want to know what?" asked Delilah.

Sighing, as if terribly distraught, Margo continued. "Well, uh . . . there's no easy way to say this, so I'm just gonna go ahead and say it. There was an accident on set a little while ago, and it's kind of your fault."

Panic flooded Delilah's body, and she sat up straight as a board. "What are you talking about?"

"What *are* you talking about?" demanded Agnes.

Margo looked at Delilah sorrowfully. "A spaghetti squash exploded during the initial rehearsal of your Florentine recipe, and it destroyed the set."

"What?" Delilah cried.

"Yeah, it seems you forgot to include that you need to puncture the squash shell before heating in the microwave. It's a complete debacle in the studio. I was just down there," Margo fibbed. "*Everything's* covered in a thick coat of slime."

"A thick coat of slime?" Agnes slowly repeated, blinking, dumbfounded. Then she folded her willowy arms, turning to Delilah. "Is this true? What is this, amateur hour? Give me a break! You know better than that."

"I *do* know better than that," Delilah desperately agreed, her heart pounding in her chest. "Agnes, I'm *sure* I included that step. This has to be some sort of misunderstanding. Why would I leave something so obvious out?" Confused, she stood and hurried toward the door. "Let me go get the recipe. It's right on my desk."

"No need." Margo intercepted her. "I have it here." She handed Darcy's clipboard to Delilah.

Well, aren't you Santa's little helper? Holy shit. Let this be a nightmare. Let me wake up right now. Time to rise and shine and be safe and sound inside my cozy bed. Delilah's stomach plummeted as she skimmed the recipe and realized, to her horror, that she was guilty as charged. She listened for a melancholy bugle playing taps somewhere off in the distance. "I . . . I . . . I don't know what to say. I have *no idea* how I could have left that out. I know I was rushing to get ten things done at once but . . ."

"The thing is?" Margo winced theatrically. "There's sort of more . . ."

"Oh God." Fear dripped out of every pore on Delilah's body.

"Rodney slipped on some squash flesh and is seriously injured. It's not good. He was rushed to the hospital in an ambulance."

"WHAT?!" Agnes flew off her chair like a rocket. "This has *lawsuit* written all over it. Dammit, Delilah!" She bounded out of her office, shouting at Julian as she zoomed past him, "Call the lawyer! See if he's available to meet later today! *Fuck!*"

Inside Agnes's office, Delilah remained in shock, but what's more, she was irritated. Her blood slowly simmering, she sat glaring at Margo.

"What?" Margo shrugged innocently, gesturing with her hands.

"You couldn't have waited? That *had* to be done in front of Agnes right here and now? This very second?"

"Well, it's an *emergency*, Delilah. I thought you'd want to know."

Hurt, Delilah narrowed her eyes into bitter slits. "Or you thought you'd make me look like an idiot in front of Agnes." She shook her head, disappointed. "Real nice, Margo. Thanks a lot," she said as she stormed out of the room, trembling with both fury and fear.

"I'm sorry!" Margo called after her. "That wasn't my intention!"

Back in the convertible, Delilah exhales dramatically. "*Thank God* it was only a sprained knee and Rodney's okay. I don't think I could have forgiven myself if he'd really been hurt."

"Anyway," Delilah continues, "I do realize Margo can be

rather tricky at times. I have no intention of letting my guard down completely around her, but there's no need for us to treat each other like sworn enemies. She's not Lex Luthor, for crying out loud. I'd just as soon avoid any more drama."

"Amen to that. So what are you gonna do, raise your Bellini glass and toast to a wonderful holiday among dear old friends?"

Delilah stares at the road ahead, considering the idea. "Why not? Sounds like a reasonable plan to me. I'll drink to that!"

Sofia rolls her green eyes. "Sweet Jesus, I was joking. But, in that case, make mine a double." Trusting Margo about as far as she can throw her (she's never tried but guesses she can hurl her at least three and a half feet), she decides she better keep close watch over Delilah's back this weekend.

Homecoming

"There's my dumpling!" Mr. Trawler, a stout and stumpy fellow, shouts as Sofia's convertible pulls up the half-mile-long cherry blossom tree–lined driveway. He has spent the past ten minutes pretending to be incredibly busy buffing an invisible spot on his sleek, black 1930 Mercedes-Benz Count Trossi SSK, one of only thirty that were manufactured and just one of the many rare automobiles in his exceptional collection. In reality, however, he's been waiting for the two girls to arrive. "Welcome, welcome!" he cheerfully calls out. Delilah thinks Sofia's father is so wonderfully darling that someone ought to mass-produce Mr. Trawler dolls. He envelops Sofia in a giant bear hug.

"Okay, your turn, White!" he shouts to Delilah when he finally releases his daughter. "Get over here and give me a damn hug!"

"Hi, Mr. T. It's so good to see you!" Delilah throws her arms around him.

"Your mother's in the kitchen putting the finishing touches on dinner. Fresh lobster and steamers sound alright to you girls?"

"Mmm, sounds heavenly," Delilah says, licking her lips.

"Your cousins took the pontoon boat out for a little spin, but they should be back any minute," Mr. Trawler informs Sofia. "Derek's starting to go bald. Don't mention it to him though because he's sensitive. He's wearing an awful lot of hair gel. Your mother tells me he's a metrosexual."

Sofia laughs. "Daddy, do you even know what that means?"

"Nope. Don't know if I want to."

"I'll fill you in later," she promises, reaching for her suitcase in the backseat. "I want to say hi to Mom."

When they reach the enormous kitchen, Sofia's mother, Blythe, stops slicing lemon wedges and greets the girls, insisting they look as gorgeous as ever, and explains that, due to the many weekend visitors, only two guest rooms remain unspoken for. She asks Delilah if she'd prefer the room with the canopy bed or the one overlooking the English rose garden. Delilah chooses the canopy bed. She doesn't particularly care for roses and their prickly thorns. She finds them ordinary. After a man gets to know her, if he gives her roses, she knows immediately that he's not her Mr. Right—if such a person exists. Mrs. Trawler beckons Consuela, the maid, and instructs her to bring the girls' luggage upstairs to their respective suites. The plump Spanish woman with rosy cheeks, dressed in a traditional black-and-white maid's uniform, picks up the suitcases and, just as she's about to exit the room, catches sight of Sofia and Delilah. "Sofia! Señorita Blanca! Buenas días! Bienvenido a casa!" She grins, walking toward them with her arms stretched wide open. "It's so good to see you!"

"Hola!" Sofia greets her enthusiastically with a hug and kiss on both cheeks.

"Consuela!" Delilah embraces her. "Es bueno verle! Cómo está usted?"

"Soy bueno, gracias. Tell me," she continues in English, "where's the third young lady who usually comes with you?"

"Margo drove up separately; she should be here soon. By the way, call me Ms. White again and I'm packing bowling balls and bricks next year," Delilah adds with a sly wink. "I'm not kidding."

"Ay caramba," Consuela murmurs as she ascends the ornate mahogany staircase covered with an elegant Oriental runner leading to the second floor.

⊰⊱

Dinner is set outside on a large cherrywood deck overlooking beautiful Lake Minnonqua, but first everyone gathers for a cocktail. Years ago, when the Trawlers were debating whether or not to purchase the pricey estate, the magnificent four-acre private beach in the backyard is what finally sealed the deal. The warm lake air is refreshing, and the rhythmic sound of the waves rolling in with the tide provides the only background music necessary for a good old-fashioned family meal. Delilah leans against the lattice-trim rail bordering the perimeter of the spacious deck, cocks her right leg behind her left, and takes in the surroundings. She feels the tension of the past month begin to slowly dissipate. Sometimes she forgets that quiet, tranquil places like this even exist. How easy it is to get swept up in the chaotic whirlwind of her everyday life in the city that never sleeps. Go go go. Rush rush rush. At times it's possible for it to escape Delilah's mind altogether that there are alternative lifestyles out there reaching far beyond the borders of shadowy steel skyscrapers, flashing lights, crowded avenues, and honking taxicabs. Gazing off into the distance at a sailboat floating languidly on the open water, Delilah realizes she's long overdue for this break.

She draws in a deep breath and slowly exhales. Next time

she's racing from one meeting to another, and she can't find a cab to save her life, and it looks like it's about to downpour any second, and some aggressive person on the sidewalk passing out pesky flyers nobody wants shoves one in her face, and her cell phone's ringing only she can't find it because her trendy purse has too many damn pockets, and a police siren is wailing, and she longs to grab a hot dog on the corner because she didn't have time for breakfast and she's positively starving but she's on a tight schedule and can't stop, and a dirty pigeon almost poops on her Manolo Blahniks, she'll pause. Stop. Dead in her tracks. Just like that. And she'll remember this moment, standing peacefully on the deck, admiring the reflection of the sun beginning to set, casting shades of pink and purple and tangerine against the rippling waves. Suddenly, the big bad city she's really in love with won't seem so mean.

"Sure is something, isn't it?" a man's voice questions, knocking Delilah out of her reverie.

"It sure is," she smiles.

"I'm Derek, Sofia's cousin from Connecticut." He reaches out his hand to greet her.

"Pleased to meet you. I'm Delilah. I work with Sofia at *Domestic Bliss.*"

"Ah, the *Domestic Bliss* connection."

"I *was* going to tell you that I'm a taxidermist," she admits, taking a sip of her pinot grigio.

Derek gives her a questioning look.

"To the stars?" she adds.

A loyal and devoted ESPN fan, Derek doesn't spend much time watching *Domestic Bliss*, but he's heard Sofia mention Delilah's name on many occasions and knows who she is. "A taxidermist *to the stars*?"

"Mostly B-list talent," she elaborates, gesturing to forget it. "Sometimes talking about *Domestic Bliss* gets a bit old, so I make up a random whopper," she admits, her blue eyes twinkling.

"Hmm, *Domestic Bliss*. Don't believe I'm familiar with it. How 'bout them Yankees?"

Delilah giggles. "So what do you do, Derek?"

"You like amusement parks?"

"I love 'em."

"I'm a carousel maker. One of the last of the old-fashioned merry-go-round manufacturers. It's a dying art, I'm afraid."

"Wow. Now *that's* one I haven't heard before. How'd you get involved in that?"

"Family trip to Disneyland when I was a kid. I fell in love with theme parks on the spot. I knew I wanted to do something where I could contribute to their magic. Sounds kinda goofy, I suppose." He finishes off the last of his scotch. "No pun intended."

"Not at all," Delilah smiles, happy to be talking about somebody else's passion for a change. "I'm the front seat of a roller-coaster kind of girl myself. The higher and faster, the better—as long as there are no loop-de-loops."

"None?"

"Nope. They make me vomit and see spots."

"I see. So you're a thrill seeker," he concludes.

"I guess." She shrugs, slowly sipping her wine.

"A ride or two can change your point of view. Stepping inside an amusement park is stepping outside the ordinary troubled world," Derek muses.

Delilah finds herself riveted by this strange and, yes, slightly balding man. "I've never thought of it like that before. Do you build other rides? Or only carousels?"

"I'm strictly a merry-go-round man. It takes about a year to complete one ride. Each one I make is unique."

"Really?"

"NOOOOOO!" Derek shrieks, startling Delilah. "I'm an accountant!" he confesses, spanking his thigh in a fit of laughter. "I crunch numbers!"

"Nice one," she congratulates him, shaking her head that she actually bought his kooky story. "You, my friend, are gifted."

At this moment, Margo Hart steps out onto the deck. Delilah politely excuses herself to say hello to Margo, her colleague at the celebrity taxidermy . . . lab? Office? Bureau? Oh, to hell with it. Derek's eyes linger a moment too long as she strolls off.

"Delilah!" Margo receives her with an embrace that catches Delilah off guard. "I'm so glad to be here. I'm sure Sofia filled you in about Preston, right?"

"She did. I'm sorry your weekend together was spoiled. I know how much you were looking forward to it. But I'm happy you're here too." Delilah grins, not quite sure what to make of Margo's abrupt one-eighty. *I think I once saw something like this happen in a* Twilight Zone *episode . . . Uh oh. If she's part robot, I'm going back to the city right now. Before it's too late!*

Margo assumes a grave expression and looks her square in the eyes. "Listen, before we go any further, can I talk to you for a moment, please?"

"Of course," says Delilah, leading her toward a quiet spot nearby. "What's up?"

"Do you think we can put this forsaken work bullshit behind us? I just have to say up front that I *know* I've behaved like a deplorable bitch, and I am *so* sorry. Seriously, Delilah, I'm not proud of the way I've acted lately. It's inexcusable." Margo cringes. "If you wanna know the truth, I still feel badly about

Squashgate last month! Let's just say I have *a lot* to learn about being a graceful contender, not to mention improving my etiquette." She sighs dramatically, looking away toward the lake. "I don't know why I act the way I do. Please tell me you forgive me. *Please.* I don't want there to be any bad blood between us. Life's too short."

Crikey! My goodness already. She's not gonna cry, is she? Overt groveling is definitely not Margo's style. Wow, she must really feel wretched. Delilah allows her to agonize for a few long, drawn-out moments. Finally, she shakes her head and narrows her eyes. "You can be such a damn barracuda!" And then, softening her expression, she smiles and gives Margo a big hug. "Now let's go find us some cocktails, shall we?" Delilah grabs Margo's hand and leads her toward Mr. Trawler, who stands toward the back of the deck behind a fully stocked bar merrily mixing Trawler-tinis (1.5 oz. vodka, ½ shot Watermelon Pucker, 1 splash soda water, watermelon garnish).

Dinner Is Served

At dinner, Mrs. Trawler introduces Delilah to the rest of Derek's primarily Connecticut-based family, including Aunt Deb, Uncle Mark, cousin Jack, cousin Samantha, and Samantha's college roommate, Lisa. At twenty-one, Samantha is at least a decade younger than the rest of the family and most of the guests attending the Trawlers' Fourth of July bash, so it seemed fitting that she bring along a companion her own age.

The lavish meal is presented buffet-style. Talk about an incredible spread! In addition to lobster and steamers, there is Caesar salad, corn on the cob, garlic mashed potatoes, asparagus with hollandaise sauce, tricolored sautéed baby carrots, and fresh baked rolls. The picturesque serving table closely resembles one that was displayed on a recent episode of *D.B.* in a segment on "How to Create the Quintessential Summer Buffet (Everything You Need to Know and Then Some)!" From the blossoming, fragrant gardenia plants stationed at each end of the long rectangular table, to the red-and-white-checkered linen tablecloth, to the silverware wrapped in gingham napkins and secured with matching red ribbon—it's all there, *exactly* like it appeared on *Domestic Bliss*. "Looks like some *wise* person has been watching the show," Margo grins, wrapping her arm around Mrs. Trawler's shoulder. She produced the segment in question and is delighted to see it practically applied. "I couldn't have done it better myself, Blythe. Everything looks stunning. Hats off to the chef."

"Thank you, honey. I forgot to cut the butter into daisy-shaped patties. I *knew* I was leaving something out. I just couldn't remember what!" Mrs. Trawler says, sipping her vodka tonic.

"I'd make a run for it, lamb. The police are coming to arrest you for committing such a twisted crime," Mr. Trawler teases. "I mean, what's a man gotta do to get some decorative butter around here, *dammit*? I want a divorce!" He bursts out laughing, cracking himself up.

Mrs. Trawler throws a warm roll at his head but misses and hits Derek smack-dab on his bald spot. Margo takes it upon herself to remove several bread crumbs caught in his well-gelled remaining hair, and they strike up a conversation.

Delilah chuckles to herself, amused. She's always gotten a kick out of the way Mr. and Mrs. Trawler interact. She hopes she can share such a playful relationship with her husband someday. *A husband . . . HA!* she thinks. *Don't get too carried away now, Delilah. Perhaps it might be wise to concentrate first on finding a decent man who's a generous tipper and not such a frisky horndog that he's inclined to play hide the sausage on the first date.* She takes a seat next to Aunt Deb and is about to untie her napkin when Sofia stops her. "Wait a sec. Come sit here next to me." She pats the empty chair on her left, beckoning her over.

It makes little difference to Delilah, so she picks up her plate and joins Sofia at the other end of the table. "I wanted to be able to talk to you," she explains under her breath. "Everything okay with Margo? I saw you two hugging back there."

"It was the strangest thing. She apologized to me about everything."

"Really?" Sofia crumples her eyebrows. "She did? Do you buy it?"

"You know, I *do*, actually. She was very upset. It seemed totally sincere. I think she knows she was out of line and honestly feels really bad about it. She seems to have realized that there's no reason why we can't keep this competition clean and fair."

"Hmm . . ." Sofia considers it. "That's good. This is an interesting development. Unexpected, but definitely positive." A bit perplexed, she tries to process this kinder, gentler version of Margo Hart. "I hope it lasts."

"Who knows. I'm just waiting for the friendship bracelet to make it official." Delilah pops a crouton into her mouth.

"Don't joke. Margo makes gorgeous jewelry! Her beadwork is impeccable. You'll fill me in on the details later," Sofia whispers, not wanting Margo to notice them conspiring. Although, at the moment, she's engrossed in a conversation with Derek. If one didn't know Margo had a boyfriend, one might think she was flirting with him.

"What am I thinking? Where are my manners? Have you met my cousin Jack?" Sofia asks Delilah, gesturing to a man seated directly across from her, going to town with some bright yellow corn on the cob.

"Your mom introduced us earlier," Delilah says, nodding hello to Jack.

"Hello again," he says in between mouthfuls of corn. "The corn is excellent!"

"What's not to love about corn on the cob?" Delilah asks.

"Seriously," he says and smiles, revealing a huge piece of corn stuck to one of his front teeth and a kernel dangling from his chin. Delilah wants to laugh, but she manages to maintain her composure. However, it's impossible to stifle her enormous grin.

"You have a great smile," Jack comments. The hanging piece of corn seems to defy the laws of gravity.

"Thank—" But before Delilah can finish her sentence, she's interrupted.

"Everybody, if I may please have your attention for just a moment," Mr. Trawler requests. He stands at the head of the table with his napkin tucked into the neck of his periwinkle whale-print shirt, tapping his knife against his crystal water goblet. All eyes settle on him as he continues, "I would just like to welcome you all to Cherry Pond and let you know how pleased we are that you could join us for our traditional Trawler Family Fourth. It's a great treat to have you all here, and Blythe and I want you to make yourselves completely comfortable. So enjoy! Sit back, relax, go for a dip in the pool or the lake, feel free to use the boats at your leisure, play some tennis, toss back some cocktails, take a snooze in the hammock, go horseback riding—you name it. Our home is *your* home," he finishes, and everyone happily clinks glasses and drinks to that.

Jack raises his bottle of beer and gently knocks it with Sofia's and Delilah's glasses. Then he tells Sofia to smile. She does. "You've got a chunk of corn stuck in your tooth," he says.

"Really?" Sofia tries to get it out with her tongue. "Which one?"

"That would be *all* of them!" Jack taunts. "Excuse me, Aunt Blythe?" he calls out to Mrs. Trawler, the resident photographer of the family, "Will you please take a picture of me and Cousin Corny?"

"Ha ha, hilarious," Sofia asserts.

"What? I think it's an attractive look for you. My Cousin Corny is very beautiful. Come on, show me that cornarific smile of yours! Who's the prettiest corn-face in town?"

"Oh, you are *so* dead!" she announces, pounding him on the arm.

Jack

As a lanky little boy, Jack Walsh could usually be found wearing nerdy glasses and a heavy dinosaur-print backpack stuffed with books. From the time he was a kindergartner, he knew what he wanted to be when he grew up: a teacher. Well, either that or a heart surgeon. As fate would have it, the sight of blood makes Jack need to lie on the floor and slowly count to ten—sometimes in Spanish if it's an especially gruesome scene. Typically, by the time he reaches *ocho*, the room has stopped spinning and he's able to feel his hands again.

Sure enough, Jack was right about his calling in life. Every day he returns home from West Elementary School, located on Chicago's illustrious North Shore, with a stack of drawings and notes from his second graders with charming little captions such as "Mr. Walsh is the best teecher in the wurld!" and "I love Mr. Walsh" and "Me and Mr. Walsh on a rainbow eating Cheetos!" He saves them all in a messy closet in his one-bedroom apartment. Even the ugly ones. The only problem is that, on his salary, he can't afford Chicago Cubs season tickets, which stinks because the Cubs are his favorite baseball team and he lives within walking distance of Wrigley Field.

Sitting across from him, Delilah thinks he physically resembles a handsome, lost member of the Kennedy/Onassis family.

With a strong jawline, thick brown hair, dreamy chocolate-colored eyes, and a dimple in his left cheek that has been known to make women swoon, he could easily pass for Jackie's six-foot-four, illegitimate child. Delilah wonders if anyone has ever told him this before.

At least three of Jack's wiser second graders plan on marrying him when they grow up. Several of their mothers have flirted with the idea themselves.

❧

"I'm hitting the buffet for more lobster. Can I get anybody anything?" Delilah offers.

"I'd love some more salad," Jack says. "Thanks."

"I'm ready to explode," Sofia moans, leaning back in her chair. "Ugh, nada más."

"Unbutton your jeans," he suggests.

"Always works for me," Delilah concurs as she heads for the buffet.

When she returns, Sofia and Jack are debating whether there's any truth behind the myth that you should wait an hour to go swimming after you eat. "Forget about it. I'm not going for a damn moonlight swim. I'll sink!" Sofia insists.

"Malarkey," Jack assures her as Delilah places a fresh plate of salad before him. "Thank you. Wanna go for a moonlight swim later on?"

"Sure," Delilah smiles. "Sounds like fun. I can't even remember the last time I went night swimming."

Jack grins triumphantly. "Sorry, cuz, you lose."

"Yeah, *you'll* lose when you drown."

"I'm telling you the same thing I tell my students: it takes the body thirty minutes to digest a meal. *Thir-tee min-utes.* Face it, cornball, I'm right."

"Are you a teacher?" Delilah cuts in.

Jack nods, taking a bite of salad.

"Mr. Walsh here is an *amazing* teacher," Sofia boasts. "Absolutely amazing."

He smiles and gently elbows her, looking down at his feet.

"My sister's a teacher. What grade do you teach?" Delilah inquires.

"Second. How 'bout your sister?"

"She used to teach fourth, but now she's teaching fifth. Do you like it?"

"I love it," Jack grins.

Delilah can tell he means it too.

Once everyone is stuffed to the point where they can't possibly eat another bite, Mr. Trawler and Uncle Mark make their way down to the beach to start a bonfire, while Consuela begins clearing the table. Mrs. Trawler announces dessert will be an interactive event involving flames.

"Uh-oh," says Derek.

Joy to the World

By the time all the guests find their way down to the bonfire by the shore, night has fallen and the temperature has dropped a good ten degrees. The crescent-shaped moon glows bright, and the smell of the crackling logs fills the crisp air, bringing Delilah back to her youthful days at Camp Birch Trail for Girls, "where the sun always shines." *At last, it officially feels like summer*, she muses. *It's about time . . .*

"What'cha thinking about?" Margo asks Delilah as they stroll barefoot in the sand, shoes in hand, toward the glowing bonfire.

"A boy and a girl in a little canoe."

"Ahhh, you too? Good ol' camp memories."

"Indeed." Delilah laughs at how, at thirty-three years old, she can still perfectly recall the fairy tale–like innocence and fun of those summers spent at sleepover camp.

"My God, it was easier back then, huh?" Margo says, almost to herself.

"No kidding. My biggest worry was grape bug juice or cherry."

"Grape," Margo says at the exact same time Delilah asserts "Cherry." They look at each other like the other one is stark raving mad and sit down on a fuzzy red blanket near the fire. For the first time since Agnes's announcement, Delilah finds herself at ease with Margo—even having a good time—and she feels as if a great, cumbersome weight has been lifted off her shoulders. *Thank God. Finally . . .*

After the way Margo attacked her during a pitch meeting the day before, Delilah was beginning to suspect their rivalry would end in the boxing ring with the bell sounding as they're forcefully pried apart, kicking and screaming. The Thursday morning weekly meeting including all *D.B.* creative staff began just as usual, with Agnes Deville in command. "Okay, everybody here?" She stood in front of a large white board, green dry-erase pen in hand, and quickly surveyed the conference room, taking a mental roll call. "Good, great, fantastic. Let's go. Who wants to start? Who's got something? Hit me with something brilliant. Make me want to give you a gold star. Who's first? Batter up!"

Eleanore from Pastry Production eagerly began, "I've been thinking . . . Coffee cakes are not getting the attention they deserve, and it's pissing me off. Consider it: this traditional and once highly regarded pastry, which has been around since the fourteen hundreds, thank you very much—*the fourteen hundreds*—has all but fallen by the wayside. It's almost a distant memory. *Think about it!* When was the last time somebody in this room enjoyed a nice delicious piece of coffee cake?"

Nobody responded.

"Well?" Eleanore waited, tapping her foot. "Somebody? *Anybody?*"

No one in the room batted a lash. Natasha from Gardening Arts nervously chewed her fingernails, wondering if Eleanore would need to be carried out of the room fastened to a stretcher.

"This is *exactly* my point. Okay, this is exciting. I've come up with a bunch of fantastic new recipes that redefine the coffee cake as we know it," she continued with frightening intensity. "I want to bring that cake back from the dead, and I want to restore it to its former glory!" Eleanore triumphantly pounded her fist on the table, making Natasha jump.

"Honey, you're scaring the kids. No more caffeine for you today. But you got me with the 'glory' part. It's going on the board." Agnes quickly scribbled "glorious coffee cake" on the white board in almost illegible cursive. "Everyone agree?" she tested, scanning the room.

All heads nodded in approval.

"I have something good," Margo volunteered, standing up. "How about a trompe l'oeil headboard viewers can easily make for under thirty dollars? It's elegant, stylish, and will completely transform the bedroom."

"I don't know," Mandy, head of Interior Design, interrupted. "Trompe l'oeil is never easy. I've done it a million times, and it's always harder than it looks."

"True," Agnes agreed, blowing a wisp of silvery white hair out of her face.

"Plus, the name alone is intimidating. People don't want to tackle a project that sounds out of their league," Delilah suggested, looking up from her notepad in which she had just jotted down *trompe l'oeil.*

"Just because it's out of *your* league doesn't mean our viewing audience can't hack it," Margo snarled. "They're quite capable. Do you have a better idea?"

Yeah, how about you lay off and stop filling me with hate? Jeez . . . "I didn't mean any offense, Margo," Delilah said sincerely, trying not to let Margo throw her. "How about something like this? We all have neighbors who on occasion can be noisy little bastards who we want to throttle with our bare hands, right?"

"I'd like to stab the aspiring actress who lives next door to me and thinks she's Ethel Merman," Peter from Carpentry Arts announced. "I'll bring around a cloud to rain on that tart's parade any day."

"Yes! That's *exactly* what I'm talking about," Delilah replied, pointing at Peter. "So, how about a fun, good-spirited, tongue-in-cheek segment on how to handle that pesky noisy neighbor *without any confrontation*?"

"I'm in," said Peter.

Glad to have someone on her side, Delilah continued, "Similar to the DO NOT DISTURB signs hotels use, my idea is to create anonymous, good-humored, premade notes viewers can easily download off the Web site, glue onto cardboard, and hang directly on their neighbor's doorknob. No harm, no foul."

"Interesting," Agnes said, chewing on her pen. "What do these notes say?"

"I have a couple ideas," Delilah smiled, feeling her adrenaline skyrocket. *Please like this*, she thought. *Realize it's a fun and whimsical project, and that's a good thing.* She cleared her throat. "IT'S NICE YOU'RE HAVING LOTS OF SEX, BUT IT WOULD BE EVEN NICER IF YOU DID IT IN SILENCE." A light spattering of laughter filled the room. "Or PLEASE BUY TOTO A MUZZLE, MY PRETTY, OR I'LL SEND MY FLYING MONKEYS FOR HIM." The laughter grew. "And then there's THE PEOPLE WHO LIVE DIRECTLY BELOW YOU LOVE YOU, BUT THEY HATE YOUR DAMN HIGH HEELS."

"Amen!" shouted Hank from Sewing Arts. "Ever heard of slippers?!"

"There will also be a blank note viewers can download and create their own messages on," Delilah concluded, more or less pleased with her pitch.

Margo raised an eyebrow, shaking her head in opposition. "No way. That's ridiculous. The idea would only appeal to people living in big cities—*if* that. What about people who don't live in apartment buildings?" she snorted. "Way too exclusionary. You can't think like that."

"This is New York City. Everybody lives in an apartment building," Delilah countered.

Agnes furled her brow and agreed with Margo, reminding Delilah that *Domestic Bliss* is a traditional television show marketed toward the thirty-one- through sixty-five-year-old demographic throughout the entire country, and edgy concepts aimed at hip urbanites unfortunately aren't proper fare.

"Isn't that in our mission statement?" Margo said, looking straight at Delilah.

After the meeting, Delilah trudged to her corner office on the forty-fourth floor feeling worthless, defeated, and, above all else, frustrated—crawling out of her own skin frustrated. Wondering why everything has to be so hard, she plopped down in her ergonomic, black leather desk chair and, needing to vent, began a fuming e-mail to Sofia, which she knew she probably wouldn't end up sending. Before she had a chance to finish composing the message, however, her morning cappuccinos caught up with her.

Hoping to rub a little salt in her competition's fresh wound after that oh-so-rough meeting, Margo Hart happened to stop by Delilah's office while she was in the ladies' room. "Knock knock," she sang in a high-pitched voice, lightly tapping her knuckles against the door, which Delilah had left wide open. Upon entering the space, Margo took a moment or two to curiously pry around—leaning toward the wall with her hands clasped behind her back to take a closer look at a framed photograph of Delilah shaking hands with the first lady in the China Room at the White House, glancing at a tall stack of manuscripts in the far corner, frowning at an open can of Mountain

Dew on Delilah's desk—and eventually decided to leave a "thoughtful" Post-it note on Delilah's computer monitor. She couldn't help seeing, and reading, the e-mail to Sofia:

> TO: Sofia_trawler@domesticbliss.com
> FROM: Delilah_white@domesticbliss.com
> DATE: July 1
> SUBJECT: SHOOT ME NOW!!!
>
> ugh . . . segment pitch meeting was a bona fide disaster—very upsetting! i feel so depressed. sometimes i can't help but wonder what i'm doing wasting my time here tolerating such unnecessary crap from moron potpies who are afraid to take a risk. so sick of it! when did it become a crime to think outside the box?! i know i joke about it, but days like today make me want to walk out that door and never come back. i might be at my wit's end with this place. really! *sigh* . . . can't wait to get the hell out of here! NOT looking forward to taping the damn show tonight. (is it time for "happy hour" yet? Calgon, take me away!)

Taking full advantage of what she viewed as a quickly closing window of golden opportunity, Margo paused—looking out the large window at the panoramic view of New York City's steely skyline—and rationalized that this situation presented itself. It's not as if she entered Delilah's office intending to read her private e-mail or commit a secret e-crime. Things happen for a reason, she reminded herself—and this was meant to be.

Then, like a jaguar moving swiftly with purpose, she bent over the keyboard and began typing at lightning speed, her slender fingers skillfully dancing across the keys. Margo erased Sofia's address from the TO: field, replaced it with *Agnes_deville*

@domesticbliss.com, and clicked the SEND button. Then, careful to cover her tracks, she immediately deleted the message from Delilah's SENT mailbox and emptied the message from the TRASH box, smirking as it disappeared, never to be seen again. And finally, clicking the PREVIOUS PAGE button repeatedly, Margo restored the computer screen to exactly the way she found it, sans e-mail. All in less than thirty seconds.

She stood up straight, smoothed her fiery hair, adjusted her pin-striped blazer, and strolled out of Delilah's office, imagining Agnes's facial expression when she reads the incriminating subject line "SHOOT ME NOW!!!" No Post-it note necessary. Mission accomplished, thank you very much.

⁂

At the bonfire, the Trawlers have all the necessities covered, including the most critical element of all: s'mores! "Everybody grab a pointy stick, stab a marshmallow, and let the roasting begin!" Mrs. Trawler directs, planting herself on a blanket next to her husband. Margo and Delilah exchange knowing glances, as this is about as "camp" as you can get. Swept up in the spirit of the moment, Margo takes a bite out of Delilah's s'more. "How dreamy is that?" Delilah asks.

"Mmmm, sooo good! I want to marry that when I grow up," Margo moans, tilting her head back. Even she can't resist the delectable delight of warm chocolate and sweet toasted marshmallow sandwiched between two flaky graham crackers. "Although, on second thought, Preston's not so bad." She winks playfully. "Poor guy's probably still at the office slaving away on his new case. It sounds like a real doozy."

"What awful timing. It's such a bummer." Delilah pops the last bite into her mouth and licks a drop of chocolate off her pointer finger.

"Oh my God, I *so* want one of those," cousin Samantha whimpers to Lisa, eyeing a s'more as if it were the Hope Diamond.

"That looks freakin' delicious!" Lisa exclaims, salivating.

"Totally!" Samantha agrees. "Like, I'm not even kidding about how good that looks. Like, literally . . ."

"For real. Right?" Lisa asks.

"They may sound like ditzy Valley girls, but these young women actually represent the crème of the crop at Berkeley," Margo whispers to Delilah. "Comforting thought, isn't it?"

"Like, *yeah*, it is." Delilah smiles.

"They've gotta be at least two hundred calories apiece, wouldn't ya say?" Sam guesses, staring at the s'more.

"Well, let's think about this," Lisa advises. "Two graham crackers are 120 calories, a Hershey bar is 230 calories, so half would be 115, and then the marshmallows are what? Probably 100 calories?"

"One regular-size marshmallow is 49 calories, so two on a s'more makes it 98," Samantha, who earned a perfect score on the math portion of the SAT exam, informs her.

"So that's a total of 333 calories. Forget it. *So* not worth it! Like, not even close," Lisa, the human abacus, concludes.

"As if! You are so right. *Thank God* you're here and can talk some sense into me!"

"Oh my God," Lisa smiles, "right back at ya, babe."

"Alright everyone, I know this is what you've all been waiting for," Uncle Mark taunts, eyebrows mischievously wiggling up and down. "Fear not, I'm here to please the masses. I do take suggestions."

"Daddy . . . No. Seriously, Father, don't do this," Samantha begs, hiding her head in her hands.

Uncle Mark puts down his Jack Daniels and whips his guitar out from behind the log he's perched on. "Try and stop me. I expect you all to join in on the chorus," he announces before strumming his guitar with great gusto and belting out, "Jeremiah was a bullfrog!"

"Oh God, Daddy! I *beg* you to stop," Samantha pleads.

"I'll pay you cash!" Derek offers. "Small unmarked bills!"

Uncle Mark isn't the best singer in the world, but what he lacks in substance he makes up for in style, and it's just a few more verses before everyone has joined in with the rousing chorus. Most everyone, that is. Delilah spies Jack mouthing the words with impressive spirit. His head bops from side to side and his lips move convincingly, but zero sound escapes them.

Uncle Mark even forces poor Consuela to get in on the act when she comes to retrieve the leftover s'mores ingredients. "Ay caramba! No, sir, I don't sing. Really," she insists.

"It's all *you*, Consuela! Take it away!" Uncle Mark commands, pointing at her.

Consuela lets out an exaggerated sigh, throws her plump arms up in the air, and in her thick Spanish accent speaks the words: "Joy to thee feeshies in thee deep blue sea."

Delilah whistles and howls. "Yeah, Consuela! You rock!"

"Joy to you and me!" She finishes dramatically with a curtsey and returns to the house, laughing and murmuring, "Está loco! Dios mío . . ."

After Uncle Mark retires his guitar for the night, Mr. Trawler asks if anybody has a good ghost story they'd like to share. Surprisingly, Margo says she's got one, but it could be too terrifying to tell. "Oh, honey, out with it!" Blythe encourages, still sipping on a vodka tonic. "Scare us good."

Margo obliges, opening her eyes wide as she speaks, and

growing more and more animated as her story continues. Sure enough, her chilling tale of the unhinged rich debutante whose perm went horribly awry—causing all her hair to fall out and her mind to snap—sends shivers down everyone's spines. Well, at least two of the women's spines anyway—and Derek's. "According to the legend," Margo, quite enjoying herself, explains in a low, eerie tone, "the unhinged rich debutante's hair never grew back. *Never.* After she bludgeoned her hairdresser and several innocent junior hair-washers to death, she escaped deep into the Catskill Mountains, where to this day she patiently lurks, waiting for her next victim with beautiful, healthy, vitamin-rich hair. If you listen closely enough, you can sometimes hear her haunting whisper: 'Salon perm? No, Ogilvy. You . . . Must . . . DIE!!!' "

Sofia, hardly amused, lets out a sarcastic bloodcurdling scream for dramatic effect, which legitimately terrorizes poor Samantha, inspiring her to shriek at decibels unhealthy to man. Lisa grabs her hand, comforting her. "Jesus Christ . . . ," Samantha stammers. "W . . . what the hell?"

"I'm sorry, sweetie," Sofia apologizes, laughing—now thoroughly entertained. "I was just trying to give Ms. Hitchcock over here a hard time. I didn't mean to freak you out."

"It's okay, Sam," Jack soothes. "Go to your safe warm place. Everything's fine."

"Oh, come on, you jerks! Leave the poor girl alone," Aunt Deb comes to her daughter's defense. "Enough's enough."

Once Sam finishes cackling so hard that 150-calorie wine cooler almost shoots out of her nostrils, she announces she's ready to turn in. It's after ten thirty and for most everyone there it has been a long day that included braving hectic holiday travel. Slowly but surely, everyone follows her lead, welcoming the prospect of a good night's sleep in the mountains.

Margo brushes the sand from her clothes and gives Delilah a big, warm hug. "I'm glad we smoothed things out. I feel a lot better about everything."

"Me too," Delilah smiles. "I really do."

"Should we head back to the house?"

"It's such a great night." Delilah exhales, gazing up at the glowing abundance of stars. It's a rare occasion, if not a Christmas miracle, that she can actually see the stars in Manhattan. Of course, there she sometimes sees stars of a different nature, though they seldom interest her. "Think I'm gonna stay out here a little while longer and enjoy this gorgeous night. I'll be in soon. See you in the morning?"

"You bet, sweetie," Margo purrs.

"Wait up!" Sofia calls out to Margo. She gives Delilah a quick peck on the cheek. "You know where everything in the house is. Just help yourself to whatever you need, okay? Oh! Consuela left you fresh towels in the bathroom attached to your room."

"Thanks, Sofe. Sweet dreams."

"See you tomorrow, D." She ambles toward the house with Margo. "G'night!"

Warming her hands by the dying fire, Delilah lets out a big yawn and looks around for her shoes.

"Behind you and to your left," Jack directs, approaching her.

"Thanks." Delilah slides into her funky rainbow flip-flops and puts on her lilac hoodie sweater, zipping it up the front.

"That was quite a yawn," Jack observes. "I hate to say it, but how about a rain check on that moonlight swim?"

"I hate to say it, but I think that's a good idea. I'm beat," Delilah admits, surprised that she's so sleepy. On a typical weeknight she's accustomed to being up until at least one in the morning working on the show. It's rare for her to be relaxed enough to feel legitimately tired at this "reasonable" hour, and she interprets it as a positive sign that her brain has sent the signal to her body that it's finally on vacation.

"A superhip Trawler bonfire will do that to ya. We do not mess around."

"Are you kidding me? I love it! Your family's wonderful."

"Yeah, we'll see what you say at the end of the weekend," Jack teases. "Shall we?" He nods toward the warmly illuminated house, extending his hand to help Delilah up.

"We shall," she smiles.

Wordplay

"Hey, what are you doing up?" Jack asks Delilah. It's one in the morning and she startled him when she tiptoed into the kitchen without making a peep.

"I woke up a little while ago and needed a drink of water," she says, bleary-eyed, hair in pigtails.

"There's some bottled water in the fridge. Help yourself."

"Thanks." Delilah grabs a bottle and joins Jack at the long rectangular kitchen table, hand-hewn of richly grained walnut wood and imported from Milan, where he sits doing the crossword puzzle and eating chocolate cake. "What are you doing up?"

"I'm always up late." He puts down his pen. "I'm not very good at falling asleep."

"Me neither," Delilah replies, now fully coherent and adjusted to the light.

"Insomnia?"

"No, not really. More like it's just hard for me to drift off. It can take hours. But once I'm out, I'm usually good to go until morning, so it's not that bad." She unscrews the cap and takes a sip of water. "How 'bout you?"

"Same here, mostly. My mind starts racing, and the next thing I know, it's three in the morning and I'm making imaginary lists."

"Yes, but are they alphabetized?"

"Only on Wednesdays," he jokes.

"Nice . . ." Delilah smiles, appreciating his wit. "Believe me, I hear ya. How's the puzzle?"

"Brutal! The Friday *New York Times* slays me every time. I don't know why I come back for more. It's sadistic, really."

She laughs. "I assume you've already filled in the standards."

"Such as?"

"Well, for starters, you can almost always count on *Ono.*"

"Lennon's wife," Jack responds, amused. "Alright . . . *Erne?*" he challenges.

"Seashore bird," she answers immediately. *"Etui?"*

"Fancy needle case," he replies, grinning. "But of course. *Épée?*"

"Fencing sword. *Elba?*"

"Exile isle!" he blurts with growing energy. "Diva's solo?"

"*Aria!* I see?"

"AHA!" Jack triumphantly hollers, smiling bright enough that the darling dimple in his left cheek appears. *"A-H-A!"*

Delilah quickly holds a finger to her lips, leaning forward. "Shhh! We're gonna wake the whole house up," she giggles. "The Trawlers'll never ask me back."

"Alright, alright . . ." He eyes her closely. "I can see I'm not dealing with an amateur here."

"Wanna go three and three?"

"What's that?"

"I answer three clues and then you answer three. We do it together until we've filled in all the squares," Delilah explains.

He considers the idea. "I've always thought of the crossword as a solitary activity, but hey, why not? Of course, this could take us until morning to finish. Let's not forget that this is the Friday puzzle."

"Nonsense. We're very bright sadists." She reaches for the puzzle and pen.

A half hour later all the squares are filled in, and Delilah and Jack are fairly confident they've made up only one—*maybe* two—words. Jack insists *qortle* is an African beach bird, but Delilah has her doubts.

Jack glances at his untouched cake. "Can I interest you in a slice?"

"Oooh, that looks tempting. Chocolate cake?" she teases.

"I'll take that as a yes," he quickly fires back, rising to fix her a plate.

Before they dig in, Delilah holds a forkful of gooey cake out in front of her. "Cheers," she says, knocking her fork against his. "So what was with the Milli Vanilli act earlier tonight?"

Jack cocks an eyebrow, impressed. "You caught that?"

"Busted. Don't worry, your secret's safe with me."

"I'm a horrible singer, the *worst*!" He makes an ugly face. "I feel like a moron when I sing—or should I say *attempt* to sing? It gives me the willies. I don't even hum in the shower. I'd scare the water."

"Come on, I highly doubt you're that bad."

"Well, that's 'cause you haven't heard me. Trust me, nobody should have to."

"Ooookay, subject dropped. You're no Sinatra." Delilah takes a sip of water and pauses a moment. "Soooo . . . What are these racing thoughts of yours about? If you don't mind me asking, that is."

"Not at all. Ask away," Jack welcomes. "I guess I'm mostly thinking about New York these days."

"Really? What about it?"

"I'm moving there in a couple weeks."

"No way! I didn't know that," Delilah exclaims, grinning.

"There's lots of things you don't know about me," he winks.

"Excellent point. What brings you to Manhattan?"

"That would be one underresourced second-grade classroom in Harlem. I'm doing the New York City Teaching Fellows program."

"Wow. That's amazing. I've heard of the program, but I don't really know that much about it." She takes another bite of cake.

"Basically, there's a huge shortage of teachers in New York, and the Fellows program takes educators from all over the country and places them in the city's most needy classrooms." Jack gulps his milk. "The pay's not exactly a small fortune, but it's a nice opportunity to work with some great kids in a different environment. Hopefully, I'll be able to help 'em some, assuming they don't terrorize me and have me crying like a baby on the first bus back to Chicago or, better yet, stuff me inside a locker and leave me for dead."

"Stop it. That's incredible. I'm a serious teacher fan," she admits. "Last September I was on *Domestic Bliss* discussing tips for packing a nutritious and delicious school lunch and I insisted on wearing a Ravinia School T-shirt, which is where my sister, Francesca, teaches. The Wardrobe Department did *not* want me wearing that shirt on air, but I made a big ol' stink about it and somehow ended up spending a majority of my segment jabbering away about my 'amazing sister, Miss White' and how extraordinary teachers are. I didn't even have time to talk about the healthy desserts kids won't want to trade." Delilah shakes her head. "I still can't believe they let me back on the air after that."

"You kidding me? How could they not?" Jack smiles, inhaling his cake.

"*And* I can't believe Sofia didn't mention you're moving to New York. I think it'll be a great move."

"Yeah, well, I just hope it's not a stupid move. It all sounded great on paper, but now that I'm really doing it—relocating, leaving everything behind, and starting from scratch in a new city—it's only now hitting me as reality. If that makes any sense. I've reached the point where nervousness is slowly starting to creep in and make me ask, 'What the hell are you doing, Jack?' Though, it'll be great to live closer to my family. Granted, I may sing a very different tune once I'm an official resident of the tri-state area and Aunt Kerri has me coming over left and right to open up mysterious glass jars of God-knows-what for her that have been in the refrigerator since 1972, and my mom keeps begging me to let her give me a haircut *herself*, and my dad—'Johnny Guitar'—forces me to keep time to the flippin' 'Rainbow Connection' with a stupid tambourine I've dreamed of lighting on fire since I was eight years old. But, what can I say? I miss being around the fools." Jack stops to breathe and notices Delilah staring at him, captivated. He self-consciously runs his fingers through his hair. "I should have given you a stun gun to use on me, or at least told you to feel free to stop me at any time."

"Absolutely not," Delilah insists, touched by his response. "Know what?"

"Hmm?"

She smiles warmly, her blue eyes sparkling. "It's gonna be wonderful."

Jack looks at her across the table, sitting Indian-style in an old faded gray Tinkerbell T-shirt and navy pajama bottoms.

"How do you know?" he asks.

"Because just listening to you is inspiring. Your new students in Harlem? They have no idea how lucky they are."

"Thank you," he says, smiling back at her. Pausing, he appears to really stop and contemplate her. "I'm sorry for going on and on like that about me me me. I never do that!"

"Ain't no thing but a chicken wing," Delilah assures him, scraping the last bit of chocolate icing off her plate. "Mmmm, yummy cake."

Jack lets out a hearty laugh. He's got no clue what's going to come out of this curious woman's mouth next. "Well, you have to let me make it up to you. Now you owe me your story. Has Sofia arranged plans for you girls for tomorrow night?"

"I don't think so. I think we decided we're gonna play things by ear."

"Do you suppose she'd mind if I steal you away for a couple of hours and take you to dinner?"

Out of nowhere, butterflies arrive in the pit of Delilah's stomach. Up until this point she had been so involved in their conversation and having such a good time that she never stopped to consider Jack as anything more than Sofia's sweet and goofy corn-loving cousin (with that ridiculously adorable dimple).

"I think she'd be pretty understanding," Delilah tells him, strangely excited by the notion of going on a date with Harlem's most eligible new teacher. She tries to wipe the smile off her face, but it's not much use. This may not be what she was expecting to happen this weekend, but she's not complaining. Not at all.

"Good. Seven thirty okay?"

"Sounds good to me." *Yes! I love seven thirty! I love the Fourth of July! God bless America!*

Jack glances at his watch and does a double take. "It's three in the morning!"

Rise and Shine

Delilah stumbles out onto the sunny deck around nine the next morning to find Sofia and Derek cooling down after their five-mile run on the beach. She squints at them in their sporty athletic gear and shakes her head in wonder. Delilah is not a morning person or a running person. If she's ever spotted running in the morning, it's safe to assume she's either late or being hunted.

"Good morning, lady. Sleep okay?" Sofia greets her.

"Good morning. I slept great," she yawns. "I can't believe you guys already went for a run. What'd you people do, get up at six?"

"Did you want to join us?" Derek asks while touching his toes, giving Delilah her first good chuckle of the day.

Sofia points out the breakfast buffet Consuela has set up, and Delilah helps herself to coffee and—*What's that? Could it be? You've gotta be kidding me. I can't believe it . . . a bowl of Berry Patriotic Breakfast Pudding.* "My Lord, does your family ever miss an episode?" she asks incredulously.

"Nope. My mom TiVos every one of them. She's a fanatic. My dad's been threatening to hire a counselor and stage a TiVo intervention. By the way, that pudding's actually delicious. I already had a bowl."

"Where is everyone?" Delilah asks, sitting down at a table with a big white-and-yellow-striped umbrella facing west toward the lake.

"Let's see . . . My mom and Aunt Deb went into town to pick up some last-minute items for the party tomorrow; Sam, Lisa, and Margo are doing water yoga in the pool; and my dad and Uncle Mark are probably on the ninth hole about now."

Delilah oh so casually inquires, "Where's Jack?"

Sofia looks at her like she knows a secret and smiles, sitting down next to her. "Jack?"

Detecting her "tell," Delilah opts not to take the bait just yet. She stretches her back and slowly sips her coffee. "So, am I the last person up this morning?"

"If you are, it would be understandable."

Delilah leisurely heaps another spoonful of sugar into her coffee. "It's nice out today. Not a cloud in the sky. I'd guess it's—what?—Probably a perfect eighty degrees?"

Sofia can't take it any longer. "Mercy! Jack's been up for an hour. I think he went for a dip in the lake," she smirks.

"It's too early in the morning for me to be coy," Delilah surrenders. "I need caffeine. Lots 'n' lots of sweet, delicious, potent caffeine."

"I need a shower," Derek announces, smelling his pits. "Whoa, man stink! Wait for me to go to the beach?"

"You bet," Sofia agrees.

Once he's in the house, Sofia turns to Delilah, crossing her arms. *"So . . ."*

Delilah double-checks to make sure nobody's around. "Perhaps I should ask *you* the same question. How come you didn't tell me about your cousin?" She smiles like a schoolgirl.

"Jack?"

Delilah gives her a look. "No, Samantha." Then she adds, "*Yes*, Jack!"

"I actually wasn't sure if he was gonna be able to make it this weekend." Sofia sips her coffee. "He's been so busy getting ready to move to New York and tying up all the loose ends in Chicago. I didn't find out he was definitely coming until yesterday."

"Yes, but you could have at least *mentioned* you have a charming, adorable cousin who happens to be moving to New York! Some best friend you are."

"Jack's the greatest," Sofia declares, smiling. "Isn't he hysterical? I had a feeling you'd like him. I'm happy you two hit it off."

"Wait. Did he say something to you about last night?"

"Not much, really." Sofia nonchalantly examines her fingernails. "Just that you stayed up late talking. Oh! And something about a qortle?"

Delilah chuckles, shaking her head. "There's no such thing as a qortle. The guy is out of his mind. So, that's it?" She stirs her coffee, tapping her spoon musically against the mug. "That's all he said?"

"Well, that and he wanted to know if I'd mind if he took you out tonight. Delilah, you have a date!"

Delilah beams for a moment, but then quickly reins it in. "Oh, please. It's no big thing. Totally casual . . . *just* dinner," she insists, having been on more than enough dates with more than enough men to know by now that they rarely amount to much more than a story to laugh about with her girlfriends over Sunday brunch. No use getting excited over somebody until at least the fourth date and a visit to his apartment to make sure he doesn't live like a college frat boy or have a girlfriend. Or, heaven forbid, *both*!

"I don't care what you say, we're still going shopping later to pick out something amazing for you to wear on your *no big thing* date tonight," Sofia declares.

"That's below the belt. And I've been doing so well too. I haven't so much as entered a department store in three weeks. You're evil."

"So, anyway," Sofia suddenly blurts, "you can just pee in your pants during the movie or play and nobody will know?! Why, that's genius! Theater Pants! Pee away! Let the river flow!"

What the fuh? Delilah has no idea what in the name of Martha Stewart is going on.

"I don't know what you women are talking about over there, and I don't know if I want to," Jack teases, walking barefoot toward the breakfast buffet.

Aha. Now it makes sense. Delilah turns around to say hello, but words suddenly escape her when she lays eyes on Jack—dressed in navy swim trunks with an iPod sticking out of his back pocket—and his scrumptiously defined six-pack. *Don't stare! Do not stare. Avert your eyes. Oh no, you're staring. You are staring up a storm. You're the staring queen. You're not drooling, are you?!* she thinks to herself, daintily wiping her mouth with her napkin. As if on cue, the butterflies return to the pit of her stomach, only this time they're dirty dancing to the song "Teacher's Pet."

"Good morning, sunshine!" Jack says to her.

Move Over, Esther Williams

Having decided to check out the action on the local waterfront scene, Delilah, Sofia, Margo, Sam, and Lisa lie on the busy public beach soaking up the morning sun.

"It's hot as Hades! Anyone want to go in the water?" Delilah asks, lying on her back with her head propped up on a pillow made of sand.

"I don't know. Do you think it's clean?" Margo asks from beneath her enormous white sun hat, which she claims once belonged to Joan Crawford.

"I've been swimming in this lake all my life. It's clean as can be," Sofia swears. "I'll go with you, D."

"Not me," Sam says. "Want to play backgammon, Leese?"

"Sure. I'm way too bloated to be running around the shore," Lisa grumbles. "I feel like a frickin' Macy's Thanksgiving Day Parade balloon. My visit from the feminine fairy's coming, like, anytime now. Care to be white or red?"

"Red, please." Sam begins setting up the board.

"Did you know backgammon has been around for almost five thousand years?" Lisa asks, positioning her white pieces. "I mean, like, can't you just see Sophocles and Euripides going head to head? Being like, πρόκειται έτσι να κλωτσήσω το γάιδάρο σας σε αυτό το παιχνίδι!"

"So true! So true!" Sam laughs. "Ο γάιδάρος μου φαίνεται τεράστιος σε αυτό το κοστούμι, είναι σκληρά γυναίκα."

"Ah, but isn't it?" Lisa replies. "I might have to quote you on that."

"Wait a second," Delilah interrupts. "You speak Greek?"

They both nod and go right back to their apparently hilarious conversation, tuning out the rest of the non-Mensa-affiliated world.

"Wow. Guess it's just us," Delilah tells Sofia, rising from her white and pink polka-dot towel.

"That bikini's adorable, by the way," Sofia compliments Delilah as they wade knee-deep in the cool water. The bright hot sun beats down on them, causing them to shield their eyes with their hands while they chat.

"Thanks. I got it especially for this weekend. I couldn't wait to put it on! This is the first chance I've had to wear a bathing suit all summer. Can you believe it?" Delilah lets out a cathartic sigh. "It feels so good to be out of the office! I hardly know what to do with myself!"

Sofia smiles mischievously. "In that case? We're goin' under."

"Ready?" Delilah grins. "On the count of three. One . . . Two . . . THREE!"

They both disappear beneath the cobalt water. Splishing and splashing around, these powerful, savvy Manhattan businesswomen are suddenly no different from the other littler kids playing in the lake.

ꟹ ꟸ

After a refreshing swim and a leisurely stroll along the water's edge, Delilah and Sofia join up with the other girls, Derek, and Jack aboard *Lola*, the Trawlers' fastest speedboat. Derek takes the steering wheel, getting a kick out of referring to himself as the Skipper. Jack, who refuses to let Derek call him Gilligan, tosses a pair of water skis overboard and dives into the water. It doesn't take long to notice that he's a natural on skis, zipping through Lake Minnonqua, giving the Skipper the thumbs-up sign to go faster. Delilah knows a thing or two about water-skiing and is impressed. Later, when Jack's back on board, she tells him all about the time she did a show skiing performance to the song "Cupid" in front of her entire camp.

"No you didn't," he laughs, trying to picture it in his mind's eye.

"Oh, I *did*—frilly costume, mint green bathing cap with big neon flowers, the whole nine yards."

Jack's smile widens. "Forgive me, but that's priceless."

When it's finally Delilah's turn to give the skis a whirl, Jack hollers from the boat, "Hey! Do your routine!"

"What?" she shouts from the water, bobbing up and down in a fluorescent orange life vest. "I can't hear you!"

"I WANT TO SEE THAT ROUTINE FROM CAMP!"

"Oh yeah? Is that a dare?" she screams back, cupping her hands around her mouth.

"Why not?" Jack yells, smiling invitingly.

She gives the Skipper the thumbs-up, *Lola*'s engine roars, and for the first time in about a decade, Delilah's up and away on water skis. *I cannot believe I'm doing this. This is crazy . . . This is completely insane. I must've fallen directly on my head as a child.*

❧

Margo, watching the impromptu aquatic entertainment from the front of the boat, wonders why a tasty morsel such as Jack Walsh is wasting his time batting his lashes at Delilah. Her eyes graze over his outstanding body, then she grabs a bottle of suntan lotion and saunters up beside him.

"I don't want to miss the big show," she says and smiles, sticking out her picture-perfect size 34C bust, which didn't come cheap and is carefully accentuated by a sexy white bikini halter top that leaves little to the imagination when wet.

"Something tells me it's gonna be good," Jack predicts without taking his eyes off Delilah.

Delilah swivels, spins, and dances with style and ease, as if she's a Vegas showgirl on skis and has been doing this all her life. Skimming along the water with the wind rushing through her hair, she feels exhilarated and free. This vacation is turning out to be far better than Delilah expected. Just what the doctor ordered.

Back on the boat, Margo slowly eyes Jack, admiring his broad shoulders, strong, capable arms, and powerful torso. "Your back is getting an awful lot of color. It looks like you might be burning. Want me to put some suntan lotion on for you?"

"Sure," he replies, tightening his towel around his waist. "That'd be great. Thanks. I didn't even feel myself burning. I don't want to end up looking like a lobster."

"No, that would not be good." Margo squirts some lotion into the palm of her hand before gently massaging it onto Jack's muscular back. "Although, lobster *is* quite delicious. You must work out. What do you do, lift weights?"

"Nah, I hate the gym. I mostly run and ride my bike around Chicago, weather permitting, of course." Jack's eyes remain fixed on Delilah, who now appears to be doing a disco move straight out of *Saturday Night Fever*.

"I love bicycling. Do you ride alone?" Margo casually inquires, hands gliding down his back. "Or do you like to ride your bike with anyone special?"

"Like with a trainer you mean? Nah, I'm really not that serious about it. I just do it for fun." Jack realizes that Margo's still slowly rubbing lotion on his lower back, making tiny circles with her thumbs. He tenses. "My girlfriend rides with me on the weekends when she has time off from teaching."

"She's a teacher too?" Margo doesn't skip a beat.

"Yeah. She's teaching summer school this session—A.A."

Margo nods her head. "She's an alcoholic?"

"Advanced algebra. That's why she wasn't able to make it this weekend."

Continuing to work the lotion into Jack's back, Margo uses her weight to knead his muscles. "I see . . . That's too bad. You must be disappointed."

"I am. It would've been great to have her here." He laughs, nodding toward Delilah.

Delilah shakes her fanny before motioning her arms as if she's pulling back and then releasing an arrow from a bow. But instead of smiling like a love-struck cherubic cupid, she frowns at the sight of Margo practically licking Jack's back. *Alright, alright, that's more than enough suntan lotion. You can stop anytime you'd like now, Margo. This is not the* Love Boat *dammit! Get your hungry paws off him! Better yet, push her overboard, Jack.* Distracted, Delilah forgets the golden rule of show skiing: pay attention to your surroundings. She doesn't even notice the zooming speedboat with a silver lightning bolt painted across its hood pass her on the right, creating mean, choppy waves. Lurching forward, Delilah bends sloppily at the waist, leaning precariously toward her left, and then toward her right. Cold water sprays her in the eyes, blurring her vision as she clings on for dear life. *Don't wipe out! DON'T WIPE OUT!!!* she commands herself, fighting to maintain balance. *"Stay standing!"*

Back aboard *Lola*, Margo grimaces as she watches Delilah wobble to and fro and then, finally, at last, gain control. "Whoa. Close call. What's your girlfriend's name?" she asks Jack, continuing to rub his shoulders.

"Carly, but people call her Cee-Cee."

"My boyfriend has to work this weekend as well," Margo adds, patting Jack on the back and screwing the cap back on the lotion bottle. "I think you're now safely protected from the sun."

"Thank you kindly."

"My pleasure. I've got your back, *Jack*," she winks.

Out on the water, Delilah—pleased to see that Margo has finally managed to stop caressing Jack—nimbly glides over the wakes. Focusing intensely, she prepares for her big showstopping finale. *You can do this. You're a giant spaz, but you're not going to wipe out. Use the force, Delilah. Be one with the towrope. Feel the towrope. The towrope is your friend*, she guides herself. Emoting as if she were dazzling a sold-out crowd, she slowly and carefully removes her left foot from the ski—leaving it floating behind her—grabs the towrope with her free foot, and gracefully extends both arms above her head like a ballerina.

Everyone on the boat goes buck wild—hooting and hollering—clapping in surprised delight.

"*Nice* toehold," Jack comments to Margo, jaw semi-agape. "Very nice."

"She's just full of tricks, that one," Margo remarks.

⁂

When Delilah climbs back aboard the boat, soaking wet and shivering, Jack greets her with her towel and a look of amazement.

"Pretty silly, huh?" She wrings out her long, dark hair, wrapping the towel around her shoulders, trying to get warm. "It's much better with the bathing cap on. Believe me."

"On a scale of one to ten, that was a twelve!"

"It was awesome!" the Skipper agrees. "You're like a mermaid."

"Totally!" Samantha chimes in. "You could, like, perform at Sea World or something! That was so cool, Delilah!"

"It's like having our own little Shamu right here with us on the boat," Margo says, grinning as if her mouth were stuffed full with SweeTarts.

"I'm such a dork!" Delilah smiles self-consciously, aware that everyone's looking at her. Her sassy pink bikini has crept up her derrière, and she'd sure love to do something about it. As a general rule, however, she tries not to pick her butt in front of an audience. *Nothing quite like showing your date for the evening your big fat giant wedgie*, she thinks to herself. *Very classy.*

This Past Wednesday

Preston, exhausted and starving, arrived home late after a grueling day at the firm to find Margo standing at the kitchen island—Cole Porter playing softly in the background, candles lit—whipping up his favorite meal, fillet of Kobe steak and béarnaise sauce. Wearing nothing but sexy-as-hell ivory lace panties, a skimpy matching camisole that revealed plenty of cleavage plus her midriff, and shiny come-hither red–painted toenails, she grinned and poured him a glass of cabernet. "Welcome home, baby."

He paused to absorb the gorgeous sight of Margo expertly dicing shallots, her red hair cascading down around her milky white shoulders, and all but forgot about his tiring day. "I couldn't be happier to be here, m'lady," he said and smiled, inhaling the invigorating aroma. "That's not Kobe and béarnaise, is it?"

"Mmmm. I wanted to make you something special."

Preston approached her from behind and clasped his hands around her waist, burying his nose in her freshly washed hair. "And why is that? What's the catch?" He slowly kissed her neck. "Because I know there's a catch."

Margo spun around and looked him in the eyes. "And how do you know that?"

He kissed her forehead. "Because I know you."

She looked away from him and sighed, her shoulders slumping slightly. "I hate it when you're right."

"What is it, gumdrop?" He kissed her right cheek. "Tell me."

"You're not going to like this," she said, frowning.

"I like this little outfit you're wearing."

Margo cocked her head to the side and grinned flirtatiously. "This old thing?"

"Mmmm, that old thing." He kissed her left cheek. "So what is it?"

She ran her hands up and down Preston's sides and removed his tie, tossing it haphazardly on the shiny black slate floor, trying to distract him. "I'm not happy about this. Trust me." She slowly traced her fingernails down his back. "It's not what I wanted."

"Say it." He kissed the tip of her nose.

"Alright. Promise you won't get mad?"

"Margo Jessica Hart, stop stalling," Preston urged with growing impatience. "You're starting to make me nervous."

"Okay, okay." She cringed before quickly blurting, "We have to cancel our trip this weekend. I can't go to Martha's Vineyard with you."

Preston recoiled, placing his drink down with a harsh clink on the black granite counter. "Dammit, Margo! I *knew* this was gonna happen."

"Knew what was gonna happen?"

"That *something* would come up for you—probably something work related—and it would take precedence over everything else," he huffed. "If I'm not mistaken, it's the fifth time this has happened in a matter of weeks."

"Baby, come on. That's not fair. You know damn well how much I've been looking forward to this weekend. I can't believe you'd even question that!"

"Are you telling me I'm wrong?"

"Well . . . *no*," she said, pouting.

"Are you telling me you haven't spent practically every night since Memorial Day working late? Are you suggesting you haven't become obsessed with landing this promotion?"

"Don't play prosecuting attorney with me, Preston," Margo warned with a chilling stare. "I'm not up on the stand."

"Half the time when I call you at the show, your annoyingly perky assistant, Caca—"

"Her name is *Coco*," Margo interrupted, still glaring at him.

"Whatever. She tells me you're not there, and then when I call you on your cell phone, you don't pick up."

"You know perfectly well that if I'm not in my office, then I'm in the studio, and cell phones are strictly forbidden in there. My God! Why are you suddenly acting suspicious? I'm trying to earn the promotion of a lifetime! You know what it means to me, baby."

"Yes, but I thought we agreed that we were going to make a concerted effort to work on *us*. Excuse me for saying, but I don't see how this qualifies. If our relationship is really worth attempting to salvage like you claim it is, then maybe, just *maybe*, we should try spending some time together. How's that for a novel idea?"

"I told you I feel terrible about this," Margo whined, stamping her foot. "*Please*, baby, let's not fight. This isn't what either of us wants. I love you. *Of course* I want to be with you."

"So what is it then? Why can't you go to Martha's Vineyard?"

Margo crossed her arms defensively. "Because I found out today that Agnes was invited to Sofia's Fourth of July party and she's going. She'll be spending all weekend in the Catskills, Preston, *with Delilah*—under the same roof. I'd be an idiot to let

Delilah have all that time alone with her. She's my only competition, and Agnes loves her. The last thing I need to do right now is stand back and let the two of them enjoy quality tea time."

Preston's baffled expression said it all. "So, just to be straight . . . You're telling me that you're ditching our vacation, which we've been planning for months, *to go on vacation with other people*? Do you have any idea how fucked up that is?" He began walking toward the foyer. "Sometimes I don't even know why I bother."

Margo sighed, chasing after him. "Do you think I *want* to hang out with Delilah White and Agnes Deville? Is that what you think I actually want?"

"You're positive Delilah's going?"

"*Yes.* She and Sofia are driving to the Catskills together Friday afternoon," Margo explained as she sashayed toward the stove to stir the béarnaise with a miniature wire whisk. "I'm telling you, baby, Delilah and I are neck and neck for this promotion right now. There's no guessing who has the upper hand. That little cake-hugger will take full advantage of the opportunity to have Agnes all to herself for three long days. She will kiss Agnes's wrinkly ass, she'll impress her with her 'brilliant' ideas, she'll cunningly position herself for executive producer, and she *will* gain the upper hand. Worst of all, I'll have let her do it. I *have* to accept Sofia's invitation, no matter how much I don't want to. Don't you see?" Her voice softened. "I have no other choice. Everything is at stake for me here. *Everything*. Please, Preston, try to understand."

"I do," he sighed, surrendering. "I do, babe. I just don't like it." He slowly came up beside her and placed a gentle kiss on her shoulder.

"Me neither," Margo groaned, leaning into him, resting her

head on his chest. "I hate it. All I want to do is to be able to spend time with you. Hell, all I want to do is to be able to spend the *whole weekend* curled up in your arms. I'm so sorry about this. I promise I'll make it up to you," she whispered, searching his eyes. "Promise, promise, promise . . ."

Unable to resist, Preston pulled her closer, wrapping his arms around her. "I understand, baby. I do. This is what you have to do to get what's yours."

Butt of Course

After lunch, riffling through the display racks at Bon Bon, a fancy-pants local boutique, Delilah finds herself thinking about Jack and how easy he is to be around. There's something different about him that she can't quite put her finger on. His thoughtful, playful nature and quiet confidence set him apart from the usual commitment-phobic Manhattan men with big dreams and even bigger egos. She typically manages to maintain a healthy sense of humor about New York City's vicious dating circuit, but every now and then she can't help but wish she were a lesbian or a nun. *Things sure would be easier*, she muses. Unfortunately, Delilah's interest in men precludes switching teams, and she's half Jewish. *Foiled again! Oy . . .*

"There it is!" Sofia exclaims, pointing across the store. "That's the one. Oh, I love it."

"Which dress? The red or the black?" Delilah asks.

Sofia thinks for a moment. "That's a good question. I have no idea. You need to try 'em both."

When Delilah exits the dressing room in the black wrap dress, Sofia whirls her straight back in to try on the red. "Too boring. But the cut's fantastic on you. I really like it."

Alfred, the leather Gaultier-panted salesperson with a peculiar accent, concurs, commanding her to "tock it off and try tha otha."

He claps his hands in approval, bouncing up and down, when Delilah returns several moments later wearing the red dress. "Mugnificahnt! You look lock a glahmorous lipstick!"

"You look great," Sofia agrees, trying not to laugh at Alfred.

Delilah feels comfortable and confident in the outfit and thinks it's just right for a nice, casual "no big thing" date. Plus, it will look sensational with her new black crocodile Hermès bag, which she waited patiently for six months to arrive and finally came last week (Margo's jealous reaction rendered it well worth the wait!). She's about to return to the dressing room when Alfred suddenly stops her.

"Wait a sawcond! Tarn around, Ms. Diva Homemakur," he instructs, swirling his pointer finger in a frantic circle. "Lot me see your backside." He scrunches up his forehead as if he's contemplating a complex mathematic equation. "Hmmm . . . No. Not so much. Not ruhlly. Negatory."

"What? You don't like it?" Delilah is perplexed by his blatant look of disapproval. "What's with that face? Oh my gosh, I'm making you ill. You're gonna vomit. I'm vile! Quick! Turn away! Don't look!"

A lightbulb seems to go off in his head. "Oooh! I know! Problem solved! Alfred's don eeet again!"

He flits to a nearby rack and grabs an overpriced black cardigan sweater. "Har you go, sweet pea," he singsongs, expertly tying the sweater around Delilah's waist. He examines her closely as though he were searching the sexy red dress for a lost contact lens. At last, he smiles with satisfaction. "Thar. Mach better. *This* I likey."

Delilah thoughtfully studies her reflection in the three-way mirror. Aside from the sweater (and harsh fluorescent lighting, which she's positive was invented by Satan), she likes what she sees. "I don't know . . . I kind of preferred it without the cardigan," she admits, hoping to avoid hurting Alfred's feelings.

"Well, interesting point, but tha sweatuh is very slimming, eef you catch my drift." He laughs semi-insanely, throwing his head back.

"Alfred?"

"Yos darling?"

"I have a butt."

"Well, yos, don't we all? Baht this way tha sweatuh makes you look more like a ten than a twolve. Eeet's all about meenimizing, you see."

Delilah looks at him deadpan. "Alfred, I've got some booty goin' on. It's okay, I'm fine with it. The way I see it, a woman trying to hide her butt with a sweater is the same thing as a man trying to hide his bald spot with a toupee: neither one is fooling anybody. *We all know* what's hiding underneath! Know what I'm saying?" She smiles affectionately, removing the sweater.

Horrified, the salesperson standing behind the cash register runs to the back of the store and disappears behind an aqua taffeta curtain.

"Oh no! I thunk Guntha hard you," Alfred frets. "He's so sahnsitive, that one!"

He flutters after Gunther—arms flailing—shouting, "Don't warry, darling, she wasn't talking about *your* toupee! Yours looks so rall! So furry and lifelike!"

Embarrassed, Delilah hides her face in her hands. "Oh, am I a jerk. Gunther hates me," she moans. "I feel terrible."

"I could tell he was wearing a toupee," Sofia whispers. "Poor guy. He should shave his head."

One Plus One Does Not Equal Two

Later that afternoon, in the dining room back at Cherry Pond, Consuela passes Sofia a sharp pair of garden clippers and instructs her to cut the tips off the ends of the French white tulips. "Now be sure to snip them on a diagonal," she stresses. "Es muy importante. I learned that from watching your show," she proudly adds.

"Got it." Sofia nods obediently. "Slantways it is. Where are these arrangements for anyway?"

"These are going in all of the bathrooms for the Independence Day soiree." Consuela drops a handful of trimmed flowers into a large silver bucket. "The professional florists are taking care of everything else. Your mother hired a massive team for tomorrow!"

"Well, this is our biggest party of the year," Sofia reminds her, raising a tulip to her nose and inhaling. "Mmmm . . . Mom lives for it."

When Mrs. Trawler had first hired Thor to plan the extravaganza, she had but one request: "This party can't be a rich, stuffy old bore; it has to be fun! A fabulous time with a capital *F*! A goddamn blast! Are we clear?" Thor had assured her that he understood—promising a celebration of America's birthday guests would be talking about for weeks, if not months, to follow—before promptly accepting her $200,000 check for deposit.

"Did you know that over two hundred invitations went out this year?" Consuela continues. "That's about cincuenta more than last year." She lifts the back of her hand to her forehead and sighs, seeming exhausted by the thought of it. "I love her dearly, but your mama's loca en la cabeza. I'm just glad the party's mostly outside. I don't want all those people traipsing around the house making a mess of things."

When the phone rings, Sofia puts down her scissors and answers it, surprised to hear Preston's voice on the other end. "Is everything okay?" she asks.

"Oh, um, yeah, yeah, everything's fine. I'm sorry to call your house. I found your number in Margo's Rolodex. Um, I'm actually just trying to get in touch with her. I've been calling and calling her cell, but she's not picking up."

"I think she's in the shower at the moment, that's probably why," Sofia deduces. "I can go get her if you want."

"Oh, no. No, you don't have to do that. Um, it isn't necessary."

"You sure everything's okay, Preston? You sound a little bit, well, frazzled. I hope your new case isn't too awful."

"My new case?"

"Margo told us about how you were assigned to one at the very last minute yesterday. I'm so sorry you had to cancel your trip because of it. I know she was really looking forward to going away with you."

For a few moments Preston remains silent, processing this information. When he speaks again, he no longer sounds "frazzled." He sounds downright suspicious. "Sofia, may I ask you something?"

"Of course." She cradles the phone against her shoulder in

order to free her hand and cuts another stem, adding it to the growing heap before her.

"Is Agnes Deville there?"

"Agnes? No."

"She's not?" he asks to be sure there's no misunderstanding.

"No, thank goodness. Can you imagine how awkward that would be with both Delilah and Margo here as well? *No thank you!* Why do you ask?"

"Let me be certain I have the facts straight," Preston states, swiftly morphing into lawyer mode. He clears his throat. "You did not invite Agnes to spend the weekend with you at Cherry Pond?"

Sofia puts down the scissors and flowers, offering Preston her undivided attention. "No, I did not. Preston, what's going on?"

"That's a damn good question," he says with a sigh. "I have no idea, but apparently we've both been duped."

"What are you talking about?"

"Margo told me *she* had to cancel our trip because Agnes was going to be at your house this weekend and she didn't want Delilah to have three whole days alone with her to win her over, which, like a pathetic fool, I believed. God I'm stupid."

"Preston, you're not stupid," Sofia gently assures him. "Margo's your *girlfriend*; of course you're gonna believe her. But wait, hold on. Let *me* make sure I've got the facts straight. You don't really have a new case? Margo told you *I* invited *Agnes* to spend the weekend here?"

"Indeed she did, and *no*, I do not have a new case. Then, about half an hour ago, who should call the apartment looking for Margo? None other than Agnes Deville herself. She asked me to have Margo call her back *at home. In the city. As soon as possible. She said it was urgent.*"

"Whoa. Whoa whoa whoa," Sofia stammers, unable to think

of anything remotely intelligent to say as she digests this news. Rising off the chair, she begins to pace around the living room.

"My thoughts exactly."

"I . . . I don't know what to say. Margo's obviously up to something, although I can't imagine what. And I wonder what Agnes could've been calling her about that's so urgent? What's so important that it couldn't have waited until—"

"Know what?" interrupts Preston. "Will you please just let Margo know I called and wished to pass along the message that Agnes phoned the apartment this afternoon looking for her *and* that Ms. Deville and I subsequently had an interesting little chat?"

"Of course," Sofia soothes him, sensing how hurt he is. "Of course I'll tell her. Preston, are you okay? I'm worried about—"

"Me?" he cuts her off again. "I'm fine . . . *fine*," he lies. "Um, but I actually have to get going. Could you please just be sure to relay the message?"

"Absolutely," she promises. "I'll let Margo know as soon as she gets out of the shower. You know, Preston, you're more than welcome to join us. The party tomorrow night's gonna be huge. I haven't seen you since the December Gala; it would be great to catch up, honestly. I can give you directions on how to get here. I can't imagine traffic will be bad right now. Why don't you hop in the car and drive up?"

"I appreciate the offer, really, but I don't feel much like celebrating. Not now."

Sofia sighs, her stomach churning. "I understand, but let me give you my cell phone number just in case." She recites the number, adding, "The offer still stands if you change your mind."

"Thanks, Sofia. Uh, I should really get going. Have a good holiday." He abruptly hangs up, leaving her flabbergasted.

Sofia's mind races as she grabs two tulips by their heads, crumpling their pale, delicate petals, and aggressively chops off their stems, horizontally, about six inches too high.

"Dios mío! Gimme those shears!" Consuela grabs them from Sofia. "No no no, that's not how we do it. Bad girl! Very bad!"

"I'm sorry," Sofia apologizes, snapping back to reality. "You better take over."

"Ooooh, you think?" Consuela snorts, shaking her head disapprovingly.

Sofia doesn't know what Margo's up to, but she does know two things for certain: she's glad she read the complete collection of Nancy Drew books when she was younger, and she has no intention whatsoever of telling Margo about Preston's phone call. No way. Not until she can manage to get to the bottom of whatever Margo thinks she has planned.

She decides to hold off on telling Delilah about this disturbing new development as well. No need to ruin her evening with Jack. She'll tell her everything first thing tomorrow morning.

Suddenly, it dawns on her that Preston might continue to try to get in touch with Margo, thus allowing Margo the opportunity to create more lies to cover up whatever she's scheming, which Sofia is now determined to uncover. She realizes there's only one thing she can do to try and prevent Preston from contacting Margo, and vice versa. And she knows she doesn't have much time to do it. Like a bat out of hell, Sofia zooms up the stairs toward Margo's suite, leaping over several steps at a time. She breathes a slight sigh of relief when she hears the shower running in Margo's bathroom and proceeds to frantically search the adjoined bedroom for Margo's cell phone. "Where are you, where are you, where are you?" she whispers. "Come to mama, you damn phone . . . Aha!" Sofia finds it on Margo's bedside table, snatches it up, and makes a run for it.

"Slow down, you move too fast," Uncle Mark sings when he catches her racing out of Margo's room.

Sofia, sweating and beet-red, stops, shoving the phone in the back pocket of her jeans. "Hey, Uncle Mark, what's going on? Did you catch any fish today? Really? That's great! Gotta go!" And she makes a mad dash for the wine cellar, leaving Uncle Mark standing in the middle of the hallway, bewildered by his encounter with his niece, the Tasmanian devil.

Meow

Margo peers over her British *Vogue* magazine and does an overt double take. "Ooh la la! You certainly look nice," she compliments Delilah as she strides into the kitchen looking all dolled up and ready for a hot night out on the town. Her hair is down and her ebony locks look shiny and smooth, not the least bit frizzy. Her eyelashes are coated with jet-black mascara, and her lips are dabbed with a sheer touch of rosy gloss that matches her sexy new red dress. A sensible pair of heels and large silver hoop earrings complete the outfit. "Don't you think it's a bit much for going to the movies?"

"Didn't I tell you?" Delilah plops her purse down on the counter. "I'm having dinner with Jack tonight."

Margo looks at her as if she just announced shoulder pads are back in fashion. "Jack . . . *Jack* Jack?"

"Well, actually, it's Jack *Walsh*," Delilah says, grinning. "Have you seen Sofia?"

"She disappeared a while ago. I think she's upstairs getting dressed." Squinting, Margo scratches the side of her forehead, plainly trying to understand. "Wait. Just the two of you are going to dinner?"

"Mmhmm."

"And you're all dressed up like that." Margo appears to be confused. "What, are you going on a hot date or something?"

"Why do you say that like it's so hard to believe? Yes, Jack and I are having dinner together, and I *suppose* it's a *date*—if you have to attach a name to it. Semantics . . ." Delilah removes a daisy from the bright flower arrangement in the center of the kitchen island, by which Margo sits, and sticks it behind her ear. "Too much?"

"Don't get defensive, doll. I'm just surprised, that's all. I like the daisy. It's cute."

"Why is it so surprising that I'm having dinner with Jack?"

"I didn't mean anything by it. I just didn't realize the two of you had something going." She gives her a subtle once-over. "You're a lucky lady."

Not about to let Margo ruin her night, Delilah ignores her snarky remark, busying herself with making sure her hoop earrings are securely fastened—something she'd already checked a few minutes ago when putting the finishing touches on her evening ensemble. "It's really not a big deal."

"Could've fooled me by the looks of that dress." Margo examines her closer, a tiny smirk forming at the corner of her lips. "Are you wearing a push-up bra?"

"No . . ." Delilah looks down at her chest, assessing her firm, voluptuous size 36C breasts, which she has always considered to be rather lovely. "Why? Does it look like I am? Am I sporting too much cleavage? Oh no, do I look like a lady of the night?" Delilah's aware that the line between looking appropriately sexy and looking like a paid professional is extremely fine, and every once in a while it can accidentally be crossed without realizing it.

"Not at all. You look very perky. *So*," Margo presses, "you think Jack's interested in something more than friendship with you?"

"Sweet Christmas, Geraldo! What's with the twenty questions? I have *no idea.* It's one meal. We're not going to pick out china or exchange vows." Exasperated, Delilah returns the daisy to its original place in the flower arrangement.

Margo thrusts up both palms in surrender. "Okay, okay, no more questions. I'm only trying to understand your situation." She resumes paging haphazardly through her magazine. "You should read this when I'm done. There's a fantastic article on—"

"Am I missing something, Margo?" Delilah interrupts her. "What's there to understand about my *situation* with Jack?"

"Delilah . . ." Margo slowly closes the magazine again, biting her bottom lip. "Honey, you *do* know that Jack has a girlfriend, *don't you*?"

Delilah stiffens slightly at the word *girlfriend*. "Pardon?"

"He told me all about her today on the boat. Her name is Carly, but people call her Cee-Cee. Isn't that a darling name? She's a teacher in Chicago," Margo adds for extra fun.

Delilah remains perfectly poised, though her voice raises an octave higher. "Jack was talking to you about his girlfriend Carly?" She wonders why she should care, one way or the other, if Jack has a girlfriend. He's certainly entitled after all.

"Oui, mon chérie."

What? What the hell? What the frickin' frackin' hell? she thinks. "What did he say?" she coolly inquires.

Margo smiles like a child on Christmas morning. "I don't know—the usual stuff I guess. He talked about how they like to go on bike rides together on weekends and how she teaches A.A. at summer school."

"Advanced algebra?"

"Yep," Margo nods. "She wasn't able to take time off. That's why she's not here. Jack seemed down about it." She watches Delilah's expression.

Rather than allow Margo the satisfaction of seeing the embarrassment and disappointment register on her face, Delilah smiles as if she's just heard the funniest joke in the universe and shakes her head, rolling her saltwater-taffy-blue eyes. "*Of course* I know Jack has a girlfriend! Come on, you think I don't know about *Cee-Cee the algebra teacher* stuck in the Windy City? Please! Don't be nutty! Of course I know!" *Dear God, I'm an idiot*, Delilah thinks to herself, hoping Margo's buying her little Academy Award–winning performance. *As in IDIOT! What the hell? Why didn't Sofia say anything? I don't understand . . . God forbid I should have a normal date with a man who's actually—oh, I don't know—SINGLE?!* "Um, where did you say Sofia is?"

Margo narrows her eyes, tapping her pointer finger against the counter. "I didn't. My guess is she's probably upstairs somewhere."

But before Delilah has a chance to find and interrogate Sofia, Jack strolls into the kitchen looking dapper and relaxed in khaki trousers and a green button-down shirt that almost makes his chocolate-colored eyes look hazel. "Lady in red . . ." He smiles warmly at Delilah. "Nice! I've never seen you looking so lovely as you do tonight."

Delilah quickly adjusts her dress, her attitude, and smiles. "You're a goofball."

"Am not." He turns to Margo. "And what's on your agenda for the evening?"

"I think we may check out a movie later on. Sofia said there are a couple good ones playing at the theater in town. I like that shirt you're wearing."

"Thank you."

Stretching across the kitchen island, Margo reaches for Jack's arm. She feels the material, rubbing it between her French manicured fingertips. "Cotton?" she inquires, as if she's utterly intrigued by the fascinating composition of his shirt's weave.

"Uh, I think so," Jack replies, as Margo gently strokes his forearm. "Hey, watch out for Samantha. She'll chat your ear off during the movie."

"I appreciate the warning." Margo grins. "By the way, have either of you seen my cell phone? I can't find it anywhere."

"You had it earlier this afternoon at the beach," Delilah recalls. "Did you check your beach bag?"

"Yeah, it's not there. I've retraced all my steps today, and I can't find the damn thing anywhere. I don't know what's wrong with me. I *never* misplace it."

"Well, it has to be here somewhere," Jack reminds her. "I'm sure it'll turn up soon. Maybe Consuela or one of the staff accidentally moved it?"

"That's a possibility. I haven't spoken with Consuela yet."

Delilah slaps Jack on the shoulder as if she were a quarterback and he, the receiver, just made a winning play. "Nice call, amigo."

"Well, good luck finding it. We are going to leave you to your girls' night out and be on our way." Turning to Delilah, Jack adds, "I made us a reservation at a great little Italian place in town called Martinelli's. They have the best lasagna on earth, I swear."

"Sounds wonderful, *pal*." Delilah smiles, resigned to try and have a nice *friendly* evening with her new *friend*, Jack Walsh. "See you later, Margo. Hope you find your phone."

"Thanks. Have fun you two. Stay out of trouble. I want her back home by midnight, young man. Or else . . ."

"You have my sacred word, ma'am," Jack pledges, placing his hand on the small of Delilah's back and leading her off.

"Ya hear that? You have my *buddy's* sacred word," Delilah reiterates, trying not to acknowledge how nice Jack's warm hand feels gently pressed against her back.

Jack gives her a curious little glance. Had he turned around for one last look at Margo, he would have seen her gritting her Da Vinci porcelain veneers.

Good Fella

Martinelli's is the kind of restaurant you'd see in a Martin Scorsese film about mobsters—just the low-key, cozy sort of spot Delilah loves. Its dark mahogany walls, overstuffed burgundy leather booths, dim lighting, and signature drippy candles on the tables and walls lend to an intimate atmosphere that's perfect for a romantic first date (or having some poor chump named Vito whacked in the parking lot). Jack, a true old-fashioned gentleman, pulls Delilah's chair out for her. And when the waiter, a gangly long-limbed fellow named Ron, arrives to take their drink order, Jack first inquires if she'd prefer cocktails or wine.

"Wine sounds nice."

"Would you like red or white?"

"A place like this calls for red," Delilah says, admiring the jewel-toned Tiffany-style stained-glass light fixture dangling above the table, casting a warm, dim glow. "Definitely."

"Cabernet or pinot noir?"

"I like pinot."

"California? Or Italian?"

Delilah tilts her head to the side, thinking. "Italian, why not?"

"Are you always this decisive?"

"Usually," she says, smiling playfully.

Jack orders a bottle of wine, unfolds his napkin, and settles his big brown eyes on Delilah. "I hope you're ready."

"Ready for what?"

Reaching for a breadstick and a pat of butter wrapped in gold foil, he casually replies, "To tell me everything."

"Everything? That's a lot to tell you. What are you talking about?"

"Well, last night you got to hear my whole sordid tale. Now the spotlight's on you," Jack says, pointing the breadstick at her, "lady in red."

Flattered, Delilah smiles unabashedly at him. "Uh, well . . . ," she laughs, not knowing where to begin.

"You really do have a great smile," he observes, leaning toward her ever so slightly with his elbows on the table. "You must hear that all the time."

She flushes a little, unconsciously flips her hair behind her shoulder, and softly says *thank you*, officially deciding to let the Cee-Cee factor slide for the evening. Bombarding Jack with too many personal questions will only make her look nosy or, worse, desperate. Besides, she has no right to expect anything from him. Jack's personal affairs are just that. *It's none of my business if he wants to date a stupid heinous math teacher with bad breath and a wandering eye*, Delilah reminds herself. While she has no way of knowing whether Cee-Cee is visually impaired or suffering from chronic halitosis, it makes her feel better to assume affirmative on both counts.

When their waiter returns a half hour later to take their dinner order, the bottle of wine is nearly half empty and Delilah and Jack are so deep in conversation that he's forced to clear his throat in order to get their attention. "Ech-ech, ahem!"

Delilah stops chatting happily about the time she was eight years old and swallowed three quarters and a Princess Leia action figure head. "May I please have the steak al forno, medium rare?" she orders.

"And I'd like the same, please," says Jack, wiping tears from his eyes from laughing so hard. "I swallowed a nail when I was six," he shares. "Which leads me to a random factoid: Did you know that, according to the U.S. Census Bureau, redoing the kitchen is the most common remodeling project Americans undertake?"

"You don't say," the waiter replies, surprised, topping off Delilah's glass of wine. "I would've guessed it was the bathroom. Possibly the bedroom. Although, bathroom makes more sense, if you ask me."

Jack smiles. "Well, I was asking the lovely lady, actually. But now that you mention it, the bathroom's a perfectly logical choice."

Delilah looks at him quizzically. "I had no idea. Where'd you pick that up?"

"I checked out the *Domestic Bliss* Web site earlier today," he confesses. "You know, to get a better sense of what you do. I've missed *one or maybe two* episodes of the show," he flubs, "and I decided to take the Test Your Domestic Savvy Quiz. I couldn't resist."

"*That's* where I know you from!" The waiter points his pen accusingly at Delilah. "I knew you looked familiar. You're from that show my ex-wife watches! That one on TV. The one with those crafty ladies who like to remove stains and make flambé and do house things and stuff." He grins, pleased with himself. "A celebrity in the house! I'm glad I'm wearing a clean apron today."

"That makes two of us," Delilah smiles.

He stands there, silent, gawking at her with a wide, goofy grin.

After a few amusing moments, Jack gives him a gentle nudge. "Uh, Ron?"

"Huh? What?"

Jack smiles sympathetically. "Were you, uh, gonna place our orders?"

"Oh! Yes! Yes, of course. I'll be back in a little later—um, in a little while, I mean. I mean, I'll be back in a little while. Later on. Um, yeah," Ron mumbles as he speeds toward the kitchen, barely escaping a head-on collision with another waiter carrying an overflowing tray of piping-hot spaghetti and meatballs.

Jack shakes his head, amazed. "That the kind of reaction you usually get?"

"*No!* Thank goodness." Delilah blushes, returning to their original subject as quickly as possible. "But tell me, how'd you do on the Test Your Domestic Savvy Quiz? I wanna know . . ." She's tickled to learn that Jack considers her examworthy.

He makes a face. "Abominably. I should probably be ashamed to admit this, but I'm a 'safety hazard.' "

"Nuh-uh, that bad?" She sips her wine.

"Let me put it to you this way: the site recommends I invest in flame-retardant apparel to be on the safe side."

Delilah covers her mouth and laughs. "Well, there's always the makeup exam."

"And a fire extinguisher," Jack adds with a chuckle.

"See? You've got it covered."

"So tell me, Delilah White, how do you like working at *Domestic Bliss*?"

Though she had resolved not to think about the show while

she was away, Delilah delves into what life at *D.B.* has been like since Agnes's announcement, and how she and Margo are competing for the executive producer position. Perhaps it's the wine and drippy candles, or maybe it's that she somehow knows that she can trust Jack—single or not—but she tells him things that she hasn't mentioned to anyone before.

Jack listens attentively, nodding occasionally, only taking his eyes off her to cut his meat. "So you enjoy working at *D.B.*, but you want to produce material that reflects your own creativity and style, which doesn't necessarily meet the parameters of the show's content," Jack sums up. "And, *of course*, you'd like to show Margo Hart who's boss."

"Exactly," Delilah says, nodding. *He gets it. He really gets it! Uh-oh. What's the hitch? He's gotta be a kleptomaniac. Or a serial killer. Or worse . . . dating a stinkin' algebra teacher! Christ I hate math!*

"And you'll be able to do just that if you're promoted to executive producer?"

"That's what I'm hoping. I'd definitely like to take the show in a funkier direction—infuse *Domestic Bliss* with a little bit of urban spirit and target it more toward the modern city man or woman. You know, the person who loves homemaking, cooking, crafts, entertaining, that type of thing, but lives in an apartment building with an economy of space and, as a result, must adopt a metropolitan lifestyle, which—let's be honest—is as different as night and day from suburban or country living."

"Absolutely," Jack munches on a sizable bite of steak. "My apartment in Chicago's the size of a shoebox."

"Are you kidding? My first place in New York was the size of a shoe!" Delilah laughs, remembering the itty-bitty Chelsea abode that she had dubbed Tiny Tim. It certainly wasn't much, but by the time she'd finished working her domestic magic, it looked like something straight out of *Architectural Digest*, and the landlord had offered to pay her to fix up several other ratty-looking units in the building.

Delilah wipes her mouth with her napkin and suddenly wonders if her mascara is running or if she has armpit stains. She had been sure to apply plenty of deodorant to avoid embarrassing sweat rings, which she's prone to suffer during the sweltering summer months. "Now look who won't stop yapping about their career!" she jokes, hoping she hasn't bored Jack to death with her domestic diva dish.

He stabs a piece of steak with his fork and chews it thoughtfully for a second. "Have you ever considered starting your own show?"

Delilah pauses, having skillfully skirted her way around this question in the past on more than one occasion. Taking a big sip of ice water and an even bigger deep breath, she considers whether or not to tell a lie. In most circumstances, she wouldn't even have to think about it. Revealing the truth wouldn't be an option. "Yes," she finally admits, avoiding Jack's gaze.

"What would your show be called?"

She's never had the courage to say this name out loud to anyone before, or even so much as allude to the fact that she's contemplated starting her own TV show for several years now. For some reason, it always seemed like a far-fetched, starry-eyed dream—one that made her feel silly to talk about. Looking at Jack, Delilah smiles shyly and softly says it: *"Heavenly High-Rise."*

Sing, Sing a Song

Once they finish their meal and exit Martinelli's happily sated, Jack mentions there's a quiet little bar located just down the block. "Feel like swinging by for one more drink?"

"I think you could probably twist my arm," Delilah replies, slightly light-headed from the wine with dinner. She looks at Jack and grins. "I should thank you."

"You're a forgetful one. You already thanked me inside," he reminds her as they begin strolling at a leisurely pace toward the bar. "And, like I said, the pleasure's mine."

"No, not for dinner. For getting me out of my damn head. I've been so preoccupied with *D.B.* lately," she explains. "I'll have you know, I managed to make it through half a meal tonight without even thinking about it once. That's close to a miracle. It's just nice to have a change of scenery and be out and about with you. Quite what I needed!" she brightly adds. She clears her throat, hoping that she hasn't said too much.

"I'm happy to be of service," Jack says and smiles at her. "Come to think of it, I haven't worried about moving to Manhattan all night." He pauses to consider it, appearing rather amazed. "*I* should thank *you* for agreeing to have dinner with me."

"The pleasure's mine," Delilah beams.

When they enter the "quiet little bar," however, Jack immediately regrets his spontaneous suggestion. "Look! It's karaoke night!" Delilah exclaims, pointing to the vibrant SATURDAY NIGHT MEANS KARAOKE NIGHT! banner dangling above the bar. "I love karaoke!"

Suddenly, Jack's pushed out of the way by a bald, beefy bouncer escorting two punch-drunk, rowdy men from the bar for lighting sparklers inside. "That's the third and *last* time I tell you fellas, NO SPARKLERS INSIDE THE BAR! It's a goddamn fire hazard! Now get outta here before I call the cops!"

"Some *quiet* little bar, eh?" Delilah grins, looking around. The pulsating joint is decked out in splashy red, white, and blue holiday decorations and packed full of hard-drinking locals. The aroma of day-old beer and peanuts permeates the air.

"Are you sure you want to stay here?" Jack stares nervously at the small stage erected in the back corner of the room, shifting positions on his feet. "Because, come to think of it, there's more than one fully stocked bar at the house. And I *know* how you feel about goofy banners," he desperately adds, stepping back to allow a perspiring bartender carrying a huge tub of ice above his head—hollering "Comin' through! Comin' through!"—to squeeze by.

Delilah giggles. "Jack, Jack, Jack . . . If the big bad karaoke machine's frightening you, all you have to do is say so. I promise you, I'll understand."

"Frightening me? *Ha!*" He folds his arms defiantly across his chest, smirking like a tough guy. "Name your poison."

"You sure? I'm only playing with you. I'm happy to go if you'd like. Really, I was only—"

"Nonsense," Jack cuts her off. "What's your fancy, sunshine?"

She eyes him closely, making sure. "I think I'll stick with red wine," she says, smiling. "Thanks."

"Fair enough. I'll find the drinks, you find real estate."

"Deal."

Delilah manages to score a small round table covered with red, white, and blue star-shaped metallic confetti and begins perusing the enormous song options binder, while a brooding punk-rocker type in ripped jeans and sunglasses takes a noble stab at Billy Idol's "White Wedding." When Jack arrives moments later with their drinks, he pulls his chair directly next to hers so he can read through the titles with her. They're seated so close together, in fact, that his left leg accidentally brushes against Delilah's right leg, causing her pulse to quicken. And then, to Delilah's delight, it remains there, nestled softly against her, shooting tiny bolts of electricity throughout her entire body. She makes a conscious effort not to move her leg a single millimeter.

Jack removes a paper American flag from his scotch and raises his glass in a half salute, meeting Delilah's eyes. "To a wonderful evening, with wonderful company."

"And to New York." She smiles, taking a little sip of her drink, trying to stop imagining how nice it would feel to have his arms wrapped snuggly around her waist. *Stop it! For heaven's sake! Now is NOT the time to lose focus and go developing feelings for some charming yet already spoken for teacher guy. No no no no no . . . There's no time for distractions. Not now. Not when I'm within a hair of landing executive producer and everything I've worked for all these years at* D.B. *Axay the growing rushcay, elilahday. Oh my God. I'm thinking in Pig Latin. Shit! This can't be healthy. This can't be a good sign. Shit! Focus. Keep your eyes on the prize. This is what I've been training for,* she reminds herself like a dedicated soldier. *But that dimple . . . For the love of all that's good and pure, that dimple!*

"To New York . . ." Jack nods, his eyes penetrating hers once again.

"Hey! That's my on-deck number flashing!" Delilah shouts. "That was fast. Be right back." She bounces up and walks off, thankful for the distraction.

"Your what? Where are you . . . ?" Jack struggles to keep his eyes on her as she maneuvers her way through the crowded floor and disappears inside the ladies' room marked DAMES in fancy red cursive letters.

⁂

The next thing Jack knows, Delilah is standing center stage, holding the microphone, belting out "Girls Just Wanna Have Fun," commanding the room's attention. Her voice is steady, strong, and, holy crap, really amazing! Shocked by her talent, he glances around the bar, wondering if everyone else is as impressed as he is. The crowd is clapping, smiling, pointing at Delilah, and whispering in each other's ears. Their enthusiasm is contagious, and soon Delilah starts dancing with a little Cyndi Lauper flair. With a tinge of pride, Jack howls along with the audience as she spins around, impassioned, belting out the chorus with sass.

"Honey! Your underpants! Fix your dress!" a tall woman in the audience suddenly shouts, waving both hands in the air to get Delilah's attention. Jack sees the woman jumping up and down, wiggling her hands with purpose. And then—nearly causing him to tumble backward off his chair—he sees the reason why she's making such a fuss. The back of Delilah's red dress is tucked into her underwear. There, right before him and everyone else in the entire pub, is Delilah's butt. Smack-dab in the center of the white-hot spotlight. Bouncing high and low, left and right, to and fro, as she sings her heart out. Jack leans back in his chair, nervously running his fingers through his hair, unsure what the ever-helpful reference book once given to him by a bitter ex-girlfriend, *A Gentleman's Guide to Manners*, would suggest as the appropriate response to this situation. He presses his hand against his forehead trying to think.

Up onstage busy mooning the masses, unable to hear anything other than her own voice, Delilah winks and waves, unaware that the pale pink satin panties, which she had purchased especially for the trip just days before at Agent Provocateur, a chic downtown lingerie boutique, are on display.

"Your ass is hanging out! Yo! We can see your ass!" a drunk guy wearing a yellow sideways baseball cap hollers at her. Jack sits at the edge of his chair, fiddling with the confetti on the table, praying that the man will capture her attention and quick!

But Delilah just blows the drunk guy a kiss and keeps on singing and bopping joyously around, inspiring Jack to emit a soft little chuckle as he watches her, with his right knee anxiously bouncing up and down.

Refusing to give up, the drunk guy removes his cap—revealing his mullet—and shakes it frantically above his head, yelling, "Yo! Butt alert! Nice panties, sweetheart! Show us your bra!"

When a sympathetic cocktail waitress eventually dashes onstage to let Delilah in on the horrific fact that the entire bar is staring at her uncovered caboose, Jack exhales a sigh of relief and tosses back the remainder of his scotch.

❧

For a moment it looks as if Delilah is about to collapse. She contemplates sitting on the floor in the fetal position, rocking back and forth, and crying. But after several humiliating seconds during which she nearly drops the microphone and runs for the door, she manages to begin breathing again. She's sure this has to be the most embarrassing thing that's ever happened to her in her whole entire life—even worse than the time she fell down the escalator at the mall when she was fifteen and spotted Mrs. Fields, the holy mother of mall cookies herself, standing, there in the flesh, behind the cookie counter on the lower level. But, as a firm believer in the theory that the show must go on, Delilah deftly untucks the hem of her dress, holds her head high, and keeps right on singing. Recalling something similar that once happened to her in a particularly vivid nightmare, she quickly scans the room for knife-wielding clowns or a giant talking panda holding hands with Mrs. Tepper, her high school gym teacher. Delilah's certain that her violently pounding heart is going to shoot right through her red dress and hit some poor sap in the face, but she plods ahead, leaving little doubt that "they just wanna, they just wanna-a-a—girls just wanna have fu-un!"

As she keeps singing, the blush slowly draining from her cheeks, people stop throwing darts, and pounding shots, and playing pool, and chatting about their daily woes to see what the feisty brunette, who just mooned the whole room, will do next.

Out in the audience, Jack shakes his head and smiles, swirling around the melting ice cubes in his glass. He flags down a cocktail waitress and orders another round.

When Delilah brings her song to a rousing finish, the room erupts into wild, alcohol-induced cheers and applause. Several appreciative patrons sway their lighters in the air, as if they were at a Rolling Stones concert. Laughing, Delilah takes a hurried, shy curtsy and scurries back to the table, thankful to have survived one of the most mortifying moments of her life.

Jack jumps to his feet to greet her. "You're a rock star! I didn't know you could sing like that!"

"There's lots of things you don't know about me," she quotes Jack from last night. "Like, say, for example, the fact that I'm about to have a heart attack and *die*!" She covers her face with her hands, shaking her head back and forth. "Oh God, Jack! I'm so embarrassed! *Now* would be a good time to call nine one one." She slowly peeks through her fingers at him, begging, "You've gotta get me out of here. Please! *Seriously.* There must be a back door around here somewhere!"

"You were amazing," Jack says. "You couldn't have handled it better. You were fantastic up there! Are you kidding? I would have *died* if it had been me on that stage!" He immediately flinches, wishing he wasn't missing that darn sensitivity chip. "Don't listen to me," he commands. "What do I know? I could never get up there in the first place—and might I remind you that I'm weeks away from being stuffed inside a locker!"

"Oh my God . . ." An alarming expression creeps across Delilah's face. Her blue eyes widen with dismay. Her jaw drops.

"What? What is it?"

Gasping dramatically as the realization dawns on her, she freezes in place. "I can never show my face in public again. I have to find an underground pod to live in. I'm the Karaoke Ass Girl!" She looks at Jack, dead serious, and declares, "I'll change my name."

He can't hold back his laughter any longer. "Delilah, I promise you, honestly, it wasn't that bad."

"It *wasn't that bad*?! *It wasn't that bad* that I *mooned* a room full of strangers?!?! Hello?! This is *EARTH*! It *was that bad*! It was worse than *that bad*! It was, it was, it was—"

"Alright, come on now," Jack interrupts her rant, placing a calming hand on her shoulder. "Technically speaking, you didn't moon anyone. You were wearing underwear. And besides, you don't hear me complaining."

Delilah considers it, twirling a dark tendril of hair around her pointer finger. "Well . . ."

"You're really talented. You're like . . ."—he tries to think of the perfect thing to say—"the next American Idol!"

"Aw shucks," she playfully concedes, adrenaline still racing through her veins, relieved she was able to turn lemons into lemonade. Incredibly indecent lemonade, but lemonade nonetheless. She lifts her hair off the back of her neck with one hand and fans herself with the other. "We don't have to tell anyone about this, do we?"

"About what? I have no idea what you're talking about. It must be the meds."

Delilah plops down in her chair, thankful for Jack's understanding. "I need a drink. A *big* one. With a drink on the side."

"Oh yes," Jack agrees. "I took the liberty of ordering us another round."

"Bless you."

"HEY! GIRL IN THE RED DRESS! WHERE'D YA RUN OFF TO?!" a highly intoxicated man wearing weathered cowboy boots, standing onstage waiting for his karaoke song to begin, slurs into the microphone, which he's holding way too close to his mouth.

Delilah shoots Jack a nervous glance.

"GET YOUR FAT ASS UP HERE ON THIS STAGE AND SING WITH ME GIRL!" He takes a sloppy swig from his bottle of Miller High Life.

The buzzing audience snickers, providing fuel for his fire.

He searches the room, trying to locate Delilah, breathing loudly into the microphone. "That's right, you heard me! Come on, beautiful. I'm askin' you nicely. Bring that glorious big fat rump of yours on up here and sing with me!"

Delilah feels as if one thousand horses just stampeded through her stomach. Still trying to recover from the usual shock that comes with accidentally flashing a room filled with strangers, she suddenly wishes she had taken Alfred's advice and gone with the black cardigan tied around her waist after all. She scorns herself for not knowing better than to challenge a gay fashionista's words of wisdom. This can't be happening. Not tonight. Not here. Not with Jack, of all people. It just can't.

She notices Jack fidgeting uncomfortably with his paper American flag.

"You got the voice of an angel, Red Dress! Don't she though?" the highly intoxicated man, oblivious that his song has already begun, asks some poor chap near the front of the stage. "I *LOOOOOOVE* ME A CHUNKY WOMAN!" He burps like an ogre, wiping his mouth with the back of his sleeve.

Delilah can feel countless pairs of eyes piercing through her. Her face begins to grow prickly flush, and her palms become clammy and start to sweat. She doesn't know where to look.

The man onstage stomps his foot, accidentally banging the microphone against his thigh, causing it to screech at a deafening pitch. "So now I coooome to yoooou with open arms, nothing to hide, believe what I say," he finally begins crooning, swaying dramatically with his hand over his heart and his eyes closed, forever ruining Journey's "Open Arms" for Delilah.

Oh God . . . Be strong. Do not cry. Say something funny. Say something clever, Delilah. Hold your head high and bounce back. You're tougher than this. Don't let anyone know you're hurt. Who cares what that jerk said? So what if he announced he thinks you're a big fat hippo to the entire bar? Delilah glances at Jack, who pretends to be terribly busy picking something off the bottom of his shoe, and she wishes she were a turtle that could simply pop its head inside of its warm, protective shell and disappear.

When Jack's big brown eyes finally meet hers, she sees a brief glimpse of pity flash across them. He slowly rises, offers a weak half smile, and politely excuses himself to use the washroom.

Delilah's heart sinks as she watches him walk away, navigating a winding path through the crowded, smoky space. And just like that, in the brutal snap of a finger, she's once again the fat little girl being teased in the school yard. *Delilah Doughnut . . .*

Her stomach muscles clench, and she feels like she's going to vomit. She just wants to get the hell out of that bar, go back to the Trawlers' house—or, better yet, Manhattan—and forget this whole humiliating nightmare ever took place. Looking around the room, which now seems to be spinning like it's closing in on her, Delilah observes that people are still staring at her, talking about her, laughing at her, judging her, perhaps even feeling sorry for her. The embarrassment is too vile to bear. Unable to spend one more agonizing second inside that room, Delilah stands up, checks to be sure her dress isn't tucked into her underwear, and quickly makes her way toward the exit, her head held low.

"Hey? Isn't that the woman from *Domestic Bliss*?" she overhears a pretty blonde girl ask a friend as she rushes by.

"Nice call! I thought she looked familiar, that's Delilah White!" the friend responds. "Oh my God . . ."

"Poor thing," mutters the pretty blonde. "She looks bigger on TV."

Fighting back tears, Delilah storms outside. She stops, leaning against the red brick wall next to the entrance—where the beefy bouncer now sits on a stool smoking a cigarette—and attempts to catch her breath, praying this story does not find its way into the local gossip page. *God would that be bad. Please let that not be the case. Talk about a nightmare . . .* The scene strikes her as both pathetic and mildly entertaining at once, prompting her to decide that if this were a soap opera, here's where the upset character would employ the ever-dramatic "wall slide" maneuver, slowly sliding her body down against the wall until at last she crumbles on the ground in a shattered heap, sobbing and either muttering, *"No! No! Nooo!"* or *"Why? Why? Whyyy?"* Trying to center herself, Delilah draws in a long, deep breath, bows her head, and covers her eyes with her trembling hands. What a disaster. *Nauseating. Completely nauseating. Get me out of here. Why did I have to sing that stupid song in the first place? I shouldn't even be here. I should be in New York concentrating on landing executive producer.*

After a few minutes, she remembers Jack, still inside the bar, probably wondering where his companion for the evening, the Karaoke Ass Girl, has run off. *All he has to do is look for her fat fanny,* Delilah figures. *According to Journey Man, it ain't hard to miss.* Embarrassed that she ran away, like a true coward, another wave of revulsion courses through her body. She rarely feels sorry for herself, but tonight is an exception.

Retrieving her compact mirror from her purse to check her face, she wishes Jack had chased after her, or at least had the decency to poke his head outside the damn bar to try and see if he could find her. But alas, nothing. No sign of Mr. Walsh. Delilah doesn't know where she'll find the guts to face him after this debacle. She hopes a firecracker accidentally lands on her head tomorrow. Figuring that she'll call for a taxi to bring her back to Cherry Pond, Delilah slowly begins walking away.

Out of nowhere, she hears a familiar, hesitant voice echoing through the loudspeakers inside the bar.

Pausing to listen, she uses the side of her finger to wipe away a tear and her dark, smudged eyeliner, which seems to be on a voyage to her chin. It's difficult for her to hear it clearly, but it sounds as if the voice is shaking and struggling to find the song's right key. Delilah tosses the compact back in her purse and begins rummaging around for her lipstick.

"You brought the sun to meeee . . ."

She looks up, focusing harder on the timid, warbling voice, craning her neck toward the bar's entrance.

"Shoot! The words are moving so fast! Where's . . . Where's the bouncing dot?!"

Delilah's eyes bulge out. *No . . . No way . . . It . . . It couldn't be.* She listens even harder still.

"*Crap!* With your smile you did it girrrrllllll . . ."

Delilah smoothes her hair, gathers her courage, holds her head high, and saunters back into the bar. *Public humiliation be damned!*

"Atta girl," the beefy bouncer says, smiling as she breezes past him.

And there before her eyes, in the middle of the stage—wide-eyed and smiling nervously—stands Jack, sweating, clutching the microphone in an awkward, white-knuckle grip, singing Davy Jones's heart-warming and goofy ballad "Girl." Singing. Out loud. In public! *For her.* Delilah's heart flip-flops into her throat. And for the first time in her life, she knows what it's like to be swept off her feet. A radiant smile slowly spreads across her face. Delilah has never felt more beautiful.

End Note

Back at Cherry Pond, Jack and Delilah stand at the bottom of the staircase like a couple of gawky teenagers—minus the acne and midnight curfews—trying to say good night. "So, uh, can I get your phone number?" he says, fidgeting with the elegant ebony banister. "You know, in case I need to call you in New York to find out how to weave a macramé pot holder, or make a pound cake or something?"

"Simple. Pound of flour, pound of sugar, pound of butter, pound of eggs, dash of vanilla, then bake," Delilah recites, her blue eyes twinkling.

"Alright . . ." Jack studies her expression. "Well, then, what if I can't resist your charm and I'd like to take you to dinner again? Or to the theater? Or to a"—he tries to think of a really good one—"a *craft fair*? I love a good craft fair."

Delilah lets out a sleepy laugh and divulges her number, which Jack enters directly into his cell phone.

"Tired?" he asks.

"A little. You?"

"A little," he says and smiles.

"I had an amazing time tonight." She smiles back.

"So did I." Jack takes a step closer to her.

"Thank you," she whispers, inching a step closer to him.

"Thank *you*," he whispers back.

Delilah's heart races. She wonders what Jack's hand gently brushing against the side of her cheek would feel like, or how his fingers slipped between hers might feel. The mere thought of his warm breath against her skin sends shivers down her spine. She wants Jack to envelop her in his arms and kiss her, softly and slowly. But instead, he gently takes her hand in his and places a tender, perfect kiss on top of it—which promptly turns her knees to wobbly Jell-O—and then walks her to her door before slipping down the hall with a whispered *good night*.

Sunday, July Fourth

After waking up at 2:00, 3:00, and 4:00 a.m., Delilah peers at the little alarm clock on her bedside table—now flashing 5:20 a.m. in bright red, hateful numbers—and decides there's no use fighting it, she best surrender. Slumber simply isn't in the forecast. As she sits up, rubbing wishful sleep from her eyes, it dawns on her that for the first time in as long as she can remember, her woken midnight hours weren't spent obsessing over the executive producer position dangling before her like a corn dog on a stick. For a welcome change, Delilah's thoughts were devoted to something else—someone else. The faintest smile creeps across her lips, soon becoming an outright grin. But then, while staring at the alarm clock lost in dreamy thought, the annoying blink-blink-blinking numbers suddenly remind her of Cee-Cee, the annoying, and lucky, math teacher in Chicago. A mean, rushing river of envy washes over Delilah, carrying her resentfully back to shore where reality all too quickly sets in. Groaning, she grabs the alarm clock and turns it away from her so that it's facing the wall. *Stupid horrible numbers! I hate numbers! Who needs 'em?!* She sighs, plopping her head back down on the feathery soft pillow. Extending her arms at her side, she gives her body a nice, long, indulgent stretch, determined not to let her disappointment get the best of her. She didn't even know the name Jack Walsh a few days ago, she reminds herself. It's silly to let him affect her. It's silly that the mere thought of him makes her heart catch in her throat. It's silly that she somehow feels a genuine sense of loss. Shutting her eyes, Delilah tries to shake off her silly sorrow, telling herself once again that she came to Cherry Pond to have a good time, and that is exactly what she still intends to do. *Well, might as well use the time for something productive*, she figures and throws back her blankets. *Wait, is that the distinct combination of coffee, bacon, and freshly cut lilies I detect? Oh yes, follow that nose . . .*

Delilah is surprised to discover the kitchen—outfitted with top-of-the-line stainless-steel appliances and gadgetry, a double-size professional range, and plenty of working space—alive with a flurry of unexpected activity, as preparation for the evening's highly anticipated party-to-end-all-parties is already well under way. A plump man wearing a messy apron cracks dozens of eggs into an enormous silver mixing bowl while a woman by his side with a smudge of flour on her forehead kneads a knot of cream-colored dough. Several assistants gathered around all four sides of the kitchen island slice a vast array of vibrant fruits from all over the world—some of which Delilah has never seen before—into bite-size pieces. And a blonde woman wearing nose-plugs crouches over a massive pyramid of crushed ice, deveining about one thousand fresh shrimp that were swimming merrily around the Atlantic only hours ago. Off in the far corner, Consuela, busy preparing a special holiday-style Sunday breakfast for the Trawlers and their guests, monitors everyone's progress like a protective mother hen.

Delilah looks out the eight-foot-tall windows above the kitchen sink—letting in the first light of the sun rising on the other side of the house and views of the lake—and spots more hired labor outside on the deck and in the sprawling backyard, where an American flag now waves atop the old-fashioned gazebo. Burly men unload folding chairs from the back of a truck and place them around big square tables that seat ten, and in a shaded area nearby, women use industrial-strength steamers to remove wrinkles in the elegant white slipcovers that will soon be draped around each chair. The party planner in charge of Operation Trawler Family Fourth, a distinguished Brit called Thor who is typically booked two years in advance, has one walkie-talkie, two cell phones, and a pager fastened to his belt—as well as a wireless, futuristic-looking headset secured around his ear—instructs his team of men to pick up the pace. "Let's put a bit of pep in our step, chappies!" He claps his hands enthusiastically. "We've much work to be done before showtime! We're pulling out all the stops for this one, mates!" Thor blows the silver referee whistle hanging from his neck. "Milo, I want you clipping the cherry blossoms in front of the house. Remember, anybody who's *anybody* in this town will be here tonight. We want everything looking absolutely shipshape *perfect.* Tom, distribute the tiki torches evenly throughout the beach. I want them bordering the perimeter, spaced approximately twenty-one and a half feet apart. Sayid, you're in charge of stringing the little twinkly white lights throughout the evergreens in the north quadrant. Pappy, my boy, you're on dog detail."

Pappy, a short Mexican teenager, the youngest member of Thor's crew, stamps his foot. "Aw man! *Again?* Why do *I* always gotta be the one to pick up the doggy doo? This shit ain't fair! When did I become Pappy the Poop Boy?! Besides, I thought the Trawlers don't have a dog."

"They don't. But their neighbors on both sides do," Thor

counters. He raises an eyebrow, giving the rebel youth the once-over. "Well, you *do* look like you have strong lungs. Perhaps you'd prefer to help blow up that large children's play castle jump thingamajig, whatever do you call it?" Thor points to the primary-colored structure crumpled in a menacing heap toward the west side of the estate.

Pappy's eyes bulge out. "Nooo way, man. You gotta be kidding me. That thing's humongous! You sure we don't use a machine to blow it up?"

"Oh, I'm sure, Pappy, I'm sure. It requires manual inflation, I'm afraid. It'll take twelve hours. I need someone who won't faint to start blowing immediately."

"No way, man! I *love* poop!" Pappy assures him as he races off.

Thor cackles. "London bridges! Messing with that lad's far too much fun," he mutters to himself.

⊰ ⊱

Watching the scene from inside, Delilah can't help but laugh. She's had a special fondness for the Fourth of July ever since she was a little girl. Each year her grandmother Violet would take her and Francesca to the annual Eagle River Holiday Pet and People Parade, which was particularly spectacular due to the fact that (A) overzealous animal owners dressed up their pets in the stupidest, tackiest-looking costumes known to mankind, and (B) people riding sparkly floats would hurl copious amounts of candy and gum at delighted onlookers lining the streets. Delilah was pegged in the head with a flying individually wrapped sweet on more than one occasion—a Bit-O-Honey in the eye almost landed her in the emergency room one year—but something about the Fourth of July has always tickled her fancy. It reminds her of her youth and makes her feel like it's really summer, which is easy to forget when you work the kind of crazy hours she does.

True, Delilah had promised herself that this weekend she wouldn't allow her mind to wander toward anything having the slightest thing to do with *Domestic Bliss*. But, as fate would have it, last night with Jack inspired her, sending her creative juices racing into overdrive. Without fail, her best work tends to come after a stimulating encounter with a provocative individual, or a particularly phenomenal night at the theater (Delilah White + The Great White Way = True Love Forever), or following a long, lazy stroll with no final destination through Central Park just as dusk is descending upon the metropolis. Infused with ideas that could possibly help land her the coveted executive producer position, Delilah can't very well let them lie dormant and slip away, which she knows is exactly what will happen if she doesn't write them down. *That* handy lesson was learned the hard way years ago after spending several frustrating days racking her damn brain trying to recall the "brilliant" concept she had come up with earlier that week while riding the number 6 train. She vowed then and there to start writing things down, and now she keeps a gallon-size Ziploc bag stuffed with ideas and messy little notes written to herself on wrinkled cocktail napkins—some sporting the occasional ketchup stain—backs of receipts, torn-off scratch paper, even the odd candy wrapper. Every now and then, usually when the bag's about to burst, Delilah dumps its contents on top of her bed and diligently weeds through the pile.

Comfortably situated in a quiet spot at the Trawlers' kitchen table with a piping-hot cup of coffee and a chocolate croissant by her side and her computer in front of her, Delilah's fingers find their familiar place on the keyboard and begin typing away.

Got Milk?

By the time the rest of the household starts their day, Delilah has completed outlines for not one, but two new segment ideas aimed to dazzle Agnes Deville. One details how to install a new showerhead—not an especially thrilling concept (*yawn*), but it's practical. After all, everyone showers eventually. Her other idea, which might not be as universal but is more interesting and inspiring in her opinion, covers how to grow a flourishing herb and tomato garden in the city *above ground* using a standard window box, sunlight, water, and the appropriate nutrient-enriched soil. The plump, red tomatoes growing outside the living room window of Delilah's seventeenth-floor Manhattan high-rise rival those nurtured in the most glorious country gardens. She recently served Agnes a Caprese salad made with fresh basil and tomatoes from her very own window-box garden. After taking a bite, Agnes moaned out loud, "Oh yes, just like that," and refused to accept that tomatoes *that* exquisite, *that* juicy and delectable could possibly grow in an urban environment. "Impossible! Hogwash!" she had stubbornly snorted to Delilah. "Believe me, White, I've tried!"

"No rest for the wicked, eh?" Margo says to Delilah as she enters the kitchen, practically the last one to rise, looking fresh and chipper in a turquoise terry-cloth Chanel sundress over a sexy black bikini. She nods toward Delilah's computer. "Working on a holiday . . . Now *that* is dedication. You've gotta be the hardest-working employee at *D.B.*"

Hoping to deter Margo, who can be quite nosy at times, Delilah quickly clicks on the GAMES icon on her computer screen. "Playing solitaire hardly counts as work," she says, grinning. "Good morning."

"Why do I always sleep like a hibernating bear when I'm in the mountains?" Margo yawns.

"It's the pure mountain air. The human body needs it," Aunt Deb, sitting across the table from Delilah, suggests. "See? It serves you working gals well to get out of the big city once in a while and give your minds a rest from all that hard work. Go get some breakfast, Margo. The buffet's in the living room."

"Beat ya to it!" Jack chimes in, coming from the buffet with a heaping plate of food. "Good morning, everyone. Happy Fourth of July." He drops a waffle on the floor and quickly swoops down to pick it up. "Oops."

Uncle Mark, seated at the head of the table, lifts his nose out of the *New York Times* "Sunday Styles" section. "Morning, son," he cheerfully says before bursting into a spontaneous rendition of "Good Morning" from *Singin' in the Rain.*

Aunt Deb's eyes remain glued to the financial section as she offers a feeble half wave. "Please tell your father no singing before noon."

Delilah smiles at Jack, trying to ignore the fact that (A) she suddenly feels like she swallowed a bowling ball, which is now lodged in the pit of her stomach, smooshing the poor butterflies, and (B) she has the wildly bizarre urge to run into his arms and pounce on him—such that he ends up holding her just like

Richard Gere cradled Debra Winger at the end of *An Officer and a Gentleman,* one of the most romantic movies of all time, as far as Delilah is concerned.

"Sleep okay?" Jack asks her, taking a seat at the other end of the table.

Delilah realizes he's addressing her, but she was too caught up fantasizing about the way he'd look in a Navy officer uniform to hear his question. "Um, a little while ago," she says and smiles, hedging her bet he asked when she woke up.

"Oooookay," says Jack, unfolding his napkin and placing it on his lap.

Delilah wrinkles her nose and sticks her tongue out at him, immediately wondering why she—a respectable, professional adult—would do such a ridiculous, childlike thing. She reaches for her coffee mug and takes a sip to create a distraction for herself.

Jack crosses his eyes and puffs out his cheeks.

Gliding into the room holding a bowl of grapefruit, Margo catches this mature exchange. "Be careful," she warns Jack, sitting down next to Delilah, "or you'll get stuck that way. My mother used to tell me that when I was young. It always terrified me—the idea of being frozen ugly."

"She started it," Jack says accusingly, pointing a thick slice of bacon at Delilah.

Delilah arches her right eyebrow.

"You two are funny," Margo grins, noticing a full pitcher of milk on the table set between her and Delilah.

"Hey, Margo, let me ask you something," says Jack. "Have you ever heard of a *qortle*?"

"Oh, not this again . . ." Delilah rolls her eyes and shakes her head.

But Margo doesn't respond. Staring at the beveled glass

pitcher, which the Trawlers had received as an anniversary gift years ago, she appears to have tuned out the rest of the world.

"I still believe it's a word," Jack tells Delilah.

"So I've gathered," she replies, suppressing a giggle.

"Qortle?" says Aunt Deb. "I don't think so."

"See?" Delilah grins at Jack.

"What does my mom know about African birds?!" Jack challenges.

Holding an empty glass in her left hand, Margo reaches for the pitcher of milk with her right hand. Her fingers grasp the smooth glass handle, but somehow, as she lifts it, she loses her grip and it slips from her hand. She scrambles to steady the teetering-tottering pitcher, trying her damndest to keep it from spilling over, but she can't move swiftly enough. In two unforgettable seconds, it's too late. The damage is done. Everyone looks on in horror as a stream of creamy white liquid cascades like a waterfall directly on top of Delilah's keyboard. The thick, clear pitcher crashes to the floor, shattering into countless jagged pieces. But nobody seems to notice. All eyes remain fixed on Delilah's drenched machine, which is now producing an odd sizzling sound.

"OH MY GOD! OH MY GOD! OH MY GOD!" Margo wails, breaking the stunned silence.

Unaware that she, too, is covered in milk, Delilah remains frozen, fighting the urge to drop to her knees Greek tragedy–style and bellow, "NOOOOOOOOOOOOOOOO!" Instead, she tries to calm Margo, who is now frantically choking back tears, dabbing the computer with her little paper napkin. "It's okay, it's okay, sweetie. It was an accident. It's not your fault," Delilah reassures her, wiping a droplet of milk off her ear with her shoulder as pandemonium breaks out.

"Turn it off! Turn off the computer!" Jack yells, jumping up from his chair, knocking his fork and knife on the ground and a sausage link onto Aunt Deb's bare foot.

Delilah gasps, struggling to process this nightmare. She hits the power button, but nothing happens. She presses the round little button again, harder this time. "Nothing's happening! It's not responding! Why won't it turn off?! Help! What should I do?!"

Consuela rushes to the computer with a roll of paper towels and starts sopping up the liquid. "Tenga cuidado del vidrio roto! *Be careful of the broken glass!*" She cautions everyone.

"Hit CTRL, ALT, DELETE!" Jack instructs, running to Delilah's side. "CTRL, ALT, DELETE! *Hurry!* The motherboard will fry!"

"I am so sorry, Delilah! SO SORRY!!! Oh my God! Look what I've done! Oh God! I'm so sorry! SO SORRY!" Margo cries.

Jack holds the power button down for several tense, drawn-out moments as everyone else in the kitchen holds their breath and stares. "Come on!" he begs the computer, impatiently tapping its side. "Shut down . . . Shut down . . . Power off, dammit!" The screen eventually turns a strange, speckled shade of gray before it goes black. Jack carefully lifts up the computer, causing the pool of milk that had been trapped beneath it to ooze off the table, and carries it to safety on the counter.

Delilah stares in shock, her eyes slightly glazed, trying to catch her breath. Her mind spins with one distressing thought after the other. *Did I have all my files backed up? No. Dammit! Why am I so damn careless and lazy?! And I worked so hard on the new organizational structure and mission statement I'll use for the show if I get the promotion. Fuck! What else have I lost? WHY ZEUS? WHYYYYYYYYYYYYYYYYYYYYYYYYYYYYYYYYYYYYY YYYYYYYYYYYYYYYYYYYYYY???!!*

As Delilah calculates the many wasted hours spent brainstorming, researching, and writing the files that are now undoubtedly lost forever, Aunt Deb, Consuela, and Margo scurry about on hands and knees, collecting pieces of broken glass.

"Ouch!" Margo whimpers, when a pointy shard slices into her left palm. "Shoot!" She rises to examine her wound.

"You okay?" Jack asks. But all he has to do is take one brief glance at the crimson blood dripping down Margo's hand, off her elbow, and onto the white marble kitchen floor, to know the answer to his question. The room begins to swirl around him, slowly at first, then faster and faster, picking up speed. The color drains from his face. His brown eyes roll into the back of his head. And he drops to the floor with a dramatic *thwack!*

"Jack!" wails Aunt Deb.

Uncle Mark sprints to his son, bending down next to him. "Everybody outta the way! Give me some room!" Having seen one too many episodes of *ER*, he rips open Jack's shirt, for no apparent reason, and grabs his wrist to check his pulse. "He's still breathing!" he announces. "I have a pulse! Jack, can you hear me?! Do you know what year it is?! Who is the president of the United States?"

"Well *of course* he's still breathing," Aunt Deb huffs. "The big baby can't stand the sight of blood!" She turns to Margo, who clutches her bloody hand to her chest. "This hysteria's too much for me. Come on, hun, let's go get you cleaned up," she says, leading her out of the room. "You don't have any cigarettes, do you? I'll pay you for 'em . . ."

Suddenly, Sofia and Derek, having just returned home from a pleasant Independence Day jog, bound through the kitchen door, laughing about something or other. Sofia shrieks and covers her mouth with her hands when she sees her cousin sprawled across the floor in a gory mixture of milk, broken glass, and blood. "Jack!" She rushes to his side, crouching down next to him. "What happened?!" She looks around the room, desperately.

As Delilah begins describing the surreal order of events, Sofia leads Jack in counting to ten. "Come on, Jack, you're okay. You're gonna be *just fine.* Count with me now," she gently urges. "Uno . . ."

"Out of nowhere he just dropped to the ground!" Delilah explains.

"Dos . . ."

"He saw the blood on Margo's hand and toppled over. Like a big tree!"

"Tres . . . ," Sofia continues. "Come on, Jack, let's count together—you can do it. How did Margo cut herself?"

"On a piece of glass," Delilah says. "There was an accident. She went to pour herself a glass of milk and knocked the pitcher over right on top of my computer. It shattered on the floor and she cut herself."

Sofia stops dead in her tracks. "Milk?"

"A *big* pitcher of it," Delilah says and shakes her head, trying to erase the horrible image of it from her mind. "And who the hell drinks *milk* with grapefruit anyway? It's disgusting! I could hurl!"

"Milk?" Sofia squints.

After a couple of seconds, Jack opens his eyes and lightly taps Sofia's thigh. "Keep counting . . . ," he sputters.

"Sorry. Cuatro . . . ," she continues.

"It was an accident," Delilah emphasizes. "It's okay. These things happen."

"Cinco . . ."

"There's no use crying about it now. What's done is done," Delilah says more to herself than to Sofia.

"Seis . . ."

"I don't even want to think about it." Truthfully, the thought's almost too much for Delilah to bear. She knows if she allows herself to really process the destruction of her computer, to dwell on her lost work, she'll start to cry. And it will be revealed, once and for all, in front of all the wrong people, that she's vulnerable. Delilah draws in a sharp breath, focusing on Jack. "And then *poor Jack*—"

"Wait a second," Sofia interrupts. "Hold on. Stop. Margo was drinking *milk*? Are you sure?"

"Uh-huh," Delilah nods. "She was going to anyway."

"You're *positive*?"

Jack lifts his head slightly off the floor, frustrated. "Two percent. *Good God!* Count, will ya?"

"Siete . . ." Sofia rolls her eyes. "Where's Margo now?"

"Aunt Deb just took her to clean her cut," Delilah replies. "About a minute before you and Derek arrived. You just missed 'em."

"Ocho . . . Is she okay?" Sofia asks, gently taking hold of Jack's hand.

"I think so. I don't know for sure. There was an awful lot of blood."

"Nueve . . . Jack, can you sit up for me?" Sofia inquires, searching his face. "What do you say we try to move you over to a chair at the kitchen table? Niiiice and easy now . . . No rush."

Jack slowly sits up, regaining his composure, wiping his eyes as he tries to focus. And then he says, "Diez," and is miraculously cured. "Thanks, cuz."

Accustomed to the drill, Sofia pats his shoulder. "Anytime." Then she bolts up, grabs Delilah's hand, and begins dragging her out of the room. "I need to talk to you."

"Now?" Delilah asks, looking back at Jack. "But what about—"

"Yes, *now*," Sofia adamantly insists, tugging Delilah toward her.

"What the heck happened to my shirt?" Jack demands, noticing that it's ripped.

"You're covered in milk, D. You need to change into dry clothes." Sofia purses her lips and widens her eyes, trying to send a nonverbal "it's important" signal to Delilah as she pulls her reluctantly along, adding, "Don't worry, he's fine."

One Month Earlier

Margo looked at her watch: 4:19 p.m. It had been nearly three whole days since her argument with Preston, and she was officially panicking. When he'd stormed out of their apartment earlier that week shortly after a Memorial Day party—wearing one blue flip-flop and one Nike sneaker (he was so upset that he couldn't bother taking the time to locate a matching pair of shoes)—he had declared that he needed time alone to think and "process" things. Right before that, he had stared into Margo's eyes and quietly suggested that she uses her sexuality as a manipulative tool. "I'm sick of it! I'm tired of watching you flirt and use your feminine ways to chat up other men because 'they may be a good contact for me to have in the future' or 'they know so-and-so who would be such a wonderful guest to have on the show.' I understand that nothing is as important to you as your precious television show, but it's not respectable, Margo, and I am so tired of it. Maybe the truth is, you're not ready to be in a committed relationship with me," he'd snapped, before stalking toward the front door. Stopping abruptly, he had turned around and looked at her, hurt. "Or maybe I just don't want to have to put up with your bullshit anymore." Margo had assumed he was being dramatic and would return home calm and apologetic after a soothing walk around their Tribeca block, just like always after one of their frosty battles. If the last two years had taught her anything about him, it was that he couldn't stay angry at her for long.

This time, however, Margo was wrong. She hadn't seen or heard from Preston since then. And that afternoon, while sitting at her desk at *D.B.* among a vast array of glitter and glue pondering the joys of scrapbooking, it finally hit her: their relationship was in serious trouble.

Later that day, when Sofia caught Margo reapplying her mascara in the bathroom, she could tell right away that she had been crying. Sofia assumed there had been a death in the Hart family or something equally devastating. She knew that Margo was too proud to shed tears in public, let alone at work where she had a tough-as-nails reputation to uphold. During all their years together at NYU, Sofia had witnessed Margo cry only once, when her family's basset hound, Root Beer, was run over by an ice-cream truck in a tragic drunk-driving accident. (To this day, Margo can't bear the sight of a root beer float.)

"Hey . . . You okay, Mar?" Sofia asked while trying to remove a piece of salmon stuck between her teeth with some dental floss. "I suggest you steer clear of the salmon paillard in Test Kitchen #2, by the way. Disgusting . . . It tastes like hate on a plate."

"Actually, no," Margo sniffled, surprising her. "I'm not okay." She returned the mascara tube to her makeup bag, zipping it shut. After taking one final look at her reflection in the mirror, she let out a sigh and faced Sofia. "Not even close. Do you have a minute?"

"Of course." Sofia noticed Margo's bottom lip was quivering slightly. "Listen, why don't we go someplace a little more private where we can talk?"

They hurried down the hall—past the Conference Room, Arts & Crafts Experimental Lab, and Beta Test Kitchen #1—toward Margo's office.

Once inside, Margo slumped down next to Sofia on the cushy brown leather sofa. For a few moments, she remained silent, wringing her hands—a nervous habit she picked up as a child watching her mother compete in beauty pageants. "Everything is so fucked," she finally declared.

"What are you talking about?" Sofia probed, worried. She could tell Margo was struggling to hide her distress.

"Preston. This job. This promotion. *Everything!* He's so angry with me all the time. He resents my devotion to the show and my ambition. He thinks it's *all* I care about, which is ludicrous. He feels threatened. Of course, he's at the firm every night until at least eight o'clock." She laughed ironically, directing her gaze outside the window. "Oh, the joys of being a prosecuting attorney."

Well accustomed to Margo's flair for overexaggeration, Sofia couldn't help but ask, "Is it really that bad?"

"He's pulling away. I know it. I've been through this before." Margo cracked her knuckles, making a loud popping noise. "*God!* I'm so stupid to think anyone will ever be able to put up with my crap." She shook her head. "No way. It never works out. You'd think I'd have that figured that out by now."

"Don't say that, you know it's not true. You're under a lot of pressure, and you're doing the best you can. Every couple goes through rough spots."

"This is more than a rough spot, Sofia. I *wish* this were only a rough spot. This is hopeless." Margo fought the lump building in her throat, looking away from Sofia. "Preston doesn't want to be with me. We had a huge fight the other night, and he walked out on me."

"Ouch." Sofia winced, realizing that Margo's condition was far more fragile than she'd first suspected and that she clearly needed to vent. During her sophomore year of college, Sofia had toyed with changing her major from business to psychology, and although business had ultimately prevailed, her interest in psychology had blossomed over the years into a gratifying passion and hobby—one that she rarely passes up the opportunity to practice. "It's more fun than analyzing my own issues," she jokes to family and friends who tease her by calling her Frasier.

"It was really bad," Margo frowned, picking at the couch cushion's seam.

"I'm sure he didn't mean anything by it, Mar. Preston's crazy about you." Sofia smiled reassuringly. "He probably just recognized that the argument was escalating to an unnecessary point and it was in both of your best interests to have a moment alone to cool off and let things fall into perspective. It sounds like one of those situations where you were both reacting to the depth of each other's emotions and the best thing to do at the time was to give each other space to breathe and calm—"

"He hasn't come back yet!" Margo blurted. She covered her mouth with her hand as if she were frightened of what might escape her lips next. Bowing her head, she allowed her gleaming red tresses to fall in front of her face and began to softly weep. "It's been *three days.* He's never done anything like this before. Never. I'm really worried."

Sofia gently rubbed Margo's back, processing it all. "Sweetie, I'm sorry. I had no idea . . ."

"What if we don't stand a chance?" Margo sobbed, finally giving in to the tears. "I'm gonna end up alone," she muttered. "I know it."

"You are not. Stop this crazy talk right now!" demanded Sofia, refusing to allow Margo to wallow in defeat. She leaned over and grabbed a tissue from the box of Kleenex on the coffee table and handed it to Margo. Though she tried, it was difficult for her to understand how anyone as gorgeous as Margo could honestly believe for one minute that she stood a chance of ending up alone—as if there weren't legions of men in every town across America who'd jump to be with a woman with supermodel looks. "Why have you given up? This isn't like you, Mar. Where's that fight you're so famous for? If Preston thinks you love *D.B.* more than him, show him he's wrong."

Margo searched Sofia's eyes. "What . . . What do you mean? How?"

"Well . . ." Sofia looked down and thought for a long moment. "You're still planning on going to Martha's Vineyard together next month for the Fourth of July, aren't you?"

Margo nodded, wadding her Kleenex into a tight little ball and then unwadding it again. "Assuming he ever comes back home, that is."

"Okay . . . ," Sofia said in a reassuring voice. "Well, think how amazing it'll be for you two to have a nice, long, quiet, romantic weekend alone together. Just the two of you . . . On the vineyard . . . Moonlight . . . Sand . . . Maybe a little champagne . . . A bubble bath . . . Think how peaceful it'll be," Sofia enthused. "It's *exactly* what your relationship needs. You can make the trip sort of like a rekindling of your romance—let

Preston know precisely how much he means to you." She looked quite pleased with her suggestion.

"That's not the worst idea," Margo admitted, dabbing her runny eyes with the crinkled tissue. "And it's only a month away. It's not *that* far off."

"The Fourth of July will be here in no time at all! You know how quickly the summer months fly by." She snapped her fingers. "Like that!"

"Thank you, Sofia," Margo whimpered appreciatively, touching her arm. "You really are a wonderful listener. Please don't say anything to anyone. I don't want people talking. You know how it is around here."

"Of course not," Sofia said.

Uninvited, Margo's bubbly assistant, Coco, suddenly sprung through the door. "Knock knock! I have two iced coffees for—" She noticed Margo and gasped, "OH MY GOD! Are you okay? What happened?!"

Wiping her eyes and quickly sitting up straight, Margo feigned an unsuccessful smile. "I'm fine—just blabbering over something insignificant. It's silly really. I'm okay."

"Is there anything I can do?" Coco asked as she approached, "aside from the drinks?" She carefully set them down on the coffee table on top of two Waterford Crystal coasters emblazoned with the famous *Domestic Bliss* logo.

"Thanks, Coco, but I'm alright. I appreciate it, though. I'm just having a bad day." Margo was too distraught to care, or even to realize, that she was allowing her assistant to see her in such a vulnerable state. She looked at her drink and frowned. "Is that milk in my coffee?"

Coco smacked herself upside the head. "DUH! I'm a fool. I completely forgot . . ."

Fortunately for the eager-to-please young twenty-something, her typically tigerlike boss had been rendered a pussycat. "Don't worry about it."

"Really?" Coco picked up Margo's beverage. "Are you sure? Let me go get you another one without any dairy. It's not a problem. Seriously. I'll be right back lickety-split!"

"No need, I could probably do without the caffeine anyway. Would you mind just giving me a few more minutes with Sofia? Then I'll come out so we can go over the list of scrapbook supplies?"

"Thanks for the drink," Sofia smiled gratefully.

"You bet," Coco obliged. "Give me a buzz if there's anything else I can do for you, okay?" She smiled at Margo before tiptoeing out of the office, quietly closing the door behind her.

"What's with this no dairy business?" Sofia inquired, stirring her iced coffee with a straw.

Margo sighed, leaning back on the couch. "Don't ask. I'm on a strict nondairy diet. It's a pain in the ass."

"How come?"

"I thought I had ulcers. Don't worry, *I don't*," Margo quickly added. "I went to the doctor, and he seems to think I'm lactose intolerant. I've been avoiding all dairy products for the past few weeks, and my stomach's actually been feeling much better, so I'm sticking to it. Who knows . . ."

"*Ulcers?* Why didn't you say anything? That's awful!"

"It's nothing," Margo emphasized, shrugging it off. "I figured it was just a physical manifestation of stress. But the pain kept getting worse, so I finally made an appointment."

Sofia looked worried. "Margo, you've really got to find a way to relax and put everything into perspective. Honestly, it sounds like a stupid cliché, but life's too short. No job is worth this level of suffering."

"Yes, it is, Sofia," Margo bit back. "Don't you understand?" She shifted her position on the couch so that she was facing her directly. "This job is all I can depend on. It *is* my life."

"Oh come on, Mar! Lighten up. You're overstating things *just* slightly, don't you think?"

"No," she insisted. "I don't. Think about it. I'm in my thirties—I have no future with Preston and no other viable prospects for a relationship. My mother's deranged, God only knows where my father is—I have no family I can count on. Don't you get it?" She paused, looking at Sofia, softening her tone. "I'm alone. What have I got going for me other than the show?" Margo didn't wait for an answer. "Nothing. This is it." She wrapped her arms around her knees and looked away. "I need to make the most of it."

Finally, it hit Sofia. Underneath that perfect exterior, Margo was desperate.

Sucker Punch

Once Delilah and Sofia retreat to Delilah's suite and are safely behind locked doors, Delilah slips into a clean pair of vintage Levi's and a pretty white camisole, which always makes her feel extra feminine and light. Sofia immediately begins pacing the perimeter of the room, purging all the troubling information she's been bottling up about Margo since Agnes's announcement. She tells Delilah about Margo and Amelia's nasty exchange in the *D.B.* ladies' room earlier that week when Margo confessed she "plans to wear her down and destroy the goody two-shoes," and all about Preston's disturbing phone call yesterday, exposing how Margo blatantly lied about the weekend.

"Wait a minute," Delilah interrupts, "you mean he wasn't really assigned to a new court case?"

"Nope. Preston's home right now, probably watching *Law & Order.* It was all part of Margo's plan."

As Delilah listens, Sofia recounts her conversation with Margo shortly after Memorial Day weekend when Coco brought Margo an iced coffee with milk in it, prompting Margo to reveal that she's lactose intolerant and that her relationship with Preston is on dangerously thin ice.

"Lactose intolerant?" Delilah leans against the antique armoire in the corner of her suite, frozen, trying to absorb this onslaught of repulsive revelations. *This isn't happening . . . This isn't happening . . .* She quickly glances up at the ceiling, just to make sure there's not an actual rain cloud hovering above her. Considering her day so far, it wouldn't surprise her. "But wait a minute . . . If Margo knows you're aware that she's lactose intolerant, then why would she drink milk in front of you? It makes no sense."

"I wasn't there," Sofia reminds Delilah. "I was running on the beach with Derek. And besides, Margo was *extremely* emotionally distressed the afternoon she told me about it—*out of her mind* upset. I'm not sure it even registered with her. She was too distracted sobbing over Preston, wailing about their relationship being over. She even let Coco see her crying! *Come on,* Margo would *never* let her see her that way if she was in her right mind. Don't you agree?"

Delilah tries to follow. "I guess. I don't know . . . This is all—this is crazy!"

"Plus, the lactose intolerance has never been brought up again. I honestly don't think she remembers telling me about it, Delilah. Oh! And then I stole Margo's cell phone while she was in the shower yesterday and hid it in the wine cellar behind the French merlots because I figured, Shit! All she has to do is talk to Preston and she'll know I know she lied about the weekend and is obviously up to something—and if she knows *I know*, well, you know . . ."

Delilah can hardly see straight.

When Sofia finally concludes, she sits down on the foot of the bed, afraid to make eye contact with Delilah. "I'm sorry I didn't say anything sooner," she says, her voice brimming with guilt. "I should have known Margo was up to something evil. All the signs were right there in front of my face. I messed up."

Suddenly, Delilah has to concentrate on breathing. She wants desperately to believe that not a word of what Sofia just said is true—that it's all a spectacularly huge misunderstanding that can be easily explained and laughed about down the line at some glamorous *D.B.* social function where everybody gets trashed and forgets they're swimming with sharks. *Please let this not be true. Margo wouldn't try to ruin my career. She wouldn't really try to "destroy" me. It's too cruel. We're mature professional adults. We're friends. How could she hate me this much? What is this, an episode of* Dynasty*?! Who acts like this?! There must be some miscommunication, some explanation* . . . Only, in her heart, Delilah knows all too well that Sofia isn't capable of fabricating such ugly lies. And thus, every last word of it must be true.

Confounded, she unsteadily eases herself onto the bed. She takes a deep breath and leans forward, resting her forehead in the palm of her hand. For the second time that day, Delilah's head spins like the time she rode the whirligig at the Eagle River County Fair when she was nine and threw up purple Hawaiian Punch all over poor Betsy Kallaway. "I don't . . . I don't understand," she stammers. "Are you telling me . . ."—she slowly puts the puzzle pieces together—"that Margo spilled milk on my computer *intentionally*? She sabotaged me?"

Sofia looks into Delilah's eyes, nodding. "I think so."

"But *why*? Why would she do that to me, Sofia?"

"I don't know. I think it may be all part of her master plan—whatever that is. I wouldn't put anything past Margo at this point. She'll do whatever it takes to become executive producer—it's the only thing in her life that she thinks she has any control over. She made that abundantly clear to me when she was crying about losing Preston. All I *do* know, Delilah, is that she'll stop at nothing, and none of this adds up."

"Holy motherfucker of pearl . . . ," Delilah says, feeling as though the wind has been knocked out of her.

"Want me to count to ten in Spanish with you?" Sofia offers, trying to infuse a teeny drop of light into the darkness.

Delilah falls into stunned silence, staring into space, blinking, trying to understand how Margo could stoop so low. And although crying is the *last* thing she wants to do—she knows Margo isn't worth it—it's entirely beyond her control. She feels the tears stinging her eyes and then slowly dripping down her flushed cheeks.

"THAT BITCH!" Sofia fumes. "The woman's evil. *Pure evil!* How could she do this to you?! How could she do this to *anyone*? I wanna throttle her, so help me God!"

Delilah wipes away a tear, her blue eyes slowly narrowing with fury and determination. "Well, I'll tell you one thing, Sofia: I am *not* gonna let Margo bring me down. *No way*. If that's what she thinks is happening, she's mistaken. She's got another thing coming to her."

In a moment of insight, Delilah realizes that although she may not like it, the rules of the game have just changed, and if she doesn't amend the way she's playing, she will be eaten alive.

Pacing around the room once more, Sofia detects Delilah's brain fast at work. "What are you thinking? What is it? Talk to me."

"I have to stop her, Sofia. *Now.* Once and for all. She's trying to ruin me! I'm not gonna let her bully me out of *D.B.* I can't let her do this."

"Good! Enough of this shit!"

Delilah rises from the bed, her face contorting in rage.

"Margo Hart is *not* going to jeopardize my reputation, my career, *my future. Nobody is.* Hell no!" In less time than it takes to bake an instant cake, Delilah's initial shock and sadness transform to anger—the good old-fashioned, blood-boiling type that makes one see red. Seething, she looks at Sofia, deadpan. Her voice drops an octave. "Are you in?"

Sofia smirks. "Do you even have to ask?"

Trawlerville

Not many families have a professional, twelve-hole, first-rate miniature golf course right in their own backyard—the kind of fancy outdoor course with waterfalls, automated parts, and blinking lights. In short, the type of course most people have to drive to and pay hard-earned cash to play on. Mrs. Trawler had a fit when Mr. Trawler shared his plan to build the miniature golf course of his boyhood dreams in their backyard over a decade ago. True, with fifty acres of land, there was plenty of space to accommodate it, but she saw that as no reason to embrace the idea. "I don't want you turning our summer home into Neverland Ranch," she said. "What's next, Jacko? A petting zoo? A go-kart track? A . . . a *moat*?" Mr. Trawler's eyes lit up and the tips of his ears turned pink, a clear indicator that his interest had been piqued. Heeding the warning signs, Mrs. T knew she had about two seconds to successfully distract her husband—either that or learn to love the family moat. "A miniature golf course sounds *wonderful! Terrific! Outstanding! Why not?!*" The moat was forgotten. "It's not like we spend *that* much time here," she added wistfully.

Call it what one will, over the years Cherry Pond has become something of Mr. Trawler's fantasy playland, and most people who visit don't want to leave. Ironically, nobody enjoys the miniature golf course more than his lovely wife. She dubbed it Trawlerville and now personally oversees its yearly maintenance and renovations. Just a month ago, she added a mechanical shark à la *Jaws* to the serene, man-made Japanese koi pond bordering the eleventh hole. The savage beast, complete with a mighty roar and razor-sharp teeth dripping fake blood, is programmed to violently burst out of the water and make like it's trying to swallow the golf ball and eat the players, if the ball doesn't roll over the hidden sensor implanted in the green indicating it's heading toward the hole. Mrs. Trawler had Jaws flown in from Munich while Mr. Trawler was away on business, and nobody, aside from Consuela, knows about it yet.

The annual mini-golf tournament—not recommended for the weak of heart, pregnant women, or elderly—is one of the most beloved traditions of the Trawler July Fourth celebration. Guests who wish to participate, including everyone lodging at Cherry Pond and a select group of invited friends, are randomly paired off and compete for a fabulous secret prize. Last year, members of the winning team scored a flat-screen plasma TV.

Once all of this year's competitors are transported to Trawlerville via golf cart with an ornate gold letter *T* painted on the hood, they each pick a number out of a hat, which Mrs. Trawler holds high above her head so nobody can cheat. She doesn't believe it would be fair to expect people to compete with the Mini-Golf Champion of the Universe, so she runs the tournament from the sidelines, serving as a most enthusiastic, and slightly spastic, emcee and referee. After everyone draws a tightly folded yellow slip of paper, she begins calling off numbers to identify teams. "Here we go, ladies and gentlemen . . . Let the games begin! Team One!" She throws her pointer finger high into the air.

Aunt Deb and Jack eagerly approach Mrs. T, giving each other a high five.

"Awww, isn't that cute? Mother and son . . . ," Mrs. Trawler coos into her bullhorn, which isn't really necessary but makes her job more fun. "They're gonna be tough to beat today, folks. Yes sirree, they surely are! Let's see Team Two, shall we?"

Sam and Mrs. Trawler's friend from the yacht club, Penelope Martin, raise their hands.

"Girl power! Eeeeexcellent . . ." Mrs. Trawler nods her head. "Alright, Team Number Three, don't be shy, show your faces why don't ya!"

Delilah and Margo simultaneously step forward. Immediately locking eyes, they smile like game-show hosts and approach one another. A showdown.

"Well, what do ya know? Let's hope the prize is a brand-new computer, huh ladies?" Mrs. Trawler teases. "Looks like we've got the *D.B.* girls represented today." She claps her hands. "This match is gonna be fierce! F-I-E-R-C-E! Woo-Wee! I can feel it! Okay then, make some noise Team Four."

Margo drapes her arm around Delilah's shoulder, beaming. "Howdy partner."

"Hey there," Delilah grins. "How's your hand? Does it hurt?" *God I hope it hurts. I hope it falls off.*

Margo snorts at her wound, now carefully bandaged and wrapped in white gauze. "It's okay, thanks. Throbbing a bit, but I'll survive. Don't worry, I have no intention of letting it ruin my game." She hugs Delilah closer. "I owe you after what I did to your computer. I'm so fucking clumsy. We're winning this tournament!"

"Damn straight we are!" *Of all the people I could possibly be paired up with, OF COURSE it has to be Margo. Why wouldn't it be? Just my luck. What's going on today?! It's like I've been cursed,* Delilah thinks to herself. *It's like somebody has a voodoo doll with my face on it! Alright, stay calm. Remain focused and kill her with kindness. For now . . .*

⊰⊱

"I really am sorry about before, Delilah," Margo says, bending down to collect her golf ball from the fifth hole. "I feel horrible."

"Don't worry about it. Accidents happen." Delilah smiles, leaning on her golf club and thinking that she'd rather stick a cocktail fork in her eye than continue with this ridiculous charade of pretending all is perfect and grand between her and Margo.

"Well, it was a dumb accident. I deserve the Clumsy Ass award."

"Please . . . What can ya do? It's not as if you meant to spill the milk," Delilah says, carefully watching Margo out of the corner of her eye as she removes the pencil from behind her ear and begins tapping it against the scorecard, appearing to mentally calculate their points.

"Of course not! But still . . . Wait, did it take me three or four strokes to get the ball in the hole?"

"Five. Remember you got a penalty point when your ball got stuck in Gumdrop Mountain?" *Nice try, cheater.*

"God damn Candy Land! I swear! This makes me hate that game even more." Margo jots down her score on the little pad of paper, and they begin moseying toward the sixth hole, leaving the brightly hued Candy Land–themed hole behind them. "So . . . I haven't had a chance to ask you about last night yet. How was dinner with Jack?"

Jack? Jack? Who's Jack? Oh yes! That's right. He's that incredible man I had dinner with last night who sang his tone-deaf heart out for me and whom I'd like to spend the rest of all eternity with . . . Delilah's harrowing day has been traumatic enough that she hasn't had a spare second to devote to Jack. Cee-Cee's so far from her memory that she might as well not even exist. Under normal circumstances, Delilah would have replayed her evening with Jack in her mind—fraction of a moment by fraction of a moment—at least 144 times by now while obsessively checking her e-mail and phone messages, and absentmindedly doodling his name on a napkin or anything she could get her hands on. She would have also found a way to rationalize why Cee-Cee, a woman she's never met, is entirely wrong for Jack and would be better off teaching math in Guam. "It was nice. I had a good time," Delilah tells Margo, though she doesn't feel in the mood for girl talk.

They arrive at the seventh hole, which is fashioned to look like the gray, rocky, porous surface of the moon.

"*Nice?* Come on, Delilah, there had to be more to it than that. Do tell . . ."

"There's really not much else to say," she shrugs, delighted to keep Margo in the dark. "We had dinner, grabbed a drink, and then came home. That was that. It was . . . nice." Delilah places her ball down on the lunar landscape, assesses the crater she's aiming for, and swings her club. The ball races past the hole, and a foam meteor seems to fall from nowhere, landing inches from Margo's toes.

"Jesus Christ! I hate the moon! I swear!" she huffs. "This is dangerous. They should have had us sign some sort of release to play this frickin' game."

Attempting to hide her smile, Delilah seizes the opportunity to quickly steer the conversation in a new direction. "Have you heard from Preston? I hope he hasn't had to spend the whole weekend at the office. What a rotten Fourth of July for the poor guy."

"You know, I still haven't found my cell phone. It's the damndest thing. I have no idea where it could be. I gave up looking for it. But, to answer your question, yes, I spoke with Preston this morning. He was at the office at seven a.m. Can you believe it? On a holiday! It's disgusting if you ask me."

Keep digging, why don't you? Deeper and deeper you go. "Yes, it is," Delilah concurs as she prepares to take her second stroke. *"Quite!"* Infuriated that Margo would look her directly in the eye and lie, she considers accidentally aiming for her head with the next shot. *Oops, did I do that? Golly gee, looks like I deserve the Clumsy Ass award! You didn't really need your right eye, did you?*

But instead, the ball zooms expertly for the hole, landing inside with a *kerplunk.*

"Yes! Hole in two!" Margo flashes Delilah a wide grin. "Nice job, partner!" She raises her good hand in the air, waiting for a high five.

"Thanks, partner," Delilah replies, tapping her hand against Margo's like a good sport. *Yeah right.*

"Damn," Margo says. "Is there anything you're not good at? Something tells me we're gonna be toasting to our win tonight."

"Frankly, I think I'm ready for a frosty beverage right about *now,*" Delilah says. "What a day . . ." Forcing a smile, she takes the score pad from Margo and writes down her points.

"I have to admit my nerves are shattered after this morning. I'm looking forward to one of Consuela's famous fauxitos tonight. Those things are so damn good, I could drink a whole pitcher! I still can't believe they're made without any alcohol. I don't know how she manages to get them to taste so authentic."

"I know," Delilah agrees. "You gotta hand it to Consuela—she puts the mojito to shame. Actually, that could be a great segment for the show."

"Funny," Margo answers. "I was just thinking the same thing."

"Ha ha," Delilah laughs awkwardly. "That is funny."

While ambling along the yellow brick road leading to the *Wizard of Oz*–themed ninth hole, Delilah is struck with an interesting idea. She tries not to smile as she recalls Margo's drunken exploits at last year's annual *D.B.* holiday party, known as the December Gala. After consuming six glasses of extremely potent eggnog and one peppermint stick martini, Margo had belligerently announced to Preston—loudly enough for most everyone in the Plaza Hotel's gilded Grand Ballroom to hear—that she was a naughty little girl and wanted to "suck his candy cane." Next, to Mary and Joseph's horror (Agnes, the consummate party thrower, had arranged for an elaborate, live Nativity scene including actors, live animals, myrrh—the whole nine yards), Margo hiked up her skirt, climbed on top of Blitzen—such that she was straddling him in a rather vulgar manner—and ordered Preston to meet her in the manger for a little "kissy kissy 'neath the mistletoe." Then she jumped off the reindeer shouting "Bye-bye donkey!" tripped over her own two feet, went flying through the air—legs splayed—and landed on top of a portly shepherd who became visibly aroused upon contact. Moments later she passed out in Preston's arms as he carried her to the car. Lining up her next shot on the green in the glittering Emerald City, Delilah's heart begins to race as the seeds of inspiration quickly sprout. By the time she exits Munchkin Land, her plan to expose Margo's guilt has fallen almost entirely into place. If executed correctly, Delilah figures it might actually work.

Suddenly, Aunt Deb's piercing shriek echoes from the eleventh hole. "Jack! MY BABY!"

"OH MY GOD!!! IS HE BREATHING?!?!" Mrs. Trawler shouts into her bullhorn. "Jack! Listen to me! It's not a real shark! Jaws is fake! That's *not* real blood!!! Uno . . . Dos . . ."

Like a Virgin

"I beg your pardon, where do you two think you're going?" Thor, hands firmly planted on hips, interrogates Sofia and Delilah upon spotting them tiptoeing through the backyard looking rather suspicious—the fact that they're wearing bathing suits and holding towels causes him alarm.

"Um . . . to the pool?" Sofia hesitantly replies. "We're gonna take a swim—"

"Not so fast . . . ," interrupts Thor at the same time that his walkie-talkie beeps loudly. "Excuse me just one moment please." Turning away from the women, he raises the device to his mouth. "Talk to me, Sayid. What's your twenty?"

Sayid's gravelly voice comes through the walkie-talkie. "I'm in front of the house, boss. Chip the Ice Sculptor just arrived and wants to know where the blocks of ice are."

Thor rolls his eyes, his patience beginning to wear thin. "They're in the ice truck. It's a big silver truck marked *Ice.* It should be the only one like it in the driveway."

"Copy that."

"Good. Meet me out front in five minutes. I want to go over the renderings one last time with Chip before he starts."

"I read you loud and clear, Thor. Ten-four," Sayid signs off.

"Down 'n' gone, mate." Thor returns the walkie-talkie to its place on his belt and focuses his attention on the girls once again. "Now, where were we?"

Sofia opens her mouth to respond. "Oh yes," he continues, clasping his hands together, "that's right: pool time. Would you ladies mind terribly if I ask you to please make it a point to stay out of my men's way? We're about to enter our crunch phase." He quickly glances at his stopwatch. "It's two p.m. now, and guests are due to start arriving at five-thirty—which leaves us with only three and half hours to complete everything, and there's still lots to be done. *Lots* to be done," he nervously repeats, eyes darting about the vast backyard taking stock of where his team is and what exactly they're doing.

"Not a problem. I promise you, we'll mind our own business and won't disturb a thing," Delilah assures him. "We just need a safe, private place where we can talk and no one will overhear us."

"What's better than the middle of a pool?" Sofia chimes in.

"Oooh . . . ," Thor smirks, eying them closely. "Sounds scandalous."

"It is," they respond in perfect unison, to his delight.

"Well, don't let me stop you two Doublemint Twins. By all means, carry on!" Thor bows and motions them off. "Cheerio! Be off with you."

They smile gratefully and saunter toward the pool where Pappy is fast at work cursing and inflating body-length red, white, and blue rectangle-shaped floats.

Thor watches Sofia and Delilah dip their feet in the water and then dive in. "My word, women are vicious creatures," he says, shuddering to himself. "I love it."

Technical Difficulties

Finished conspiring, Delilah and Sofia are drying off by the side of the pool, just about to head inside and get dressed for the party, when the twinkly melody of Delilah's cell phone alerts her that she has a new message. "Huh. I didn't even hear it ring," she remarks, surprised.

"Reception's dodgy in this part of the mountains. I can never get a signal on my phone. You're welcome to use a land line inside if you want," Sofia offers, stepping into her flip-flops.

"Thanks," Delilah says and winks, while punching in her access code to pick up her new voice mail.

After a few moments, she lets her towel drop to the patio floor as the color drains from her face. About to lose her balance, she slowly lowers herself onto the edge of a nearby deck chair, clutching the phone to her ear.

"What's wrong?" asks Sofia, alarmed by her look of panic. "What's the matter, D?"

Delilah waves her hand and shakes her head no, ignoring her, listening carefully to her message, with her brow furrowed, knee nervously bouncing up and down at about a hundred miles per hour.

Finally, after what feels like an eternity, Delilah hands her the phone. "Listen for yourself . . . ," she stammers. "I have no idea what's going on!"

Perplexed, Sofia sits down next to her, grabs the phone, and hears: "Delilah, it's Agnes calling at about noon on the Fourth of July. I hope you're having a nice holiday. I'm not. I just opened your e-mail with the subject line: 'Shoot Me Now.' Delilah, I had *no idea* this is how you feel about your job and the show. I'm . . . I'm *floored*, to say the least. I'm sure you can understand how stunned and upset I am to read something like this. After all these years you *know* you can talk to me about *anything, anytime*, sweetie. Don't you? I don't understand why you didn't come to me sooner to address your issues and dissatisfaction with the show directly. It isn't something I should have to read about in an e-mail. Look, I don't know what's going on, but we need to sit down and discuss everything face-to-face first thing on Tuesday morning. I want to get to the bottom of this. I . . . I can't believe I'm saying this, but if *Domestic Bliss* isn't the place for you, it's something I need to know immediately so that I can make the right decision regarding executive producer." Agnes heaves a forlorn sigh. "Shit. Call me if you want to; I'm on my cell. Otherwise, I'll see you bright and early on Tuesday. I hope you're okay, Delilah. I'm worried about you."

Astonished, Sofia clicks the phone shut and hands it back to Delilah. "What the hell did you send her?"

"NOTHING! I didn't send Agnes anything!" she moans, feeling like she's going to be sick.

"So what's she talking about then?"

"I have no idea!" Delilah throws her arms up into the air. "I don't know how she got it. I don't . . . I don't . . . I don't even . . . I don't . . . I . . ."

"Alright, calm down," Sofia gently urges. "Take a deep breath and just try to relax a little bit. Relax . . ."

Panting, Delilah obliges, closing her eyes, trying to catch her breath. She can feel her heart pounding throughout every inch of her body as the ground seemingly crumbles beneath her feet, opening up, threatening to swallow her whole.

"Good. Now, I'm just trying to understand," Sofia patiently probes. "You *didn't* write Agnes an e-mail?"

"I *did* write the damn e-mail, but it wasn't to her. It was to *you*. Never in a million years would I send Agnes a message like that!"

"A message like *what*? I didn't get an e-mail from you."

"Yes, I know you didn't. That's because *I didn't send it*! I just needed to vent, and then I deleted it. Or at least I *think* I deleted it. I could swear I deleted it . . ." Not quite sure what to do with herself, Delilah gazes up at the cloudless sky, trying desperately to think back to that terrible morning in her office. "I'm . . . I'm pretty sure I did. I remember hitting the DELETE button. *I think*. Unless I'm completely making that part up and I somehow accidentally sent it to the wrong person without realizing it. I don't remember seeing it in my SENT mailbox. It'd be there if I sent it, right? Oh God!" Delilah groans, raising both hands to her head. "Who knows?! It doesn't even matter at this point. Agnes has the e-mail!"

Sofia's about ready to push her in the pool if she doesn't reveal what the devil was in the mysterious correspondence in the next five seconds. "Alright, D, you're gonna have to tell me what it said before I go crazy."

"I wrote it Thursday morning after the segment pitch meeting when Margo crucified me *and* both of my ideas—tore 'em to shreds in front of everyone and completely had Agnes in her corner. I looked like a big idiot. I was frustrated and upset and discouraged, and I got back to my office and wrote you a stupid, impulsive message talking about the meeting and bitching about everything and everyone at *D.B.* Oh Jesus, I did not hold back." She hunches over her knees, cradling her head in her hands, rocking back and forth. "This is bad. *So bad* . . ."

Sofia grimaces. "Stay calm. Did you mention anybody specific?"

"No. I didn't have to. I insulted the entire staff." Delilah curses herself for being so damn impetuous. "I was just so aggravated at the time!"

"Oh Delilah . . . What exactly did you say? Dare I ask?"

"I don't even know!" Delilah closes her eyes, spinning out of control, trying once again to recall the specific contents of the message. "I . . . I can't remember exactly. Something about how I'm sick and tired of taking inane crap from people at the show who are afraid to think outside the box, and how sometimes I feel like walking out the door and never coming back."

"Is that it?" Sofia prays that's it. "Please let that be it."

"I'm not sure . . ." Delilah stares at the bottom of the deep end of the pool, which suddenly seems like an excellent place for sinking, and sighs. "I think I also might've mentioned being at my wit's end with the show and having no desire to tape that night. Oh!" She cringes. "And I called the staff a bunch of moron potpies."

Sofia shoots her a questioning glance.

"I was *really* upset."

"Moron potpies?" Pressing her lips together, Sofia stifles her laughter. "Can I just ask you? Where do you come up with this stuff? Who says that?"

Delilah somberly shakes her head, softly confessing, "I ate a chicken potpie the night before. The kind you buy frozen and then just heat in the oven." Her blue eyes spill over with fear. "What am I gonna do, Sofia? I know how Agnes thinks. There's no way she'll let this slide. This changes everything. My credibility and integrity have been shot to hell. What am I supposed to say to her now?"

Stumped, Sofia hopes this is a rhetorical question. Never before has she seen Delilah this shaken. Suddenly, out of nowhere, she's hit with a terrible thought—a thought that causes her to freeze in place. "Wait a minute, Delilah. I just remembered something . . ."

"What?" Delilah looks at her. Helpless. Disheveled. Apoplectic. "Do I even want to hear this?"

"Something Preston said yesterday when he called . . ." Sofia covers her hand with her mouth. "I can't believe this . . . I don't know why it only just dawned on me now."

Apprehension shoots up Delilah's back. "You're scaring me, Sofia. What is it?"

"He mentioned that when Agnes phoned the house looking for Margo, she asked him to give her the message that it was *urgent*." The minute Preston said the word it struck me as unusual that Agnes would be making *urgent* phone calls on a holiday. Know what I mean? What's so imperative that it couldn't wait a couple days until after the break? Now I'm wondering if it might've had something to do with your e-mail."

Delilah looks, and feels, like she's been hit by a Mack truck. And then stepped on. Before being kicked in the head for good measure. By an angry T. rex. "It's over. I lost my shot at executive producer," she softly mutters.

"You don't know that," Sofia points out, trying to mask her growing concern. "Let's not jump to any conclusions."

"I might have lost my *job*," Delilah realizes, slack-jawed. She can feel the panic taking over.

"That's ridiculous and you know—"

"After all these years at *Domestic Bliss*," she interrupts. "All the hard work . . . Everything I've done . . . Every ounce of devotion . . . It was all for nothing. There's no chance now. I . . . I blew it. I can't believe what I've done . . ." Overwhelmed, Delilah's head droops forward, like an old rag doll, and she begins to cry—her body involuntarily racked with deep, heavy, gut-wrenching sobs—aware that she's shed more tears this weekend than she has all year combined. "And the worst part is, Agnes is the last person I'd ever want to hurt or betray. She's been incredible to me! I'd take a bullet for that woman!"

"Delilah, it's gonna be okay." It rips Sofia apart to see her best friend—one of the *good* guys in the truest sense of the word—shattered to this degree. But then, she's gripped by yet another unsettling, though hopeful, thought. Grabbing Delilah's arm with both hands, inspired, she nearly shouts her ear off, "Wait! Hold on a second! Is there any possibility that Margo's behind this?"

Delilah shakes her head, hot tears streaming down her face and off her chin. "No. I already thought of that, but there's no way. How could she send an e-mail from my account? This is my fault, Sofia. I'm to blame. *Me*."

"Well, e-mail mishaps do happen," Sofia concedes, "especially when people are in highly emotional states and not thinking clearly. Remember Francesca's friend who referred to her boss as a *parsimonious fuck* in an e-mail, which she intended to send to Francesca but accidentally sent to her boss instead? Ended up getting herself good and fired."

"*I know.* That's exactly why I'm worried," Delilah sniffles. "I mean, I guess I must've sent it to Agnes by accident." She squeezes her eyes shut and clasps her arms over her head, covering her face. "Arghhhhh! It's just such a stupid fucking mistake! How could I do something like this?! What have I done?!"

"Alright, the good news is the damage is not irreparable," Sofia—ever the optimist—points out. "You'll talk to Agnes, explain things, and this'll all get worked out in the end. I know it will. You have a long history together, and she's a very reasonable person."

Delilah appreciates Sofia's positive spin on the situation. Under ordinary circumstances, she, too, would be able to see the glass as half full. But the way she sees it now, the glass itself is pulverized. The trouble is, she did write that letter, and the consequence of doing so remains the same whether or not she meant to send it. The fact that she intended to delete her words doesn't make them any less true. They're out there, and there's nothing she can do to retract them.

Her mother, a particularly socially conscious woman, once relayed a haunting anecdote to Delilah when she was just a small child—too young and fresh to be able to grasp its simple yet staggering truth. But it has been turning over in her mind ever since, and now she understands the wisdom behind her mother's words: "It takes years to build a reputation and seconds to destroy it."

Wiping away her tears with the back of her hand, Delilah attempts to pull herself together. Though she's never had an out-of-body experience, she's willing to bet this is what it must feel like. "I'm gonna go inside and call Agnes right now." She stands up—her legs feeling shaky and weak—resigned to address, and hopefully settle, this matter as soon as possible.

"What will you say?"

"No idea." She shrugs, defeated. "I just know I have to talk to her." Delilah retrieves her towel from the ground, haphazardly ties it around her waist, and runs her fingers through her tangled, wet hair. "Is my skin all red and splotchy?"

"A little bit," Sofia fibs, holding up her thumb and pointer finger with about an inch of space between them, realizing it's best to downplay the fact that Delilah resembles a white-and-pink-spotted leopard with a giant booger in its left nostril.

"Well," she says, then slowly exhales, puffing out her cheeks, "time to face the music. Wish me luck."

"Good luck." Sofia smiles reassuringly as Delilah slowly trudges toward the house, shoulders slumped. "It's gonna be okay! Wipe your nose! And no more tears! We can't have you looking all red and splotchy for Jack tonight!"

Jack? Jack? Who's Jack? "Ha! The least of my worries right now," Delilah hollers without looking back.

Lost and Found

Consuela knocks on Sofia's bedroom door five times before Sofia finally opens it, with toothbrush in hand, wearing a plush white bathrobe and slippers, hair wrapped in a towel. "What took you so long?" demands Consuela.

"I was washing my hair."

"Well, I've been looking all over for you. Do you recognize this phone?" She holds up Margo's cell.

Sofia grabs Consuela by the shirt collar, quickly yanks her into her bedroom—causing her to shriek with surprise—and promptly locks the door behind them.

"Dios mío, child!"

"Who else have you shown that phone to?" Sofia demands, wielding the toothbrush like a weapon.

Consuela looks at her like she's insane. "Nobody. Why are you giving me whiplash?"

"No one else knows you have it?"

Consuela thinks for a moment. "Uh, noooo." She keeps her head perfectly still while her eyes nervously scan the room. "Why did you lock the door?"

"Margo hasn't seen it?"

"Noooo. Like I said, *nobody* has. Why are you pointing your toothbrush at my head?"

"Thank goodness." Sofia breathes a sigh of relief, gingerly placing the toothbrush down on a nearby shelf. "Sorry about that." She smooths out Consuela's wrinkled uniform and smiles sheepishly, patting her on the shoulder.

"You're acting weird," Consuela observes.

"No I'm not."

Consuela crosses her arms, sniffing the air like a bloodhound. "Are you smoking the weed?"

Sofia chuckles, assuring Consuela that, no, she is not stoned. "Listen, Delilah's in serious trouble and needs your help. We both do." With no doubt that Consuela will be more than happy to lend her valued assistance to the cause, Sofia decides now is as good a time as any to recruit her and make her a member of the team. "You might want to take a seat," she says, motioning toward the chair at her mirrored vanity table. "There's a lot to fill you in on to get you up to speed."

Que Será, Será

Delilah slowly composes herself, both mentally and physically, as she takes her time preparing for this weekend's main event, the big Fourth of July party. The past three days feel like a surreal cross between a dream and her worst nightmare, and she wonders for a minute if any of this could really be happening. How could her life be turned so upside down and in such genuine peril of collapse since leaving New York only seventy-two hours ago? With everything at stake, it doesn't seem possible, and the fact that it is only further boggles Delilah's mind.

It requires concerted effort, but with the help of a long, relaxing, hot shower, a calming cup of tea, a healing pep talk from her sister, Francesca, and the perfect amount of under-eye concealer blended just right, she manages to pull herself together nicely. She exits her suite just after 5:45 p.m., looking vibrant and beautiful in a chic black classic Armani dress with spaghetti straps that falls tastefully just below her knees. Appearing calm and poised, Delilah descends the staircase—the material of her dress billowing slightly, hugging her curves in all the right places—having put the disturbing events of the day behind her and ready to thoroughly enjoy what promises to be the most memorable social gathering of the summer.

To her dismay, she failed to connect with Agnes, despite having placed three phone calls to her—trying desperately to reach her on her cell, at home, and then finally at *Domestic Bliss*. After leaving a long-winded, emotional message on her initial call, filled with what she's sure must have sounded like the ramblings of a madwoman, she decided it was probably best to hang up after the beep on her two subsequent calls. Lest things get *really* ugly and Agnes opts to use the incoming recorded messages as evidence against her in a court of law someday.

Reaching the bottom of the staircase, Delilah turns left, breezes down the hallway and through the kitchen—smelling of warm, fresh-baked, crusty bread, buzzing with activity and noisy racket—with a gleam of determination in her ice-blue eyes.

She exits the kitchen through the open double-glass doors leading directly to the backyard, where the celebration is already off to a lively and impressive start, and strolls onto the festively decorated deck. Focused. Ready. Determined. A predator in a pretty black dress.

She'll figure out how to deal with Agnes tomorrow when she gets back to the city. For now, she knows there are more urgent matters to tend to—matters that deserve her undivided attention. After all, her covert operation has officially been set in motion. The bell in the boxing arena has secretly been rung. No turning back now.

The Great Trawler

When a handsome waiter in a tuxedo with a red, white, and blue Burberry print bow tie and matching cummerbund glides by Delilah carrying a sterling silver tray of champagne, she helps herself to a glass, smiling *thank you*. She scans the crowd for Margo as casually as she can, trying not to look as paranoid as she feels. Hoping that perhaps the drink might help take a slight edge off her nerves, she sips from the crystal flute, noting that it is fine champagne. Then, for no discernible reason, she breaks into a wide, unprovoked grin, remembering that a critical part of the scheme is to appear to be having a wonderful time at the *wonderful* party. Offering the slightest hint of preoccupation or sending a signal that something's stored up her sleeve could jeopardize the whole mission, and Delilah knows she cannot afford for this to happen. There's simply too much at stake. Lifting her chin several degrees, she forces herself to focus on the sun slowly beginning to set over Lake Minnonqua, tranquil and deep blue, just starting to show the faintest sign of dusk on the horizon. It's breathtaking. A popular swing band from Manhattan plays in the gazebo and is also broadcast over loudspeakers peppered throughout the backyard, filling the eighty-degree night air with a smooth, jazzy, upbeat tune. Delilah enjoys the music as she watches a man dressed like Uncle Sam walking around on stilts stop to bend down and twist a balloon into the shape of an elephant for an excited child with a chunk of cotton candy stuck to his cheek. She can see there's good reason why the *Catskill Gazette* referred to the Trawlers' annual Fourth of July fete as "a grand, lavish, Gatsby-like affair where decadence knows no bounds." Sofia had pointed out the little blurb written up in the daily paper earlier that morning over breakfast.

"Delilah! Delilah! Over here!" Uncle Mark calls out to her, capturing her attention and waving her over. "I want you to meet Mary Noble, an old friend of mine from Greenwich, and these are her sisters, Marsha and Barbara. They're all big fans of the show."

"I love love love *Domestic Bliss*," Mary says, smiling at Delilah. "Pleased to meet you!"

"Nice to meet you too," Delilah says and grins, shaking their hands.

"You are such an inspiration," Mary confides, sipping a frosty piña colada. "I know I sound like a blabbering fool, but I have to tell you, your influence can be seen all over my house."

"Well, thank you." Delilah smiles warmly. "That's always really nice to hear."

"I can't believe I'm about to do this, but . . ." Mary squeezes her eyes shut, as if she's about to say something truly embarrassing. "Can I please ask you to sign my napkin for me?" Her eyebrows rise in hope. "Is that an annoying request?"

"Not at all. It's my pleasure, though I have to tell you, I'm not sure it's worth much."

The gaggle guffaws, unaware that Delilah's modesty is sincere.

"Us too?" Marsha asks.

"Of course," Delilah says, nodding.

Mary fishes an expensive pen out of her purse and hands it to her along with a white linen napkin bearing a gold letter *T* embroidered in the bottom right-hand corner. "Thank you, this is great."

Sofia, standing across the deck with a bunch of her dad's patent and trade associates debating which is a better invention, the light switch or the Clapper, sees Delilah signing autographs and joins the group. "Hello, everybody. Happy Fourth of July," she says, adding, "You look gorgeous," to Delilah. "Completely refreshed. How'd you do that?"

"Thanks," Delilah smiles, handing Marsha her signed napkin. She shoots Sofia the subtlest of glances accompanied with a barely visible shake of the head.

Sofia receives the message loud and clear. "Didn't reach Agnes?" she confirms under her breath.

Without breaking focus on her admirers, Delilah shakes her head no.

When the last napkin has been signed and she is able to politely excuse herself, Delilah and Sofia set off across the west lawn in search of Margo. Meandering past the inflatable jumping castle—where sugared-up children's squeals of delight bounce off the walls and onto the wind, emanating throughout the backyard—Delilah explains her calm new take on the Agnes crisis. Having accepted that her hands are temporarily tied with regard to addressing it, she has redirected her energy toward something that *is* within her power of control: exposing, and stopping, Margo Hart, the blight of *D.B.* "Now *that's* bliss!" she mutters, rolling her eyes with a slight quarter grin, demonstrating for the first time that perhaps she does have a microscopic sense of humor about the situation. "*So*, you spoke with Consuela and the waitstaff about everything? We're really doing this?"

"We're really doing this," Sofia confirms. "Everybody's totally up to speed on the plan and willing to participate. I held a private, impromptu 'staff meeting' in the dining room right before the party began and explained everything in *very* specific detail to ensure nobody makes any mistakes that could possibly blow our cover. They'll be serving Margo the real-deal mojitos until she's seeing quadruple."

"Believe me," Sofia continues, "by the time she realizes something's askew, she'll be too far gone to figure out what the hell is going on. She'll be punch-drunk and disarmed."

"Right where I want her," Delilah adds, keeping an eye out for Margo. "And then, when she least expects it, I bombard her with everything all at once and trick her into admitting she's trying to sabotage me."

"Exactly. But don't forget you have to wait and make sure I'm there to witness it," Sofia reiterates. "It's imperative for there to be someone who can back you up in front of Agnes if it comes down to a situation where it's her word against yours. You know Margo'll do everything within her power to make herself look innocent."

"Oh God, I'm about to have a heart attack," Delilah remarks, placing her hand on her chest. "I feel like a fucking criminal! How do we know we can trust the staff? How can we be sure they won't accidentally, or even intentionally, spill the beans to Margo?"

"One, they'll probably lose their jobs if they get caught. *And*, two, for added security I promised them an especially generous tip at the end of the evening *if and only if* the mission's a success."

"No," Delilah says, shaking her head. "*No way*, Sofia. It's not fair for you to have to *pay* these people to be a part of my sick ruse."

"*Our* sick ruse," Sofia interrupts, daintily smoothing her honey-blonde hair with her fingertips. "Nothing about this situation is *fair*, Delilah. Besides, my dad's gonna give 'em a massive tip anyway; he always overpays the staff. I think he feels badly that they have to work on a holiday."

Still apprehensive, Delilah can't resist checking one last time, "And you're absolutely sure they were all happy to comply with the plan?"

"Believe me, D, Margo's nonalcoholic 'fauxitos'"—Sofia gestures quotation marks—"will be chock-full of real live powerful rum."

Game On

"I would like to propose a toast," Margo—dressed in a flirty, shimmering light peach party frock—declares, holding what she mistakenly believes to be a nonalcoholic fauxito up in the air. On cue, Delilah and Sofia raise their champagne glasses, grinning affectionately at her. "Not to the great television show that brought us all together," she begins, "but rather to the great friendships that came about as a result of it. You know, I just want to say that I'm really glad to be here with you," she humbly adds, staring at the ground by her feet and fidgeting with her fingers. "So . . . *to friendship*." Margo beams, smiling lovingly back at her companions. "There's no greater gift in life."

"So true," Delilah concurs, gazing straight into her cold eyes. Ready to vomit. *And the secret password is . . . diabolical. Have you no moral center?! What's the matter with you? What are you planning? Tell me! Tell me now, dammit! What the hell are you up to?!* she wonders to herself. It blows her mind that mature adults are capable of such pitiful behavior.

"To friendship," echoes Sofia, taking an unladylike gulp, her emerald eyes shifting back and forth between Margo and Delilah.

A long, awkward silence ensues. All three women, each conducting their own inner dialogue, stand amid a flurry of activity on the west lawn—beside an intricate ice sculpture of an American eagle soaring majestically above the U.S. Declaration of Independence—regarding one another with big, wide, duplicitous grins stretched tightly across their faces.

"Well," Sofia breaks the silence, "I don't know about you girls, but *I* for one plan to celebrate tonight. I'm ready to *paaartay*!" She downs a giant sip of champagne, kicking up her leg behind her. "Happy birthday, America!"

"Happy birthday!" repeats Delilah, shooting Sofia a subtle glance to take it down a notch, worried she might set her drink aside in order to do a round-off flip-flop. She crosses her fingers that Margo isn't picking up on Sofia's unease.

"Here here! To the American dream," Margo toasts, raising her glass once again. "Hell, it's a holiday, ladies. I think I might even have a real mojito next."

"No!" Delilah gasps. "A *real* mojito?! Why, whatever are you thinking, Ms. 'I'm Lettin' My Hair Down Tonight' Hart?" she taunts with a thick, and very bad, Southern accent. *That's right, you're gonna have a real mojito next. You better believe it.*

Sofia's jaw drops. "You must be going mad! *Mad*, I say!"

All three women break into anxious laughter.

"Oh you two!" Margo coos. "What am I going to do with you? Do not let me have more than one drink. Seriously. Okay?"

"Don't worry," assures Delilah, finishing off the rest of her champagne, "we won't." She searches for the nearest waiter floating around the grounds. "Who's ready for another?"

Sofia's hand skyrockets into the air.

Two-Step

Dusk officially settles in, pulling night closer, blanketing the backyard in an inviting, burnt-orange and amber glow as the sun sinks farther and farther into Lake Minnonqua, its sapphire water rippling peacefully. *Not exactly the Hudson River*, Delilah marvels, resting her hands upon the deck's lattice-trim rail, now woven with twinkly white lights and charming little paper lanterns, which are also hanging from evergreen trees sprinkled throughout the property. *I bet there's not one corpse floating in that lake. Too bad Margo's not floating in it. Of course, she wouldn't need to be all the way DEAD, per se—that's not very nice—but maybe just a little bit injured? Maybe an acute head trauma would help straighten her out*, Delilah reasons. *In fact, that could be exactly what Margo needs. Hmmm . . . I might be onto something here.*

"There you are," Jack says, approaching her from behind, a bottle of beer in one hand, something hidden behind his back in the other. "I haven't seen you all day. I was beginning to think you disappeared."

"Here I am," replies Delilah, banishing all homicidal thoughts as she turns around, leaning comfortably against the railing, legs crossed at the ankles.

"Here you . . . ," he swallows a gasp, "wow."

Delilah smiles radiantly and looks down, keenly aware of

Jack's eyes on her, making her feel stunning. Wearing blue jeans, a classic black short-sleeved polo shirt, casually untucked, and Birkenstocks, she can't imagine that he'd look any more handsome if he were all dressed up in a formal tuxedo. But it's his big chocolate-brown eyes, eyes that somehow seem able to really see into her, that thrill Delilah most.

"This is for you," Jack quickly murmurs, and presents her with a balloon twisted into the shape of a red flower with a long green stem.

Touched, Delilah reaches for it, glowing, allowing her hand to gently skim against the side of his hand for a moment or two. Long enough to feel the heat of his skin and notice how it affects her, summoning the butterflies, causing her stomach muscles to tighten, in a good way. But then, almost instantly, she's smacked with a clashing wave of guilt, and they clench in a bad way. Her brain is aware that Jack is unavailable. Lord knows, every time she sees a damn number (to her astonishment, numbers are *everywhere*! Who knew?), she's reminded of that unhappy fact. Still, her stubborn, rapidly pounding heart doesn't seem to get the message. "How'd you know that balloon flowers are my favorite?" she asks, still smiling.

"You don't exactly strike me as the type of woman who prefers roses. No offense . . ." Jack shoves his hands in his pockets and looks out toward the lake.

"None taken." Delilah grins, tilting her head to the side. She's pleased that someone knows her well enough to make this spot-on distinction. She's extra pleased, for some reason, that this person is Jack.

"May I ask you something?" he inquires.

"Sure." *Anything . . . What's my favorite color? Red. What's my favorite food? Cheeseburgers. Do I want you to break up with Cee-Cee? Yes. Why not? Am I crazy for having such thoughts? Probably.*

"Those shoes you got on"—he nods toward her strappy black heels—"they comfortable shoes for dancing?" He takes a sip of beer, eyeing her.

"These?" She examines them, front and back. "These shoes were *made* for dancing," she exaggerates, recalling that the first time she wore them they gave her feet such horrific blisters that her neighbor's three-year-old had burst into tears, shrieking, "Owie! Owie! NOOO!" upon wandering into Delilah's apartment while she was changing her bandages.

"Good. Come on." Jack grins, gesturing with his hand. He begins walking toward the big hardwood dance floor set up on the lawn in front of the gazebo, where the band—bathed in red and blue light—is now playing a slow, velvety romantic rendition of "Don't Get Around Much Anymore."

Delilah follows a foot or two behind Jack, stopping for a brief moment to give her flower to a rather attractive waiter, whom she asks to please bring it inside and be sure to leave in a safe place. "You're Delilah, right?" he whispers, glancing warily from side to side.

Delilah nods.

"Just so you know"—the waiter's lips hardly move—"Vulture's on 'fauxito' number two." He stares at her, tapping his fingers on the underside of his tray.

I gather I'm supposed to say something now. Um . . . Okay . . . Well . . . She nods again, less obvious this time, whispering *thank you* before the waiter speeds off with her balloon flower. Sofia, bless her heart, had insisted that all good secret operations require code names. *Vulture* seemed like a perfect fit for Margo.

"Hey! You coming or what?" Jack calls back to Delilah.

"I'm coming, I'm coming!" she says and smiles, hurrying to catch up to him, hoping that her exchange with the waiter passed under his radar.

Jack leads her onto the dance floor, past Samantha, tucked comfortably in the arms of a tall and dashing science-fiction writer named Tim, and Lisa, who is dancing nearby with a Wall Street tycoon, eventually coming to a halt near the center of the floor. Delilah glances around, trying to locate Margo. "Looking for someone?" Jack inquires.

"No," she immediately replies, covering her tracks with a flirtatious smile, which she immediately regrets when an image of what she pictures Cee-Cee to look like (wearing a tight bun, a necklace with a number sign, and holding an enormous algebra book) pops into her mind. *Ahhhhhhh! My brain! My brain! And I thought things at* D.B. *were complicated! Holy crap! This is exhausting.*

"Good," Jack says, smiling at Delilah. He takes her right hand in his left and delicately puts his other arm around her waist, softly saying, "Come here."

That old familiar feeling of her belly clenching and pulse rate soaring grips Delilah as she looks up into his big brown eyes and smiles back. Jack pulls her closer, taking in her warm, sweet scent, and they begin to dance, slowly, easily, gently swaying to the music, as if they have been dancing together like this for years. As the song continues, Delilah's nagging worries eventually begin to slip away, and she relaxes into Jack, relishing the way he makes her feel. Every now and then his legs and stomach brush against hers, sending a sensation of pleasure skyrocketing to her brain, and she wonders how it's possible for Jack to feel so good to her. So right. Inexplicably right. She lets out a soft little sigh, resting her head against his chest, and he wraps his arm farther around her waist, holding her body close to his, feeling her warmth, swimming in it. Forgetting they're surrounded by at least fifty other people on the dance floor, the rest of the world disappears as they fall deeper and deeper into one another.

They both fail to notice when the song ends and a new one begins.

But, when Delilah is overcome with the desire to softly press her lips against Jack's, her body suddenly stiffens. She had been so thoroughly swept up in the intensity of the moment that she had somehow managed to allow Cee-Cee's regrettable existence to slip from her mind. Yet again. *Shit! Oh God oh God oh God . . . What am I doing?! For all I know, Jack's madly in love with her! Shit! This is wrong. Wrong wrong wrong . . . My life is problematic enough as it is . . .* Shaking her head, as if literally trying to straighten the jumbled thoughts, Delilah realizes she has no choice but to learn the truth about Cee-Cee. Right now. Before she's in too deep and crosses over the point of no return with Jack. Although, in her heart, she knows she's already well past that point. She must know, one way or the other, whether Jack's heart belongs to another woman. There's no way she's about to let herself become entangled in a messy affair. Absolutely not. Even if she hasn't felt this way about a man in a really long time, or even ever before, and has secretly started to give up hope that she ever would. Delilah inhales a slow, deep breath and pulls back from Jack, smiling softly. "I have to ask you something . . . ," she stammers, gathering her courage and fighting the urge to throw her pesky ethics out the damn window and just plant one on him.

"What is it?" Jack brushes a wisp of ebony hair away from her eyes with his finger, allowing it to trace behind her ear and then meander softly down the side of her neck.

Hungry for more, much more, Delilah can hardly manage to get the words out. But she forces herself. "Listen," she tentatively begins, when all of a sudden she notices a short little man with a thick brown mustache fast approaching. If she didn't know any better, she'd say it was Mario from *Super Mario Bros.* himself.

"Excuse me," interrupts the man, tapping Jack on the shoulder. "May I please cut in?"

Ever the gentleman, Jack obliges, politely allowing Mario to step in and assume his position. "Of course," he says. Smiling at Delilah, he adds, "Don't lose that thought," before walking off the dance floor, turning around to look back at her.

Pee Is for Pizza

Mr. Trawler gazes up at the mighty seven-foot-tall ice sculpture of his famous Pizza Protector bathed in a spotlight, the remarkable centerpiece of a colossal pizza buffet—one of five extravagant food stations set up at the soiree—paying homage to his great invention. Staring proudly at the frozen symbol of his humble beginning, he pops a piece of pepperoni in his mouth and snaps a quick photograph of the behemoth with the digital camera dangling around his neck. Ambling beside the buffet table, threading his way through chattering guests, he notes the white plastic Pizza Protectors of all heights and sizes holding various flavored pies and extra toppings, as well as the dozens of standard industry-size Pizza Protectors with red, white, and blue tea-light candles placed on top, adding a nice flammable touch to the presentation.

After finishing her dance, Delilah arrives at the buffet to take a closer look at the spectacle. *Thor and his crew certainly outdid themselves tonight*, she thinks to herself. *Talk about thinking big . . . King Kong would approve.*

Mr. Trawler slides his arm around her shoulders. "Goddamn . . . huh?" he says, head tilted back, peering up at the giant mass of carved ice.

"Now *that* is what I call an ice sculpture," she marvels without taking her eyes off of it. "My Lord . . ."

"Don't you just want to lick it?"

Delilah nods, laughing. "Yeah, I have to admit I do."

"That's why I love ya, White." He squeezes her tighter. "That's why I love ya!"

Smiling affectionately, she leans her head on his shoulder, still staring at the jumbo sculpture. "Feeling's mutual." Suddenly, she remembers. "Hey! I almost forgot. I have an invention for you."

"That right?" His curiosity is immediately roused. Being a good inventor means entertaining the "novel" ideas of amateurs on occasion; being a great inventor means sincerely enjoying such fodder. Stanley Trawler is one of the greats, and his passion for invention runs as deep as his very blood. The fact that it's Delilah who wants to talk shop makes it that much better.

"Mmhmm. I've been meaning to tell you about it. Ready for this?"

"I'm all ears."

Delilah's blue eyes sparkle, and she grins as she faces him. "Theater Pants!"

Mr. T tosses another slice of pepperoni in his mouth and crinkles his eyebrows. "Theater Pants?"

"Theater Pants!" she repeats, punctuating her words with jazz hands.

"I heard you the first time. What is it?"

"Designer underpants you wear to a movie or play that you can pee in at your leisure and nobody'll ever know. They're high-end, comfortable, undetectable, *and* odorless. But, most of all, they're useful and very convenient."

Concentrating hard, Mr. T cranes his neck to the side, pointing his finger. "This is good." He wags his finger up and down, shaking his wrist. "Seriously. This is not bad, White."

Delilah chuckles, pleasantly surprised he didn't tell her it was a load of crap. She helps herself to a cocktail napkin and a bite-size cheese calzone. "Make no mistake, these are *not* adult diapers. Not at all. These are for the savvy, sophisticated theatergoer who doesn't want to miss any of the show. Feel like you need to go during a movie or play? Go! Don't give it another thought. Concentrate on the entertainment you paid for instead. Welcome to your own personal urination station—"

"*That's* an excellent tag line," Mr. T interrupts with growing energy. "Outstanding!" He contemplates it seriously, tapping his hand against the side of his thigh as if he were playing a tiny set of bongo drums. "Your own personal urination station . . ."

"Ha! Nobody'll ever know you're wearing 'em, guaranteed. *And*, thanks to today's superior dry-weave technology, you'll stay dry as a desert." Delilah tastes her calzone. "Hot!" She gently blows on it, fanning it with her hand. "Theater Pants give people back the precious experience of uninterrupted viewing pleasure," she concludes, serious as a heart attack.

"Empowering the theatergoer . . ." Mr. T picks up where Delilah left off, the tips of his ears turning hot pink. "Realistically speaking, you can't fight the pee. The pee always wins. Can't cost much to produce," he rationalizes out loud to himself, rocking slightly back and forth. "Opportunity for a considerable profit's there. Need for the item clearly exists. Easy to sell and supply. We're talking about a completely untapped market," he reasons, growing more animated with each passing moment. "I feel it! The spirit of the Theater Pants moves me!" He grabs her shoulders. "Delilah! Listen to me very carefully. This is going to be HUGE."

"Excuse me," interjects a tuxedo-clad waiter, walking by with an empty tray. He appears to have just stepped off the pages of an Abercrombie & Fitch catalogue. "Can I get either of you a beverage or anything?"

"No thanks," says Mr. T.

"I'd love a vodka martini with blue cheese–stuffed olives, please—if you have them," Delilah requests.

"Yes, we do," the waiter informs her. "Anything else?"

She shakes her head. "No thanks, that should do it."

"I'll be right back with that for you." He smiles and takes a few steps forward, but then comes to an abrupt stop, slowly turning back around. "Also, I thought you'd like to know . . . I just brought your *friend*"—he locks eyes with Delilah—"her third 'fauxito' of the night."

She nods inconspicuously in return.

With that, the waiter spins around on his polished black heels and briskly walks off. An operative in the field. One among many this evening. Delilah considers how wise Sofia was to suggest directly involving the staff in their trickery, and she certainly appreciates the terrific job she did assembling the team—all brave members who were sworn to secrecy.

Fortunately, Mr. T doesn't bat a lash—not that he'd have noticed if a pizza had sprouted limbs, come to life, waved hello, and started smoking a cigar. "Give me two months and you'll see a sizable sum of money in the bank. Mark my words," he assures Delilah.

Of course, she assumes he's only kidding. *He's got to be kidding. He IS kidding. Isn't he?* "Mr. T, it's all yours. Seriously. If you like the concept and think there's something you can do with it, *please*, feel free. By all means! Inventions are your area of expertise, not mine. I'm sticking to the domestic arts," she says and beams, flattered. She eats the rest of her mini calzone and wipes her fingers with her napkin. "That was delicious."

Mr. Trawler happily agrees to handle all the work himself, but insists that Delilah remain a silent partner, sharing 50 percent of all net profits. After all, it's her idea. He runs through the basics of Inventions 101, giving her the abbreviated two-minute version of the mystifying yet lucrative business of patents and trademarks. "I'll have my lawyers call your people on Tuesday, and we'll get this all worked out on paper and go from there. Don't look at me like I'm nuts, White."

"I don't think you're nuts." *Oh yeah, he's nuts. He's lost it. Absolutely bananas . . . B-A-N-A-N-A-S.*

"Good. 'Cause I know what I'm talking about. You don't have to believe me now." He smiles warmly, munching on a slice of pepperoni. "You'll believe it when the money's in the bank. I'm telling you, *two months*."

Night Falls

An incandescent full moon now hangs in the dark night sky—sprinkled with glowing stars—reflecting off Lake Minnonqua and onto the Trawlers and their guests. "Did we luck out or what? Talk about a perfect evening for a party!" Thor, feasting on a plate of spicy tuna tartare with a pair of chopsticks, raves to Consuela. "Jolly good weather!" The two wallflowers stand at the back of the deck near the entrance to the kitchen—a carefully chosen spot that provides an excellent vantage point for watching the festivities, otherwise known as spying.

"Do you happen to see Margo Hart anywhere?" Consuela asks, scanning the shore, peppered with partygoers. An impromptu game of beach volleyball has started up, and Derek is playing on one of the teams.

"I'm not sure where she is. I think that child's drunk." Thor points to an eight-year-old boy holding a dark brown bottle of root beer, having a lively conversation with an imaginary friend who is clearly pissing him off.

"I don't see Margo anywhere." Consuela crosses her arms, distracted, turning her attention to the packed dance floor where the band is playing a snappy, patriotic medley.

"Do you need her for something?"

"Sí, I have to ask her a question," Consuela lies. The truth is, she hasn't seen Margo in well over an hour, and it's making her nervous. The last thing she wants is more trouble for Delilah, but she's got this awful feeling in the pit of her stomach that some sort of mischief is brewing. Her aunt Marisol on her mother's side was psychic, and Consuela has always felt that she, too, possesses *el regalo* (the gift), though she's never been able to prove it. "Will you help me try to spot her, por favor?"

"Sure," says Thor. "Everything okay?"

"Ay caramba. Let's hope, amigo. You check the north lawn, I'll check the south."

"Yes, ma'am!" he salutes, and heads off to search his section of the estate.

After a heavenly meal of grilled soft-shell crabs smothered in butter, Roquefort potato pie, and spinach salad with lemon saffron dressing—for which she must get the recipe to share with *D.B.* viewers, statistically proven to be big fans of vinaigrette according to the results of the latest call in and vote for your favorite salad dressing viewer poll—Delilah decides it's time for another Margo checkup. Last she saw Margo, which was a little over an hour ago, she was consulting with Aunt Deb about the number of red, white, and blue jelly beans inside a huge glass jar that will go to the winner of whoever guesses closest. Margo was tipsy (she guessed "one million" and insisted that was her "final answer") but still had a considerable way to go before reaching official inebriation.

Walking along the lush green grass looking for a tall, gorgeous, and maniacal redhead, Delilah mentally runs over a few things she'd like to say to Margo when she eventually confronts her. For example, she'd like to tell Margo how stupid she was to underestimate her, and what an unnecessary shame and waste of energy this whole disgraceful fiasco really is. She moseys past the swimming pool, all lit up in the dark—where children with closed eyes, who have *not* waited an hour to digest their food, are running around with wet limbs flailing everywhere, screaming "Marco! Polo!"—and heads toward the north side of the house. She spots Jack standing by the seafood buffet between a tank of live black goldfish swimming around a miniature statue of Mount Rushmore and an enormous mountain of caviar served in an ornately carved basket made of ice. Instantly, Margo vanishes from Delilah's mind. Like magic, or a really bad romance movie that would typically make her want to lose her lunch, everything else seems to fade into the background.

Approaching Jack with a steady gait, she smiles warmly and feels her heart vroom up to double time the way it usually does whenever he's around. "Hey there . . ."

He peers up from the buffet and grins, his dimple emerging. "You disappeared again." He helps himself to a heaping portion of Iranian beluga and a dollop of crème fraîche. "You need to stop doing that."

"*You're* the one who disappeared," she accuses. "I was eating dinner with Mrs. T and some lovely musicians from the Philharmonic over there in plain view." She points left toward the dinner tables. "See? Right over yonder."

"Ahhhh, I thought over yonder was *that* way." Jack points toward the right. "That explains it." He grabs a couple of toast triangles.

Delilah glances at the pile of pigs in a blanket on his plate. "Cocktail wieners and caviar, eh?"

"A famous combination . . ." He suddenly points a finger at her.

"What?" She tucks her long, black wavy hair behind her ear.

"If memory serves me correctly, you were about to ask me something on the dance floor earlier this evening. Before we were interrupted by Luigi from *Super Mario Bros.*"

Whoosh! Delilah's stomach plummets, becoming a mosh pit for the butterflies. "I can't believe it," she smiles, stalling, "I thought he looked like Mario!"

"DELILAHHHHH!" Margo squeals without warning, barreling toward them, with a "fauxito" in hand. "Hey! Hi, Jackaroni!" She leans in and gives him a quick peck, leaving a crimson lipstick print right in the middle of his cheek, which she promptly takes the liberty of wiping off for him.

"Greetings!" he replies, giving her a look.

"You look sharp tonight. Great party, huh? The Trawlers have outdone themselves this year. Don't you think?" Margo notices the caviar. "Ooooooh beluga. Now we're talking."

"It's delicious. That's the good stuff right there," Jack smiles.

"You have to hand it to the Trawlers, they certainly do know how to entertain," agrees Delilah, relieved to see that Margo has unknowingly hopped aboard the Punch-Drunk Land Express—making all stops and arriving just in the nick of time to save Delilah from having to question Jack about Cee-Cee, whom she would suddenly prefer to pretend doesn't exist for another hour or two longer. Or maybe just until the end of the night. Or possibly next Christmas?

"Let me ask you something," she says to Delilah. "Will you taste my drink, please? It's supposed to be a *fauxito*, not a *mojito*." Margo hands it to her. "Tell me if you think there's alcohol in it. I don't know, I feel like there might be. Consuela just gave it to me."

Having already anticipated and carefully rehearsed this moment in her mind, Delilah reaches for the glass. "Here, let me see." *Hum-dee-dum-dee-dum . . .* She takes a small, prudent sip, pretending to consider it before reaching a final conclusion. *One Mississippi . . . Two Mississippi . . . Three Mississippi . . . I wonder why people count using Mississippis. Four Indiana . . . Five South Dakota . . .* "No. I don't taste anything. Definitely not," she assures Margo, returning the glass to her. "That's a nonalcoholic drink, to be sure."

"Are you?" She furls her brow. "I don't know, I feel like there might be liquor in there," she repeats. Confused and less than willing to accept Delilah's diagnosis, Margo forces her glass upon Jack. "Here, you try. Tell me what you think. K?"

"Alright," he kindly obliges, accepting the drink. "Let's see . . ."

Shit! Shit! Shit shit SHIT! CRAP! With no time to spare, Delilah—on the verge of a conniption—quickly steps backward, positioning herself directly behind Margo, and begins frantically shaking her head back and forth, violently waving her arms above her head, mouthing "NO! NO! NO!" repeatedly to Jack, terrified that he'll accidentally blow her plan to bits. *PLEEEEEEEASE say no.*

With a puzzled expression, Jack slowly lifts the glass to his lips and samples the beverage.

Delilah holds her breath, gritting her teeth, her hands clasped together as if she's praying, desperately urging him to say NO!, her hair swishing from side to side as her head shakes.

He takes another thoughtful taste.

"Well?" Margo waits for the verdict, staring at Jack. "What say ye?"

He finally shrugs. "Nope. I don't taste any alcohol either," he lies, and hands back the glass, shaking his head. "That's a virgin if I've ever." He eyes Delilah.

THANK YOU, she mouths appreciatively, ready to slump to the ground.

"Oh, I bet you've ever," Margo grins with the seductive look of a woman on the prowl. *"SPARKLERS!!!"*

"Excuse me?" says Delilah. What she really wants to say, of course, is, "Stop flirting with him, whore! Step off!" But that wouldn't be very polite, especially in front of Jack.

"Oh! I *love* sparklers!" Margo stretches her long arm in the air, bouncing at the knees, waving with determination. "I forgot how much fun the Fourth of July is! Over here! HERE! We want some!" She beckons giddily to Consuela, who is now zigzagging throughout the guests, passing out bundles of sparklers tied up in red-and-white-striped satin ribbon.

Jack and Delilah exchange a curious glance.

"We gotta get some of those," Margo declares. "Come on, let's be patriotic!" She's still sober enough to recognize that there's far too much noise and activity for Consuela to be able to hear her voice rise above all the commotion. "Don't worry, I'll go!" she volunteers, and suddenly darts off, exclaiming, "Ooooh fun!" all in the name of festive little sticks you light on fire.

Once she's out of ear shot, Jack turns to Delilah and looks at her questioningly, lifting his eyebrows to the sky.

Delilah braces herself, fully aware of what's coming next.

He takes a couple steps closer, planting his hands on his hips and lowering his voice to a whisper. "Margo's drink is clearly spiked with rum. You wanna tell me what's going on?"

Swallowing hard, she shifts her feet uncomfortably, her blue eyes holding a pleading look. "I would just like to start off by saying I'm fully aware of how nefarious this must seem—and well, actually, it is—but this is *not* as bad as it looks. I *assure* you,

I've never done anything like this in my life before, and I *highly* doubt I'll ever be forced to do anything like it again, but this *really* is an extreme situation, Jack. I don't want you to think I'm some sort of deranged psychopath nut on the loose. I'm only doing what I absolutely *must* in order to save my job and my reputation and everything I have worked so hard for all my life so I don't end up a poor disgraced hobo living in a van down by the river eating cans of Spam and selling my hair and talking to imaginary—"

"Hey hey hey," Jack interrupts, smiling, bending just slightly at the knee so that his eyes can be level with hers. "I'm not questioning your moral integrity, Delilah." He places a steady hand on her shoulder.

She draws in an enormous deep breath, filling her lungs with much-needed oxygen. "You're . . . You're not?"

"No." Jack gently squeezes her shoulder. "Of course not."

Smiling gratefully, she puts on a brave face. "Jack—"

"And something tells me you're never going to be a poor disgraced hobo," he cuts her off again. "Whatever's going on here obviously has you distressed, to put it mildly, so it must be important," he concludes, concerned. "I want to know what it is. But first, tell me, are you okay?"

No, you tell ME. Could you be any more thoughtful? What is this? Some kind of sick damn joke?! "Yes . . . Yes, I'm fine," she assures him, smiling sheepishly, hoping that she hasn't made herself look like a complete emotional wreck. She closes her eyes and collects herself. "I'm sorry. I'm not usually like this. Ask Sofia, I'm normally pretty sane."

"Ask Sofia, she'll probably tell you I'm nuts," Jack counters.

Lifting a hand to her forehead, Delilah chuckles, grateful Jack's . . . well . . . *Jack*. Then, wasting no more time, she launches into a detailed explanation of why she needed him to lie about the drink, chronicling the entire convoluted series of events involving Margo. When she finally finishes describing the plan she and Sofia devised to thwart Margo from sullying her name and ruining her career—making sure to include that it's already in full swing and much of the waitstaff are actively involved—she stares at Jack, waiting to see how fast he runs in the opposite direction from the *c-c-c-crazy* domestic diva.

Appearing rather stunned, he grabs his beer off the caviar table and takes a swig. "Jeez . . . That's significantly fucked up." He returns the beer to the table, shaking his head in disgust. "My second graders know better. They know right from wrong. They manage to understand how to treat each other with respect and kindness. Maybe I'm an idealist, but you'd think if eight- and nine-year-olds can—"

"I know, I know . . ." Delilah motions for him to stop. Deeply ashamed of herself, she considers running in the opposite direction to save Jack the trouble. "I'm not proud, Jack," she quietly murmurs, looking away for fear she won't be able to bear his disapproving expression much longer. "Like I said, Margo's got me backed into a corner." Though she tries to suppress it, a harsh feeling of disappointment at having shattered Jack's opinion of her makes her stomach turn.

"Well," Jack says, taking another sip of beer, "count me in if you need an extra hand."

Delilah can hardly believe her ears. "W . . . what?" She slowly raises her eyes until they meet his. "Really?"

"Of course!" Jack replies. His tone suggests this response should hardly come as any surprise. "What? You think I want that horrible woman to destroy your chance of getting what you deserve? I know what this means to you."

"Oh Jack!" Delilah gratefully throws her arms around him. "Thank you!" She hugs him closer without giving it a second thought, whispering, "You're wonderful!"

"I take it you can use the extra hand." Jack grins, hugging her back.

Hocus-Pocus

A series of impressed gasps emanates from the small, rowdy group gathered on the tiki-torch-lit beach around Miss Beata, renowned psychic to the stars—and hired party entertainer—who just predicted Derek will soon open his own accounting firm. "H . . . how'd you know I'm an accountant?" Derek, entirely spooked, demands. "Did my brother"—he points to Jack standing to his left—"tell you or something? He told you, right?" He elbows Jack in the ribs.

"Hey! I didn't say a thing," Jack proclaims. "Honest!"

Miss Beata smiles and slowly shakes her head, causing the little gold bells sewn to the sheer swath of lilac fabric draped around her waist-length hair to jingle. "Emily informed me," she reveals in a soft, calming voice.

"Emily," says Margo, looking around, confused. "Who's Emily?"

"My spirit guide," Miss Beata explains, gazing up toward the round, glowing moon and winking.

"Your *spirit guide*?" Sofia repeats, hardly disguising her disbelief.

Miss Beata bows her head and fingers the long, clear crystal dangling around her neck. "Yes. Emily helps me to see and better understand that which I seek from *beyond* . . . " She makes a wide, fluid gesture with her hands, which are decorated with ornate Indian mehndi that runs all the way up to her shoulders. Then, returning her attention to Derek, she foresees his new firm will be "a great success."

"Way to go, bro!" Jack proudly knocks his beer against Derek's, inspiring the rest of the mesmerized group—including Delilah, Lisa, Sam, and a few interested passersby—to raise their glasses and joyfully drink to Derek's future triumph.

Delilah deliberately clinks glasses with Vulture, who's on her fourth "fauxito." So far, her plan seems to be working like a charm, and she estimates it shouldn't be much longer before Margo's in a vulnerable enough state to be confronted—especially if this mystical "drinking game," whereby everyone drinks to Miss Beata's predictions, continues.

"What's this?" Miss Beata questions, rolling her head around her neck. "You . . . ," she says, indicating Samantha. "Look behind your bedroom dresser. You will find a lost treasure."

"Really?" Sam asks, slack-jawed. "Like, seriously?" She gasps. "Oh my God! Is it my ThighMaster?"

Closing her eyes, Miss Beata touches a smaller amber amulet hanging from her neck and hums a low note. "This I cannot detect. But look and you will find something precious you had thought to be forever gone."

Staggered, Sam nods obediently. "Wow . . . Thank you . . . I totally will. Like the *minute* I get home! I thought my ThighMaster was gone forever! This *has* to be it!" She giddily claps her hands, bopping her head from side to side.

"To Sam's ThighMaster!" Sofia lifts her champagne in the air. A rambunctious chorus of "Here here!" erupts from the lively group. Sofia touches glasses with Margo, who happily downs a big gulp.

Next, Miss Beata points at Sofia, prophesying, "You will also soon experience a significant change in your professional work."

"Me?" Sofia presses her hand to her chest in an exaggerated manner. "Who *me*? No . . ." She shakes her head in doubt. "Nuh-uh . . ."

"Yes, Emily, I see it too," Miss Beata says to the moon. "Your new venture will be a risk, but it will bring you much . . ."—she pauses for a long moment—"*bliss*. Of this Emily and I are both sure," she tells Sofia.

Sofia's green eyes, having bulged at the mention of *bliss*, appear frozen.

"Do not be afraid," Miss Beata cautions, detecting her trepidation. "I sense it will turn out to be heavenly." She dramatically bows her head.

"Yahoo!" Derek cheers loudly with his beer held high.

"Nice!" Jack purposely taps his drink against Margo's. He looks at Delilah as the rest of the group hoots and hollers.

Delilah meets his eyes and smiles. *Thank you, Jack.* The fact that he's aiding and abetting her plot warms her heart, and she can't help but feel flattered by his interest in her welfare.

"I hope, sir, you do not suffer from claustrophobia?" Miss Beata tells Jack, causing him to drop Delilah's gaze.

"Um . . ." He scratches his head. "Why is that?"

The clairvoyant shrugs casually. "You will soon be trapped in a small, confined space." Raising her pointer finger to her lips, she thinks for a moment. "Not for very long. Perhaps in a trunk? Or large case?"

"Jack!" Delilah covers her mouth with both hands. "The locker!" She's soon laughing so hard she's nearly doubled over.

Just seeing Delilah's amusement makes Jack laugh too, although he certainly doesn't look forward to being stuffed inside a Harlem locker—that's for sure.

"It seems you were right!" Delilah sputters, cracking up. "Hey! Maybe *you're* psychic!"

"Will somebody please tell me what's so funny about being trapped in a confined space?" Sofia demands with a dumbfounded expression, which only inspires Jack and Delilah to laugh even harder.

"Are you guys like totally wasted or what?" Sam wonders aloud.

"Nobody better drink to that!" Jack advises the group with a finger in the air between giggles, grinning at Delilah.

Suddenly, Miss Beata begins to sway and chant softly in Latin. "Tantum ergo sacramentum veneremur cernui . . . I fear you're right, Emily," she stammers in a low, ominous voice. "Et antiquum documentum novo cedat ritui . . ."

The group immediately falls silent. The repetitive sound of the waves crashing against the shore mixed with Miss Beata's jingling gold bells pervades the night air.

The soothsayer's intense gaze eventually lands on Delilah. "Please, may I hold your hand?" she requests in an eerie tone.

Frightened, though not quite certain why, Delilah slowly extends her hand. "Is . . . Is everything alright?"

Miss Beata frowns, then closes her eyes. "A dark force surrounds you."

"I think that means *no*," Derek interprets for the group.

"Shhhh!" Jack elbows him, riveted.

Derek smacks his younger brother upside the head.

"This negative force . . . it's strong," Miss Beata foretells.

Although it's eighty degrees outside, an icy chill creeps down Delilah's spine, and the hair on the back of her neck stands straight up. *Alright, just stay calm . . . Stay calm . . . Don't let the freaky woman scare you to death. Oh my God. What if she can read my mind right now? Miss Beata? Can you hear me? Um . . . If you can, I'm sorry for just thinking that you're a terrifying freaky woman. I'm sure you're really quite lovely. You need to understand I'm on the verge of having a nervous breakdown.*

"You have a formidable foe," Miss Beata continues, still gripping Delilah's hand. Her head quickly shoots up and her wild eyes spring open. "Danger abounds!" she whispers. "You will be betrayed—"

"Whoa!" Derek brashly interrupts, stepping forward. "This is getting creepy."

Her concentration broken, Miss Beata releases Delilah's hand.

"I'll say," Margo promptly snorts, glaring at the psychic with her nose in the air. "Tituba's starting to give me the willies."

Miss Beata whips her head around and stares at her.

"Actually," Margo smiles nervously, "I'm ready for a refill." She holds up her empty glass, defiantly, as if to prove she's not lying. And suddenly, a loud boorish belch erupts from her mouth, vibrating, seeming to take her by genuine surprise. She quickly covers her lips with her hand. "Oh my!" She grins at Jack, blinking demurely. "Pardon moi!" She glances down at the sand, and when she raises her keen eyes again, they immediately zoom in on his empty beer bottle. She nods toward it. "Looks like you could use another as well. Come with me?" Jutting out her hip and lowering her jaw a bit with a sly smirk, Margo waits for his response. "How's about it, Jackpot?"

"Uh, yeah . . . sure . . . ," he replies, distracted, looking at Delilah with concern. "You okay?" he asks her.

"I'm fine." She forces a merry note into her voice, nodding subtly, "Go with Margo." *Hopefully her toxic burp breath won't kill you.*

"Don't let this hocus-pocus *garbage* scare you," Margo says pointedly, patting her on the back. "It's a load of crap."

Delilah watches her slip her arm around Jack's waist as they stroll off together.

You Pick Yourself Up, Dust Yourself Off, and Start All Over Again

After her revealing encounter with Miss Beata, which she won't soon forget and has completely altered her belief in the unknown, Delilah leaves the beach and heads directly for the nearest bathroom. Walking speedily toward the Trawlers' house, shaking sand from her high heels and concentrating on holding her bladder, she realizes yet another sensible use for Theater Pants: they'll come in quite handy during spooky-as-hell psychic readings that compel one to wet their pants.

Approaching the gazebo, brightened by glittering white lights, she hears the familiar melody of one of her favorite songs—a song that can make her smile on even the dreariest and meanest of days—"When You Wish Upon a Star." Years ago, a Walt Disney–deploring date Agnes had set her up with had laughed in her face—accidentally spraying oyster crackers (he was eating clam chowder) all over her—when she told him she found the tune to be "achingly beautiful." He'd posed the always charming and original first-date question, "If you were stranded on a deserted island and only had five songs to listen to for the rest of your life, what would they be?" Though he rudely poked fun at her response, Delilah saw no need to mock his questionable penchant for Little Richard or to accept his invitation to lunch in Central Park the following afternoon.

The band's rendition of the song is airy and romantic, and she can't help but pause to enjoy it for just a second or two, even if her bladder is about to burst. Crossing her legs, she peers out onto the dance floor, crowded with happy couples gliding around in each other's arms, and happens to spot Jack. Though he's got his back toward her, she'd recognize his handsome, sturdy six-foot-four frame from any angle, in a heartbeat. And what the mere sight of that handsome frame does to her! Delilah's heart flutters, and the smile that instantly curls her ruby lips upward somehow manages to form on its very own.

She's about to turn around and dash for the bathroom when she suddenly notices the hands of whomever Jack's dancing with slide over his broad shoulders and comfortably—perhaps a bit *too* comfortably—settle at the base of his neck, her fingers sensuously entwining in his chestnut brown hair. And before Delilah has a chance to blink—much less rub her weary eyes to make sure that what she's witnessing is real and not some terrible figment of her imagination—Jack and this woman are kissing! Passionately. Sumptuously. Their bodies are pressed together like butter on a pancake. Delilah, staring at them, cannot repress a gasp. Frozen, she first catches a flashing glimpse of fiery red hair. And then, a violent split second later, when Jack angles his body toward the left, she discovers—to her horror—that his lips are locked with . . . Margo's.

Delilah's chest constricts as she spins around, stunned, knocked breathless by the feeling that someone just hurled a heavy brick at her gut and tore right through her. *Jack . . . and . . . Margo? Margo . . . and . . . Jack? W . . . wh . . . what?* She finds herself unable to move. Her throat clogs with confused emotion and a thick prickly lump begins to form. But

Delilah forces herself to swallow it; her pride demands it. She feels pathetic and humiliated enough as it is for having developed real feelings—the sort of feelings that make her heart feel heavy and ache—for someone who was nothing more than a sad fantasy. The last thing she's going to do right now is embarrass herself further by crying like a big disappointed baby about it. Though her eyes begin to blur, she fights and manages to rein it in, all the while her mind reeling, wondering, how could she have suffered such a significant lapse in character judgment? And why does she feel so profoundly betrayed by Jack? Reminding herself that she has no logical claim on him—that he is *not* her boyfriend, *nor* have they ever shared even one single solitary itty-bitty kiss and she ought not feel so devastated about something that never was—only makes Delilah feel worse. And crazy. Very crazy. *Dear God! Get a grip. You're losing it! Think of Martha . . . Think of Martha . . . Cool breeze . . . Martha would not crumble. She would stand tall. She would prevail. She'd write a book about it! YOU'RE IN CONTROL. THINK OF* D.B.

Caught in a hurricane of deep thought, Delilah begins to tremble as it slowly dawns on her that perhaps Jack and Margo have been conspiring together all along, and she just happened to be the weak and naive fool who leaped into their trap. Delilah releases a long, slow breath as her shoulders simultaneously deflate. No longer certain of which way is up, or which way is down, it hits her that if her suspicions about Jack and Margo are correct, she's in even more trouble than she thought. Choked with paranoia and an odd sensation of ungrounded weightlessness, as if somehow she might just float away, she knows that for now she must forget about Jack—the rotten son of a bitch who deserves to get stuffed inside a fucking locker—

and concentrate on the one thing that matters most: stopping Margo and saving her career, assuming it's not too late.

Delilah's heart feels as if it's sinking as she wanders off in a daze, numb, with no real direction, and having completely forgotten that she needs to use the restroom.

That's Entertainment

"Like, the man believes he's Wayne Newton," Samantha grumbles, sitting around a dinner table drinking coffee with Lisa, Sofia, Derek, the inventor of the Swiffer, and a few others, watching her father perform. To her dismay, he has joined the band onstage in the gazebo for a stirring rendition of "Mack the Knife" and is dipping the microphone stand low to his left side, suavely snapping his fingers, crooning his heart out for the Trawlers and their very lovely guests, whom he has referred to several times as "my babies." "No more! No more! I can't watch!" Sam declares, burying her face in her hands.

Sofia laughs, leaning back in her elegant, white slip-covered chair. "Oh, come on, cuz. Look at him up there! He's on cloud nine. I think it's sweet."

Pointy daggers aiming for Sofia's head shoot from Sam's eyes.

"Admit it!" Lisa cajoles. "He has the gift of song." Watching swaying couples on the dance floor grooving to Uncle Mark's debonair styling, she adds, "Like, I'm not even kidding—he should have his own show on the Vegas strip."

"Throw a couple lions in the act, and he'll be golden!" Sofia winks at Lisa.

"Oooh! *That* I'd, like, pay to see!" Lisa high-fives Sofia, giggling.

"So not funny, you guys." Sam rolls her eyes, taking a sip of coffee. "Like, seriously. You don't even know . . ."

"For once my sister's right," moans Derek, grabbing his bottle of beer and rising from the table. "I don't want to hear about it if he starts dancing. I'm gonna go play around with my new Segway people mover I won at the mini-golf tournament today—see how fast it can go. Anyone want to come check it out with me?"

The Swiffer inventor, commonly referred to as Swiff, shoots his hand in the air. "I'd love to," he says, standing up.

"Come on," Derek motions. "I'll show you how it works. It's out in front of the house. Wait till you see this thing. It's awesome!"

"Can I disassemble it and put it back together?" Swiff asks hopefully, rubbing his hands together in anticipation. "Bet I can do it in under an hour."

"Not happening, Swiff, my boy." Derek grins, patting him on the back as they wander off, passing Delilah. "But I *will* let you clean her after you take her for a spin. You can give her a nice thorough swiffing."

"Wait for me!" Sam calls out, saying a quick hello to Delilah as she runs after her brother and Swiff.

Delilah spots Sam's empty chair next to Sofia and slumps down into it with a worn-out sigh and thud, dejected, feeling as if she's trapped in a wildly bizarre alternate universe where, at any moment, night could switch to day and the party guests could all morph into talking anchovies wearing monocles, and she wouldn't be in the least bit surprised. Obscuring her emotions has become something of a natural reflex since arriving at Cherry Pond, and Delilah has once again resolved to rise above her complicated feelings in order to get through the rest of the evening in one piece—preferably without losing her sanity, crying, or flashing her fanny at anyone, and hopefully with her job and reputation in tact.

"Jesus . . . ," Sofia mutters at Delilah's miserable expression. "What . . . What is it?"

Staring at a pink lipstick stain on Sam's half-empty coffee cup left on the table in front of her, Delilah slowly shakes her head. "I don't even know where to start." Part of her longs to unload her problems and tell Sofia everything about Margo and Jack and how terribly confused and hurt she is right now, but the more sensible part of her brain cautions her not to submerge herself in those dangerous waters just yet, for fear they might drown her and compromise her whole meticulously structured scheme. Trapping her enemy must remain Delilah's only focus, and that won't be possible if she allows herself to succumb to a devastating emotional tailspin, which she can already feel brewing in the pit of her belly, bubbling ominously below the surface, threatening to break free. She folds her arms on the table and slowly lowers her head down.

"Oh my goodness . . . Delilah, what's the matter?" Sofia presses, her expression growing more alarmed. "Is it Margo? Has she done something?"

"Señoritas! Señoritas! There you are!" Consuela strides toward them with a gleam of fiery determination in her eyes. "I've been looking all over for you." Her knees crack as she crouches her plump frame down between Delilah and Sofia, wasting no time getting to the point. "The train has left the station."

"Pardon?" says Delilah, lifting her head from the table and squinting as if someone's shining a flashlight in her eyes.

"What is this? Nap time?" Consuela gives her a look, wiggling her eyebrows up and down. "The Eagle has landed." She nudges with her elbow, overenunciating the words. "Come on! Chop chop!" She snaps her fingers in Delilah's face. "Did you hear what I said?"

Confused, Delilah glances at Sofia, who shakes her head, not quite positive what Consuela's talking about either.

"Qué pasa? Is she drunk?" Consuela asks Sofia, pointing, unamused, at Delilah.

"No," Sofia answers, "not at all."

"Bueno, because we have liftoff, NASA. *All systems go!*" Consuela impatiently winks, waiting for a response, staring at them like they're a couple of half-wits. "Comprende? *I saaaid*, all systems go," she slowly repeats.

"Yeah yeah, okay okay . . ." Delilah gestures for her to stop. "I think I get it, but can we drop the code, please, just to be sure?"

Consuela sighs. "Alright . . . fine. Have it your way. *She's* the one who insisted on using code names in the first place." She nods at Sofia as she stands up, straightening her crisp, black-and-white uniform. And then, pausing, she finally notices Delilah's pained expression. "Mi hija, what is it? Are you okay?" she asks in a gentle tone.

"I'm fine. I'm fine," Delilah repeats, more for her own benefit than for Consuela's. "It's just been a hell of a night." Her best attempt at a smile is weak and unconvincing. "I'm really okay . . ."

Detecting that she's really not okay, Consuela places her hand on top of Delilah's and smiles kindly. "Listen . . . I just brought Vulture her sixth"—she holds up six fingers—" 'fauxito.' She said *I love you* when I gave it to her and then told me that I'm her *best friend*." She cocks her head to the side, giving Delilah a knowing look. *"In the whole wide world."*

BAM! It's as if someone just poured twelve cups of espresso directly into Delilah's veins, awakening every last nerve in her body. *"She did?!"* Sitting up straight as a board, present and alert, Delilah confirms, "Are you *sure* Margo's ready?"

"Oooooh sí." Consuela nods dramatically. "She called me Cornelia. You got Vulture right where you want her. Believe me, honey."

Sofia covers her mouth with her hands, hiding her smile.

"What's so funny, Sonya?" Consuela demands. "Eh?"

Delilah draws in a deep breath, ready to get this much-anticipated show on the road at last. Now, officially famished for this carefully constructed confrontation, merely considering tearing into Margo and knocking her off her corrupt high horse causes Delilah's jaw to clench. But, *first things first*, she reminds herself, focusing her attention on Consuela. "Thank you for all of your help tonight," she says, smiling. "I can't tell you how much I appreciate everything you've done for me, Consuela. I wouldn't have been able to do any of this without you."

"Aw . . . De nada, mi hija." Consuela tenderly cups Delilah's chin in her hand. "You just go get her." She holds up a tight, threatening fist, grinning supportively. "Make that leetle beach pay."

"Where is she now?"

"On the south lawn by the Statue of Liberty ice sculpture talking to the governor of Nueva Jersey."

"Alright . . ." Delilah turns to Sofia, pounding her palms against the table, causing the crystal salt and pepper shakers to bounce, her energy skyrocketing even higher. "This is it. Let's do it! Give me fifteen minutes alone with Margo and then come find us. Fifteen *regular* minutes, Sofia, *not* Sofia Time Conversion. Do you understand me?"

"I *promise* you, I'll be there in fourteen regular minutes,"

Sofia vows, her serious green eyes open wide. "You have my word."

After forcing Sofia to synchronize their watches down to the second, and then thanking her for being her dearest friend, Delilah explains, "I'll try my best to keep Margo right next to the Statue of Liberty. Okay? We won't be far from there. And I've got my cell phone in my purse just in case."

"Me too," says Sofia, touching her little black satin handbag and anxiously repeating, "Okay, so I'll meet you by the Statue of Liberty." She nods, sitting on the edge of her seat. "Right. Okay. You got it. I'm there. Delilah . . ." Sofia hesitates, casting her gaze toward her lap. "You realize you're calling down the thunder. Are you *sure* you're ready for this?"

Delilah thrusts her chair backward and rises, her fists clenched—though she doesn't realize it. "Trust me, you have *no idea* . . . ," she answers in a low, calm tone. Stretching her arms out in front of her, Delilah cracks the knuckles on her right hand and then her left, rolls her shoulders, and finally exhales a long, controlled breath—prepared to duck under the ropes and enter the boxing ring for the fight of her life. Determined. Unyielding. Silently seething. "I'm *beyond* ready."

"I'll say! You just gave me chills," Sofia admits, impressed, as Delilah stalks off. "*Good luck! You can do this!* I'm right behind you. Fourteen regular minutes!"

"Keep your wits about you!" Consuela advises. "Oy vey! Dios mío . . ." She places a reassuring hand on Sofia's shoulder and crosses herself with the other, watching Delilah melt into the multitude of guests. "Elvis has left the building."

Eye of the Tiger

Delilah marches across the south lawn—adrenaline pumping, adding more fuel to her already flourishing fire—hunting her prey: an evil conniving tramp in vintage Valentino. What surprises her most is that she's not afraid. She's not even the slightest bit nervous. Not at all. Quite the contrary, she's excited. Weaving to avoid a cluster of intoxicated guests posing for a picture with Abe Lincoln and George Washington impersonators, Delilah considers how in the past she has always been one to shy away from serious confrontation, opting to remain silent with her feelings bottled up safely inside, rather than risk upsetting another person or having to defend herself. Inhabiting the unfamiliar role of aggressor for the first time in as long as she can remember, it dawns on her that she's a hell of a lot stronger and braver than she had previously thought.

"*WATCH OUT!* Careful!" urges a waiter bearing a striking resemblance to Prince William, just barely escaping a head-on collision with Delilah.

"I'm sorry!" she gasps. "I almost plowed right into you!"

"Yeah, I noticed!" he says, smiling. "Good thing *almost* doesn't count. Close call though . . ."

Hands tightly pressed against her cheeks, Delilah grimaces. "Sorry about that. I have tunnel vision at the moment. I didn't even see you there!" Now alert, she takes in her surroundings, bouncing uneasily on her toes. "Guess you can say I'm a wee bit clumsy."

"Listen . . ." Prince William inches a step closer to her, lowering his voice. "I'm glad we crossed paths. You should know . . ."—he speaks out of the corner of his mouth—"I think your girl is intoxicated. I'm not sure she needs much more to drink."

"That's what Consuela said. She just brought her 'fauxito' number six and then came and found me straightaway. I'm on my way to confront Margo right now."

"Margo?" questions Prince William.

Delilah cringes, having forgotten to use her pesky code name. "I mean *Vulture. Vulture . . .*"

"So her name is Margo . . ." Prince William nods thoughtfully. "Sofia said it was best if we didn't know such 'classified' information," he quickly explains. "But we don't have time for small talk right now. You should get going before she passes out. In fact, you might wanna hurry."

Delilah frowns. "Why? What do you mean?"

"Uh . . . I hate to tell you this, but I just brought Margo another 'fauxito' as well," Prince William informs her. "So I guess that makes it—what? Drink number seven, actually."

"Oh crap . . ." Delilah rubs her forehead. "I would've just given her some hot milk and read her goddamn *Goodnight Moon* if I wanted to help ease her to sleep. Crap! Margo's not gifted at holding her liquor," she adds.

"Don't worry, she's still coherent," Prince William assures her. "In fact, now's probably an ideal time for you to have your talk."

"Lord have mercy." Delilah shakes her head at the absurdity

of it all. "Let's hope." Smiling gratefully at him, she lets out a little chuckle. "Listen, thank you for everything you've done to help me tonight. I appreciate it. I hope you don't think I'm a threat to society."

"Not at all." Prince William smiles. "Everyone has a dark side."

"No kidding," Delilah mutters. "Hey, will you please be sure to thank the other waitstaff for me?"

"Of course. It was our pleasure. Let me tell you something." He leans in, as if he's about to share a dirty secret. "It made working this event a lot more interesting. *This* sounds awful, but some of the waiters even have a bet going on how many 'fauxitos' they think she can drink. I'm out," he sulks. "I guessed only five."

"Oh dear," Delilah winces, shielding her eyes with her hands. "Well, I suppose I should hurry before Margo's face-down." Delilah's blue eyes twinkle at Prince William as she begins backing up.

"And I should probably make the rest of this champagne disappear"—he nods at his tray lined with full glasses—"before Thor has my head on a chopping block. Best of luck with Margo, I'm pullin' for ya."

Raising both hands in the air, Delilah crosses her fingers, turns around, and rushes off.

"Hey! You're something else, you know that?" he calls after her.

Delilah turns around and smiles, giving a little salute goodbye.

Neither she nor Prince William notices Margo, lurking drunkenly around a cherry blossom tree a few yards away from the Statue of Liberty ice sculpture, watching them conspire.

Heartless Hart

Delilah arrives at the Statue of Liberty ice sculpture armed and ready for battle; however, to her dismay, Margo is nowhere to be seen. Delilah looks right. No sign of Margo. She turns her head left. No trace of Margo there either. *Hmmmm* . . . She rotates a complete three hundred sixty degrees, meticulously combing the cheerful party grounds for a six-foot-tall (Margo's wearing heels, of course), drop-dead gorgeous redhead in a shimmering peach gown, with a bandaged left hand—not exactly a dime a dozen. Thank the Lord. *Where are you? Where the hell are you? I know you're around here somewhere. I can feel it* . . . Rising up tall on her tippy-toes—triggering unpleasant memories of Madame Mariska, her childhood ballet teacher who had the worst tuna-fish breath on the planet—she stretches her neck high, reinspecting the immediate vicinity. *Come on* . . . *Where are you, dammit? Come out come out wherever you are* . . . Frowning, Delilah squints her eyes, as if somehow this might help make Margo appear.

"What'd you say to that waiter about me?" Margo suddenly demands from behind Delilah's back.

Delilah spins around to find her leaning casually against a wide weeping willow, arms folded at her chest—'fauxito' in hand—staring at her with big glassy eyes. Expressionless.

"What are you talking about?" Delilah asks, hoping, praying, that Margo didn't hear their conversation.

"You and that attractive waiter who looks like Prince William." Margo takes a long, leisurely sip from her straw. "You were talking about me. What were you saying, Delilah?"

Delilah's pulse rate soars. Inhaling a sharp breath, she decides to walk right on through the door Margo so graciously just opened for her. With pleasure. "Alright, since you asked . . ." She straightens her spine. "I ordered you a White Russian."

"You *what*?" A drop of spit flies out of Margo's mouth as she eyes her suspiciously.

"I figured you didn't get to have your recommended daily allowance of milk this morning, so I thought I'd help you out and get you some nice, dairy-rich milk. Doesn't that sound delicious and good?"

"That's funny," Margo sneers. "Because the way I saw it, and I should probably remind you that I am a *professional* lip-reader, you were discussing how many fauxitos I've had tonight." She hiccups, covering her mouth with the palm of her bandaged hand. "Isn't that right?"

Delilah glances at her watch: 9:15 p.m. Sofia will be here soon. *To hell with this passive tango. Here goes nothing . . .* Raising both hands in the air, guilty as charged, she surrenders. "What can I say, Margo? You got me. You're right."

"So what's this White Russian business?" Margo demands, arching her eyebrows. "What the hell are you talking about?"

Meeting her stare, Delilah exerts every last ounce of energy she has left to remain calm and poised. "I'm talking about how you intentionally dumped your glass of milk on top of my computer this morning. I'm talking about your mission to sabotage me. Sound familiar? Does this ring any bells?"

"Sabotage *you*?" Margo laughs with an exaggerated expression of shock that makes Delilah want to ring her perfect swan-like neck. "HA! That's rich. Very clever . . ." She claps her hands facetiously, a seasoned drama queen. "*You're* the one who sabonaged *me* tonight. Yeah, that's right, Delilah. I know there's mojito in my fauxito." Pointing at her glass as if she were shooting a soda commercial, a look of smug satisfaction crosses Margo's narrow face. "Isn't there? Bet ya had me thought you going . . . So what are *you* talking about, Delilah?" She settles back against the tree, pleased with herself, her head lolling from side to side. "Huh?"

"Maybe we should ask Amelia Miller. She'll probably recall your conversation in the *D.B.* ladies' room where you told her that you—and I quote—*have every intention of wearing me down and destroying me*." Delilah shakes her head, sickened, hurt. "Why would you feel compelled to take it to that level? I don't understand. I really don't. Are you that insecure?"

"Are you drunk?" Margo snaps, hiccuping crudely.

"No." *Nice try, ace. Think again.* "Are you?"

"Noo!" Margo bends her chin down to take a sip from her straw but misses, and it shoots up her left nostril, causing her to yelp in pain like a wounded hyena. "Why are you acting like such a bitch, Delilah?" She sloppily wipes her nose with the back of her hand. "What'd I do to you?"

At an honest loss, Delilah raises her arms questioningly. "That's a good question. I'm not even sure I have the complete answer to it yet." She shrugs. "For all I know, you've kidnapped Francesca and planted contraband in my desk at *D.B.* I wouldn't put it past you. Hell, I wouldn't put *anything* past you." The nauseating image of Margo and Jack kissing on the dance floor bombards Delilah's tangled mind for about the fiftieth time.

And though she certainly has a comment or two to make on the issue, she remains silent. Determined to cling to what little shred of dignity she has left, she has resolved that she will not, under any condition, give Margo the satisfaction, the joy, of knowing that she witnessed their vile smooch. Alas, nothing would be gained by revealing this information. Instead, Delilah lifts her chin several degrees and forces herself to remain on task, continuing, "You know who'd probably have some insight about what you've done to me? Preston. We should call him at the firm—interrupt his hard work on that *big important new case* of his—and get his thoughts. Oh wait!" Delilah smacks herself on the forehead—rougher than she'd intended to. "I forgot! Preston doesn't have a new case." She pauses. "Does he, Margo?" She glances at her watch again.

Astonished eyes blazing at Delilah, a vein begins to throb in the side of Margo's neck. "Big mistake, lady. You just crossed the line!" Her voice swells, attracting the attention of a cluster of politicians standing a few yards away discussing the advantages of the electric car. "How *dare* you call me a liar? Who do you think you are?" It takes Margo several puzzled seconds to figure out that the ice-cold liquid trickling down her pale arm and off her elbow is her drink, which, unbeknownst to her, she's holding slightly slantways.

Staring back at her with eyes like granite, Delilah coolly replies, "I *know* who I am. Unlike you, I'm a decent person. And I am not going to tolerate your crap anymore or let you get away with this." The fact that Margo sincerely believes she's superior to her makes Delilah want to scream like a savage beast and scratch her eyes out. But, instead, she sucks in a deep breath, calming herself, quietly saying, "Answer me this: Are you lactose intolerant?"

"Are *you* lactose intolerant?" sasses Margo, defiance dripping from every word.

Delilah stares at her quizzically, shocked by both her infantile response and the manner of its delivery. "No." *What is this?* Romper Room? *Would you like a juice box and a little snack bag of Goldfish crackers before your nap?*

A waiter bearing a remarkable resemblance to James Dean ambles along, stopping in front of them. "Hello, ladies, can I interest anyone in a mini grilled shrimp tostada with pineapple-jicama salsa?"

"No!" they simultaneously yell.

"*Well*, alrighty then." He quickly skitters away.

"News flash: This just in! I don't have to answer to you, Delilah. So there!"

"No, you don't. But you will have to answer to Agnes." She can't resist, *"So there."*

Margo makes a repulsive face. "Is that a threat?"

"Call it whatever you want, Margo. I don't care."

Suddenly, Margo's not just laughing, she's doubled over cackling, absolutely howling with amusement. She raucously slaps her hand against her toned thigh, gasping for air, as if she's never heard anything funnier in all her thirty-four years.

"What's so hilarious?" Sofia arrives on the scene, panting, surprised to discover Margo in such a merry spirit. She had braced herself to witness a bloody massacre, not a laugh riot. Her eyes dart back and forth between the two competing producers as she fans herself, trying to catch her breath. "What? What'd I miss?"

"Well, well, well . . . Look who's here!" Margo hollers, standing upright again, causing a few more guests to turn her way and stare.

Sofia and Delilah exchange glances.

"Fancy meeting you here!" bellows Margo.

"I live here," Sofia reminds her.

"Yes, you certainly do," confirms Margo, turning her attention to Delilah. "So I spilled some milk. I SPILLED! I'm guilty of spillage! Go run and tell Agnes. Oops! I'm clumsy and I had an accident. I apologized again and again to you, Delilah. I'm sorry. I really am! How many more times would you like me to say it? It was an *accident*. It happens. *Sue me!* Last time I checked, spilling isn't exactly a criminal offense."

"Alright!" Delilah raises a finger to her lips. "Shhhhh! Let's try not to make a scene, okay? Can we please just try to keep it down?" She smooths her ebony curls, embarrassed. "I'd like to understand, then . . . What were you doing drinking milk when you're lactose intolerant? Because Sofia"—she points to Sofia—"vividly recalls you explaining how your doctor advised you to avoid dairy products at all cost. I believe Coco can verify this as well."

"And *I* believe I don't need to stand here and take your abuse. You better believe Agnes is gonna hear about this, Delilah. Damn right she is . . ." Margo faces Sofia, hurt. "Some friend you are. What did I do to you?" Sadness gleams in her eyes. "What have I ever done to you, Sofia?"

Wanting no part of this, Sofia thinks for a moment. "Margo—"

"No," she interrupts, shaking her head. "*No!* I am *through* listening to you!"

"But I haven't said anything yet," Sofia stammers.

"Well guess what? No need! It turns out, I'm *NOT* lactose intolerant. I can have *all* the dairy I desire. I can suck on a cow's udder if I choose! Would you like to know why?" Margo doesn't wait for a response. "Because I have an ulcer. An *ulcer*, Solia. Not that it's any of your damn business. *Either* of you!" She shoves her way past them, murmuring, "To hell with you both," and hurling her "fauxito" on the ground as she lumbers across the lawn.

Undeterred, Delilah stalks right after her, following close on her rancid trail with Sofia a few steps behind. "Run all you want, Margo. Do you really think I'm giving up that easily? See, *that's* where you're mistaken. That's where you have grossly miscalculated and underestimated who I am all along." Her grip on the reins of control begins to loosen. "Stop and listen to me, Margo!" Delilah stamps her foot like an impatient child who wants a lollipop.

Pivoting around with her hands firmly planted on her hips, Margo faces her. Though appearing quite calm and speaking in a milder tone, the look of unadulterated hate that crosses her face is plain as day. "What? What is it that you want from me, Delilah? Tell me."

Beginning to go pink in the cheeks, Delilah lowers her voice, positively shaking with ferocity, wishing she had the courage to walk up to Margo and smack the condescending smirk right off her infuriating face (the face that she, once again, can't help but envision kissing Jack on the dance floor). "You may think that you have the upper hand, Margo—that you're gonna walk all over me, 'wear me down' if you will, and swindle your way into this job with your lousy deceit, and your bullying, and your flagrant manipulation. But I am telling you flat out that you're *wrong*." Delilah takes a step toward her competition, blind to the growing number of guests who are now watching the drama unfold, like sands through the hourglass. Consuela stands next to the frozen Lady Liberty, biting her lip, appearing to exercise utmost restraint not to march straight up to Margo and punch her square in the jaw. Delilah can feel droplets of hurt and fury pumping through her veins, filling all corners of her body, spurring her on as she continues toward Margo, embracing her newfound strength. "You are *not* gonna tarnish my name or jeopardize my career, which you better believe I'm entitled to! You are *not* gonna run me off *Domestic Bliss* with your dirty tactics and nasty lies. Not a chance," she whispers fiercely.

"When have I lied to you?" An outrageously loud and long hiccup that sounds like the cry of a baby velociraptor pummels out of Margo's mouth. "WHEN?! Tell me! Know what? Better yet. *Don't!*" She stumbles a few sloppy steps forward—appearing to almost fall down—before catching her balance, adjusting her shimmering peach dress straps, and storming off again.

Delilah and Sofia look at each other, pause for a few puzzled moments, and then dart off at the exact same time, racing after Margo—across the south lawn, onto the patio, past the bar and a large group of enthralled guests having their fortunes told by Miss Beata. "Out of my way, please! Excuse me! Pardon me!" Margo barks, trying to squeeze past the tight cluster.

"Evil surrounds us!" Miss Beata suddenly predicts, clutching the crystal around her neck. "Danger! *DANGER!*" she warns, inciting mass panic. She bursts into an impassioned Latin chant, swaying all over the place with her arms in the air, her little gold bells jingling furiously. "Genitori, genitoque laus et iubilatio, salus, honor, virtus quoque, sit et benedictio . . ."

"Will you friggin' people move, dammit?! Coming through! EXCUSE ME NOW, PLEASE!" Margo finally manages to maneuver through the pack of frightened guests. "Thank you!" she singsongs, striding off.

Zooming by the swimming pool on her rampage, she accidentally rams into an elderly, gray-haired gentleman, knocking him and his walker into the deep end with a giant splash.

"TRUMAN!" shrieks the shriveled little old lady who was standing by his side. "Help! Somebody save my husband! My Truman can't swim!" She clasps one hand to her little white bun atop her head, plugs her nose with the other, and jumps into the water with her little old-fashioned granny purse still dangling around her elbow and all.

Not one but three fully clothed guests simultaneously dive into the pool after her to save poor Truman from drowning.

Without looking back, Margo continues cutting across the lawn.

Sofia hits Delilah in the arm as they hurry to catch up with her. "Did you see that?! She's fucking *nuts*!"

"Fucking *lethal* is more like it," Delilah mutters, slack-jawed, her hair bouncing up and down on her back. "Margo, will you please stop and listen to what I have to say for a minute?" she begs, wiping her brow. "*Please?* Before anyone else gets hurt? You're leaving a wake of terror, for God's sake! This is ridiculous! And you're making me goddamn sweat!"

Finally, after almost breaking the heel off one of her expensive Prada demi-pumps, Margo acquiesces, grinding to a resentful halt in front of the bright, inflatable jumping castle. "I've heard enough. I'm done." Her head teeters on her neck like a bobble head doll. "D-O-N, done!"

"Well, I'm *not*. This ends here tonight. Do you understand me, Margo?" Delilah notices Jack jogging toward them and quickly looks away.

"These are serious accusations you're making with no proof," Margo fires back, striking an indignant pose. "You're paranoid and delusional. Do you understand *me*?"

Delilah stands there with her mouth open so wide you could

throw a small cantaloupe in it. She tries with all her might to ignore Jack, who has now joined the growing pack of interested onlookers with a worried scowl plastering his face. "You're pathological."

"You're fat!" Margo yells.

Several of the onlookers gasp.

"What are you, in eighth grade?" *This nitwit ought really to be kept in somebody's garage.* "Why did you tell Preston you had to cancel your trip to Martha's Vineyard? Why did you tell him Agnes would be here this weekend when she was never invited?"

"*Preston* is the one who canceled our trip, Delilah, because *unfortunately* he had to work! You have no idea what you're talking about. You should shut your fat trap—"

"That's not what he told me yesterday when he called looking for you," Sofia interrupts, unable to remain silent for one second longer. "Shoot! Did I forget to tell you that he called? I'm so forgetful. Oh, consequently, I don't think he's very happy with you."

Margo's face turns fire-engine red, and for a minute there it looks as if her head might actually implode. "When did—*what*? Preston called and you . . . Do you have my cell phone, Sofina?!" She violently swats at a mosquito buzzing around her face.

"No," Sofia casually replies. "Consuela's got it. She found it by the pool."

"Oh, *by the pool*!" Margo mimics acerbically, still swinging at the mosquito.

"The pool," Sofia repeats.

"THE POOL!" Margo spews again.

"The pool," Preston calmly reiterates, stepping suddenly from the crowd of onlookers.

Thirty Minutes Ago

As soon as Delilah left Sofia and Consuela behind at the dinner table, charging toward the Statue of Liberty ice sculpture in search of Margo, Sofia's black satin handbag immediately began to vibrate, as if on cue.

"Is there a sex toy in your purse?" Consuela gasped, her brown eyes expanding as she watched it gently buzz about on the white linen tablecloth, moving at a snail's pace away from Sofia.

"No!" Sofia stretched for her purse. "Jeez, get your mind out of the gutter." She unsnapped it, retrieved her cell phone, glanced at the window display—PRESTON WILLIAMS—flipped it open, and raised it to her ear in one fluid motion. "Hello?"

"Sofia?" Preston's baritone voice quivered.

"Yeah?" She heard screaming in the background on his end.

"Remember when you said that I was welcome to drive up and join you if I changed my mind?"

The distressed cries of terror in the background sounded awfully familiar to Sofia. "I remember," she said, plugging a finger in her other ear to block out the throbbing party noise. "Preston, where are you? What's all that shouting I hear?"

"I changed my mind," he said emphatically. "I'm in front of your house. I just gave my car to the valet. And that screaming's coming from a man who seems to be stuck on one of those two-wheeled people mover vehicles. It looks like he's spinning out of control." Preston couldn't repress a short chuckle. "I think the poor bloke's in trouble."

Sofia heard her "poor bloke" of a brother's desperate wailing—"HEEELLP!!! HOW DO YOU GET THIS DAMN THING TO STOP?!"—in the background and closed her eyes, lifting her hand to her forehead. And then it registered that Preston was there! At the house! Right now! And she never told Margo that he called to relay Agnes's *urgent* message. And Margo's three sheets to the wind! Only she doesn't know it yet! Quickly looking at her watch, Sofia calculated that she had only thirteen minutes and twelve seconds to get Preston up to speed and be standing at the Statue of Liberty ice sculpture waiting for Delilah, like she had promised, or her best friend would quite possibly never forgive her. "Preston! Don't move!" she commanded into the receiver. "I'll be there in seven seconds!" Snapping her phone shut, she threw it into her purse, stood up, hiked her dress above her knees, and took off sprinting toward the front yard.

"Hey! Where you going?" Consuela called after her, hands on hips and eyebrows scrunched.

"Emergency!" Sofia hollered back, leaping over a small topiary bush as if it were a hurdle on a racetrack.

When she arrived in the front yard two minutes and ten seconds later, out of breath and beginning to perspire, Derek was still spinning out of control on the Segway. "Thank God you're here!" cried Swiff, eyes filled with panic. "Sofia! Tell me you know how to stop this blasted death trap!"

"Sorry, Swiff! No time now—I'll explain later!" She hurried past him toward Preston.

"Soooooffffiiiiaaaaa!" Derek bellowed, spinning wildly in

dizzy, topsy-turvy circles. "I'm gonna beeee siiiiiiick! Heeeeeelp!"

"I'm so sorry!" she yelled, saddled with guilt.

With his hands shoved in his pockets, Preston approached her. "Hi . . . I apologize for barging in on you like this. I hope I'm not intruding."

"Not at all. Don't be silly!" Giving him a quick hug and a kiss, Sofia glanced at her watch again. "Shoot! I don't have much time."

"Time for what?" Preston inquired, confused.

"Okay, just listen to me and don't say anything because I'm not kidding—I only have three minutes."

"Alright . . ." Preston blinked, seeming to sense that her urgency involved him in some way.

With Derek spinning in maddening circles, Swiff running helplessly around him shouting useless suggestions on how to stop the "blasted" machine, and Preston chewing anxiously on his fingernails, Sofia explained everything to him as best she could—including why she wasn't able to give Vulture his message—while the second hand on her watch continued to tick-tick-tick its way around the dial.

Preston seemed embarrassed and at a loss for words. "I'm sorry, Sofia," he said, looking off toward Mr. Trawler's fancy car collection.

"Reeeessscccuuueeeee meeee!" Derek begged in the background.

"*You're* sorry? For what? What do you have to be sorry for? None of this is your fault. You're not responsible for Margo's actions. Listen, *I'm* sorry that you had to arrive to such a nasty, convoluted drama." Sofia touched Preston's wrist.

"I'm seeing quadruuuuuuuuuuuple!" howled Derek.

"And I am so sorry, Preston, that we had to resort to such drastic measures to stop Mar—SHIT!" Sofia pointed to her watch. "Gotta go!" Smiling apologetically, she lunged toward the backyard, hollering, "We'll be somewhere near the Statue of Liberty ice sculpture. Ask someone and they'll point you toward it! Oh!" she remembered her manners, like a good hostess, "Glad you could make it! Welcome to Cherry Pond! Make yourself comfortable!"

Fairy Tales Can Come True

Silence befalls the expanding group of onlookers as all eyes land on Preston, the surprise witness. He stands several feet behind everyone, next to a carefully pruned topiary tree, arms dangling limply by his side, hair slightly mussed. The dark circles under his eyes reveal that he likely hasn't slept in days, and judging by the look of his wrinkled khakis and navy button-down shirt, it's been a while since his last shower and change of clothes as well.

Margo cocks her head to the side, paralyzed with confusion. "Pres . . . Preston?" She teeters a bit, trying to pull her body up straight, and smiles broadly in an attempt to behave as if all is perfectly swell. "Hiiiiii, baby! Why are you . . . What are you doing here?"

Delilah is nothing short of astonished to see Preston's gorgeous, fabulous, wonderful, fantastic, beautiful face. She could kiss him! She could bow at his feet!

"You're drunk," he states flatly.

"No . . ." Margo shakes her head back and forth in an exaggerated fashion, her red hair flying. Noticing her dress strap dangling around her elbow, she deftly slides it back up to its proper position on her shoulder. "I'm not. I'm really . . . not even. I was surprised 'cause—and then suddenly I heard your voice, and then . . . *Hiii!!!*" She grins, as if starting their conversation over from scratch. "It's so good to see you! Happy Fourth of July!"

"Looks like I arrived just in time for the fun," Preston remarks, glancing about embarrassedly at the many pairs of curious eyes. "What happened to your hand?"

"What, this?" Margo lifts her bandaged hand up close to her face, examining it. "Oh, it's nothing—just a li'l boo-boo." She pouts her lips absurdly. "Will you kiss it and make it better?"

Preston hardly seems amused. "Where's Agnes?"

Tucking her hair behind her ears, Margo looks around. "Um . . ." Another gigantic hiccup pours from her mouth. "Excuse me," she says, daintily raising a hand to her mouth. "I've got gas."

"No games, Margo. Don't even try it. You told me Agnes would be here. Don't make this harder than it has to be. *Where is Agnes Deville?*"

"I don't . . . I don't know, baby." She shakes her head, flustered. "I haven't um . . ."

"It's a simple question. I'll ask it again. *Where is Agnes Deville?*"

"I can't . . ." Margo swallows, lifting her shoulders to her ears. "I don't see her right now."

"Because she wasn't invited!" Sofia interjects. Her emerald green eyes squeeze shut, and she freezes, whispering, "Did I say that out loud?" to Delilah, stunned.

Laughing inwardly, Delilah closes her eyes and nods, allowing a tiny quarter smile to sneak through. This keeps getting better and better.

"I meant to think that to myself." Sofia smiles uneasily, befuddled. "Sorry 'bout that. Don't mind me. I'll just be shutting my mouth now." She gestures that she's "zipping" her lips.

Wedged into a corner, Margo looks from Sofia to Delilah before turning her attention to Preston and then all the other riveted guests who have now circled around her, like she's a caged attraction at the zoo. Trapped, she clutches her hands to her head and suddenly spins around, making a desperate dash for the blow-up castle and leaping inside its canary yellow domed entrance.

"Hey! No shoes allowed!" cries the white-haired gentleman in charge of the attraction.

"Alright ya little Mexican jumping beans, EVERYBODY OUT!" Margo, a dead ringer for Mommy Dearest, drunkenly roars at the hopping children—black mascara smudged around her eyes, fiery red hair splayed everywhere, arms flailing. She falls on her side and bounces directly back up in one fluid motion, scurrying to grab hold of the black netting windows to steady herself, wailing all the while like a beast. "Goddamn frickin' no-good heels," she mutters, bending over to remove them. "Get off!" She ferociously hurls them out the entrance door, accidentally knocking herself onto her back with her own force. Her legs shoot straight up in the air and over her head, flipping her body around. "How do you stop this damn thiiiiiiing?!" She flies all over the place, rolling around the castle floor, wildly out of control. It requires serious concentration and physical dexterity for her to manage to clamber back up onto her feet, discombobulated and irate, clinging desperately to the netting. She shakes her head, trying to center herself, spitting a wisp of hair out of her mouth. "ADULT SWIM! ALL KIDDIES OUT! *NOW!* ONE-TWO-THREE!" she shouts, scaring the poor children half to death. A little blonde girl with pigtails starts screaming in terror. A darling Asian boy begins to cry. "It's a monster!" a chubby, freckle-faced boy shrieks, wetting his overalls. The children hurry to escape, hollering bloody murder as they pile out of the castle.

Outside, the adults remain frozen, unable to take their eyes off this fast-moving train wreck.

"I'm going in," Preston announces, mortified, his jaw tightly clenched. He slides his loafers off, nodding to the castle keeper.

"No pushing or horseplay allowed inside. Keep it safe and enjoy!" the castle keeper gleefully instructs, saluting Preston as he climbs aboard.

"Goddammit, Margo! What the hell are you thinking?" He bounces toward her unsteadily.

"Leave me alone!" she barks. "I don't want to talk to you!"

"Believe me, I don't want to talk to you right now either." He stretches forward, reaching for her, but loses his balance and ends up belly-flopping onto his stomach.

"Then what are you doing in here?" She yanks her dress up over her knees, ripping the hem, and jumps away from him, toward the opposite side of the castle.

Frustrated, Preston rises on his knees, his arms extended like the wings of an airplane to maintain balance. "I had to see for myself what you were doing up here—what kind of sick trouble you were concocting. Sitting around the apartment wondering and wondering—letting my imagination get the best of me—was making me crazy! *Crazy!* So here I am," he announces, making a sweeping gesture with his arms, "on a *trampoline.* Trying, with all of my might, to catch you." He says this not to Margo, but to the air, as if it's now just dawning on him how ludicrous this situation really is. He carefully stands up, leaning forward, and says, "I should've known you'd play dirty and pull a stunt like this. You have problems, Margo, *serious* problems . . . ," then lunges for her again, to no avail.

"Hey! It's not *my* fault that pudgy cake-hugger brutally attacked me! You weren't there, Preston. You didn't see! I can't believe you'd automatically go and blame me like this. What happened to *innocent until proven guilty*? You're just being mean," she pouts. "*I* don't have problems!"

"Like hell you don't. Will you *please* stop?!" He wobbles around precariously, trying not to fall.

⊰ ⊱

Outside on the lawn, Delilah stares at the yellow domed entrance, biting her bottom lip, wondering how long it will take for Preston and Margo to emerge. Tapping her fingers against her thighs, practically bursting with anticipation, she waits for the opportunity to question Margo about her questionable activity with Preston standing at her side. Certainly the truth will have to come out then—in front of a nice, big, captivated audience no less. *Now, THAT's bliss*, Delilah thinks to herself. She jumps when she suddenly feels someone's fingers tighten around her elbow.

"Sorry." Jack smiles, sliding in next to her, "I didn't mean to startle you."

"No problem," Delilah mutters, focusing straight ahead and jerking her elbow away from him. Feeling her breath turn shallow, she takes a pronounced step forward, crossing her arms and praying he'll go away.

"You okay?" He scoots up to her.

Unnerved, her heart beats so fast and furiously that she can barely hear herself think. "Fine." Nor can she bring herself to even glance Jack's way, for suddenly the mere sight of him is unbearable. His ulterior motives flash in her mind like the bright lights on a blinking billboard, making her skin crawl, and she berates herself once again for being a pitiable enough fool to have believed that he actually might care.

"Well, looks like you've got Margo now. Wait till Agnes hears about this, huh?" Appearing pleased for her, Jack tenderly nudges Delilah's side. But when she ignores him, a growing look of concern and confusion clouds his big brown eyes. "Hey," he says softly, trying to get her to look at him. "What's the matter?"

"Nothing," she lies.

"Come on . . ." Jack inches closer to her, but she angles her body away from him again. "One word answers aren't your style," he notes apprehensively, pressing, "What is it, sunshine?"

"Leave me alone, Jack," Delilah warns. "And don't call me that."

With a slight flinch his face tightens, and he steps away from her, appearing hurt. "Why? What's going on? Why won't you look at me?"

"What don't you understand about *leave me alone*?" Delilah hopes and prays that he'll turn around and simply walk in the opposite direction. "Get away from me and *stay* away from me," she snaps harshly, hating the way it feels to be forced to hate him like this. "Okay?"

"No," Jack protests, sounding flustered and upset. "It isn't. I don't understand, Delilah." He gently reaches for her arm.

Blocking his hand, Delilah finally brings herself to turn and look into his eyes. "Don't touch me." Her voice trembles. "Please, don't you even think about it!" And the next thing she knows, she's racing away from Jack, as fast as her legs will carry her—operating on autopilot—heading straight for the inflatable castle to finish her business with Margo, once and for all, so she can return to Manhattan as soon as possible (if not sooner).

Pulling off her high heels, she turns to the castle keeper, announces she's "goin' in!" and hoists her body through the domed entrance.

"No horseplay allowed inside. Keep it safe and enjoy!" says the castle keeper, smiling and waving her on board.

"We're having a private conversation if you don't mind," Margo hisses through clenched teeth, as Delilah bounces into the castle.

"Go right ahead," she invites, losing her balance and plopping backward. She quickly bounces back up, surprised, feeling the air rush below her pointed toes. "Whoooa!"

"It helps if you keep your arms extended," Preston offers, wobbling on his knees. "Like this." He tries to demonstrate but collapses almost immediately, bouncing onto his side with a yelp. "Think I broke a rib that time!"

"Thanks! You okay?" Delilah bounces up and down. "Jeez! I didn't expect it to be so, well, *bouncy*!" She stretches her arms at her side but loses her footing when Jack suddenly leaps through the door. "Ahhhhh!" she wails, flying headfirst into the wall like a cannon.

"Glad you could make it, Jack!" Margo smirks, bouncing onto her forehead and rolling into an accidental somersault.

"Delilah, will you *please* tell me what's going on?" Jack stammers, remaining on his hands and knees and crawling toward her. "Talk to me," he pleads. Cringing, he stops and holds up a hand. "And let me just add that I have a sensitive sense of equilibrium, as made evident by the few times I've fainted today, and being bounced around doesn't usually make me feel very well."

"That's comforting. I really can't get into this with you right now," Delilah tells him, glancing over her shoulder at Preston, who appears to be doing the splits. "I'm sure, considering our *current company*, you can appreciate and understand why."

"No." Jack frowns, sounding frustrated, endeavoring to slowly stand up. "I can't. I don't understand. Not at all." He bounces toward her, imploring, "That's the problem. So, *please*, just explain it to me."

"Do not talk to me like I'm one of your second graders, Jack," Delilah grumbles, leering at him and hopping away. "Honestly!"

"Then stop acting like one. How about that?"

Insulted, she pauses to look at him, losing her balance and flopping flat on her back.

"What the hell is going on, Delilah?" demands Jack. "Why are you so upset with me? What have I done? *Please*"—his eyes desperately search hers and his voice grows tender—"just tell me . . . Why are you suddenly acting like this?"

"Like what?" she snaps, still on her back, her chest heaving as she tries to catch her breath.

"Like you want nothing to do with me." He collapses onto his stomach next to her with the full force of his weight, which, in turn, springs Delilah directly back up onto her toes.

"Bingo! Ya got that right!" she yells, bending forward, out of control, so that her palms are pressed flat against the vibrating floor, her fanny's sticking straight in the air, and she's flashing Jack. Yet again. Delilah wants to laugh. Only it's not funny. "And you better not be looking at my underwear!" She rolls onto her side, glad she decided to leave her favorite, most comfortable pair of granny-pants with the tiny bleach stain in Manhattan.

"Hey!" Margo yells at Preston, wagging a finger at him. "You better not be looking at her undies either! Perv boy!"

A bullhorn suddenly blares, prompting everyone to hush and freeze as the castle keeper pokes his kind, raisin-like face inside the entrance. "This here's a kiddie attraction, folks. It has a maximum capacity of four hundred pounds. I'm afraid it can't handle all yer weight; somebody's gonna have to hop off. Come on now." He beckons with his free hand. "Before it explodes. Right this way."

"I think he's talking to *you*, Delilah," Margo snorts, panting.

"*Margo* . . . ," Preston, sprawled flat on his belly, warns in a threatening tone.

"What?" she protests. "You heard what the man said. The castle can't hold all this unnecessary blubber." She stares directly at Delilah.

"Enough!" Preston asserts, pounding his fist against the floor, causing everyone to bounce up and down. "That's enough!"

"Uuuuuggghhhh . . . ," Jack moans, looking rather ill.

"Actually, I *have* had enough," Delilah agrees, releasing her white-knuckle grip on the window netting. She steals a hurried glance at Jack splayed across the floor with a dime that must have fallen out of someone's pocket stuck to his forehead. Bouncing past him as if he were invisible, she pauses at the entrance to smile politely at Margo and say, "I'll just wait for you right outside." And she slips out the door with a defiant little wave.

"Well," Jack says and turns to Margo and Preston, scrambling onto his feet—knocking the dime off his face—and hopping toward the entrance, "I'd like to say this was a fun time we all shared." He reaches the domed archway, smiling uncomfortably and clutching his stomach. "But it wasn't. And I have to go throw up now." His skin a pale shade of olive green, he darts out the door and runs past Delilah with both hands clasped tightly over his mouth.

Preston and Margo remain standing in the center of the castle, facing each other with knees bent and arms outstretched, balancing like tightrope walkers. "You're making a monumental scene, Margo. This is worse than the December Gala. This is completely humiliating. *Please, I'm begging you*, let's get off this thing now!" Preston lunges after her, bouncing up and down on the royal blue castle floor.

"Or what?" Margo chides, plopping onto her side and springing back up. "You're gonna throw me to the lions out there?!" She points toward the entrance, aghast.

Preston shakes his head, sadly. "Mar . . . You're the only lion around here." He quickly pounces his body on top of her, managing to clasp his arms around her narrow waist and hoist her over his shoulder, grunting, "The sooner you figure that out, the easier your life will be. I promise."

"Yeah? Well, if I'm such a *lion*, what are you doing here with me?!" she presses, violently kicking her legs in protest as he bounces her toward the castle's exit, outside of which Delilah and the crowd of curious onlookers are waiting.

Gently placing Margo down on the grass, Preston gazes at her, dejected. He pushes her shimmering peach dress strap, now draped around her elbow, up onto her shoulder and untwists a wiry strand of red hair knotted around her dangling diamond earring. "Excellent question." He walks toward his loafers and slips them back on.

Eager to conclude her conversation with Margo and get the hell out of Cherry Pond, Delilah stands next to Sofia, watching them intently, waiting for the right moment to interrupt.

"I'll start looking for a new place tomorrow," Preston says. "You can have the apartment. I don't want it." He sighs and looks at Margo sorrowfully. And then, after several long, excruciating moments, he shrugs. "Can't think of anything else that needs to be said. See ya around, I guess . . ." Turning to Sofia, embarrassed, he softly mutters, "I'm sorry about the scene," and slowly trudges off.

Margo responds with a delayed, sarcastic laugh. "Preston? Baby?! Where are . . . But, where are you going?!" she yells, tilting her head to the side. "Preston? Get back here! *NOW!*" She stamps her heel down on a sharp pebble hidden in the grass. "OUCH! Mother *fuck*! What the . . . Where my shoes are?" she asks no one in particular, hopping drunkenly around on one foot, searching in circles like a dog chasing its tail, slurring, "IknowIwaswearingshoestoday." Then, returning her attention to Preston, she wails his name again, savagely, hunching over with fists clenched tight, demanding, "Where are you going?! PRESTON?! *Squiggle Muffin?!*"

He keeps right on walking, hands tucked deep inside his pockets, head hanging low, failing to pay her any mind—seeming to block out the very sound of her voice.

When he doesn't show any sign of response, Margo viciously turns to Delilah, hands digging into her hips, and begins swaggering toward her, baring her teeth as she growls with a quiet ferocity. "Happy? Yeah, I'll bet you are . . . I'll bet you're *thrilled*!" She leans into Delilah aggressively and pauses, her eyes filled with shallow puddles of alcohol. "Well, *SHOOT ME NOW!!!* Aren't *I* a *MORON POTPIE!!!*"

The sudden quietness of the still backyard seems to echo *moron potpie! Moron potpie!*

Sofia's face registers astonished anger as she reaches for Delilah's shoulder, grasping on to it as if to steady herself, and whispers hoarsely, "She . . . She did it, D."

It takes several shock-filled moments for the staggering realization to sink in. And when it finally does, it has the same effect as if some great and powerful being with unfathomable strength had violently kicked Delilah in the gut, knocking the wind right out of her: Margo sent the e-mail with the subject line *Shoot Me Now!* to Agnes. There was her confession, leaving very little room, or need, for interpretation. Whether she's aware of it or not, Delilah isn't sure, but irrespective of her intentions, Margo just came clean to anyone with two good ears who was listening at the time.

Forgetting to breathe, Delilah stares at Margo, standing belligerently in front of her, teetering unevenly from side to side, forward and back—barefoot, obliterated, a complete and utter wreck—and what she feels isn't hatred or spite. Rather, Delilah feels pity for Margo, most sincere pity. A single teardrop spills from her eye and rolls down her flushed cheek, leaving a narrow wet streak that reflects in the moonlight. "You're pathetic," she sadly mutters, before turning her back to Margo and slowly walking away, without any real direction.

"PRESTONNNNN!!!" bellows Margo, chasing after him, flopping all over the place like an overboiled noodle.

Delilah Gloop

Warm, creamy, rich, melted gourmet chocolate cascades over Delilah's fingers, but she's too trapped in her own conflicted universe to notice. Standing beneath the starlit mountain sky, lost in a trance with her caramel square suspended in a massive chocolate fondue fountain—referred to by Thor as the pièce de résistance of the dessert buffet—she wonders why the satisfying sense of relief she had assumed confronting Margo and reclaiming her power would bring has somehow escaped her. She wonders when she'll be hit by that glorious rush of elation she had imagined time and time again she'd feel when she finally beat Margo and won the golden executive producer position, which she assumes will be hers officially when Agnes learns of Margo's corrupt, perhaps even criminal, activity. Delilah wonders why the sick, burning feeling in the pit of her stomach refuses to go away. If anything, she feels worse now than she has all weekend.

"Thcuse me! Thcuse me, mith!" says a little orange-haired girl in the pink puffy-sleeved party dress.

Delilah doesn't blink.

"Thcuse me!" she repeats, louder this time, wrinkling her freckled nose. "Hello?" Looking confused, she peers up at Delilah, mouth agape, running her tongue along the bare space of her top gums where her two front teeth used to be, seeming to think long and hard.

Delilah remains paralyzed, clutching her messy caramel. Floating . . . Melting . . . Spinning at a maddening pace into a chocolate black hole . . .

"I THAID *HELLOOOO!*" The little orange-haired girl yanks on Delilah's dress, finally winning her attention.

"It ithn't thanitary to have your hand in the fountain." She points at Delilah's hand, shaking her head. "I think you're thup-pothed to uthe one of thothe thpearth over there." Sticking out her tummy, she points to a silver bucket filled with wooden skewers to the left of the fountain, beside a tantalizing array of mouthwatering fresh fruits, marshmallows, cream puffs, pretzels, cookies, caramels, ice-cream balls, and other tasty treats suitable for spearing and dipping in a chocolate fountain that looks like it was created by Oompa-Loompas.

Glassy-eyed and dazed, Delilah glimpses at her hand and is stunned to discover it, sure enough, submerged in melted chocolate. The little girl's telling the truth; her hand really is in the waterfall! Who knew? And the spunky spitfire's right; it's not very sanitary. Delilah finally slowly withdraws her hand.

"I wonth thtuck my hand in a pot of mashed potatowth! Gotta find my brother! Thee ya!" Showing off her toothless grin, the little orange-haired girl waves good-bye, grabbing a glistening chunk of melon from the buffet as she gallops off.

Delilah tries to smile. But she can't. A drop of chocolate splatters on top of her big toe, and she realizes she's dripping all over the place, making a giant mess. Blinking her eyes, trying to orient herself, she glances around for something, anything, to wipe her hands on.

"If I'm not mistaken"—Sofia saunters toward her from behind, grinning from ear to ear—"I'm looking at the new *executive producer* of *Domestic Bliss*! Holy crap!" She emits a loud, happy squeal, bouncing up and down. "You did it, D!" She reaches for Delilah's arm, bubbling with elation, and exclaims, *"YOU DID IT!"*

Jerking forward, as if struck by a bolt of electricity, Delilah gasps and drops her caramel in the grass.

"Oh, I'm sorry!" Sofia smiles. "Thought ya heard me." But her expression soon darkens when she sees her chocolate-covered best friend. "Oh my," she utters, her eyes widening. "Yikes! You need a napkin. Here, take mine." She shoves it at her, popping a last bite of cookie into her mouth and sprinting toward the far end of the buffet. When she returns a few moments later, clutching a sizable stack of red, white, and blue cloth napkins embroidered with the familiar golden *T*, she discovers that Delilah hasn't moved an inch. "D?" Sofia softly says, examining her closely. "What is it? What's . . . What's wrong? Why do you look like someone just shot Martha Stewart?"

And with a sharp intake of breath, the storm finally breaks, and Delilah's silent tears pour down.

"Oh, D, no . . . It's okay . . . ," Sofia soothes, gently placing a steadying arm around her, wondering what on earth could possibly have Delilah in such a miserable state considering her thrilling triumph over Margo. "Come on . . . Come with me." She nods toward the house off in the distance, troubled and frowning. "Let's get you inside and cleaned up and away from all this crazy"—she seems to search for the correct word, spinning her free hand in a rapid whirling gesture—*"to-do."*

Clinging to Sofia like an anchor, Delilah begins walking slowly, awake but dreaming. Ready to be carted off to the nearest triage center. And fast.

Independence Day

A little while later, locked in a spacious guest bathroom inside the house with Sofia, Delilah finishes drying her hands and returns the fluffy gray towel to the marble countertop, shuddering as she catches her ragged reflection in the mirror, which covers the entire wall before her. "Look at me . . ." She pauses, staring, entranced, unable to help noting that being bounced around the castle like a damn popcorn kernel had definitely not done wonders for her hair. "This face"—she slowly raises a finger to her cheek, as if lifting it through thick, gummy molasses—"could be a Halloween mask. Sure scares the hell outta me. You know, I've never cried this much before in my life. I was not aware that my body is capable of producing this many tears. Turns out I'm a veritable Cathy Cries-a-Lot doll! Who knew?" she marvels with an inspired shrug, still lost in her own image, crumbling and tumbling down. *"DAMMIT!"* she yells as she slams her palms against the countertop and hunches over, gripping its ledge.

Sofia flinches.

Then, turning away from the mirror and shaking her head, Delilah quietly confesses, "I don't know what's wrong with me. I don't know anything anymore."

"*Why?* What do you mean?" Sofia squints her eyebrows, intensifying the look of confusion contorting her face. "I don't get it. I'd think you'd be ecstatic. You nailed Margo! You *won*!" she reminds Delilah. "There's no way Agnes will promote the Fang Lady now. To be honest, I'll be shocked if she doesn't fire her. Don't you get it?" Sofia smiles, trying to help her friend understand. "The position's *yours*, Delilah. *Executive producer!* This is everything you've worked for; it's your dream come true!"

Slowly crossing the lilac-scented room, Delilah lowers herself onto the edge of the elegant claw-foot bathtub beside her, too emotionally exhausted and raw for anything but the simple truth. And so she admits it out loud: "The thing is, I don't think it is." Swallowing hard, she looks into Sofia's emerald eyes. "This can't be my dream come true, Sofia."

"But *why*?" Leaning forward, she places a worried hand on Delilah's arm. "What are you talking about? Why not?"

"Because . . . I don't want it," Delilah answers in a most decisive manner, to her own amazement. And then, just to ensure that she's not hallucinating, she says those four simple little words a second time: *"I don't want it."*

Crinkling her forehead, Sofia remains silent for what feels like a very long time, gawking at Delilah, appearing to struggle to try and process this astonishing, seemingly inconceivable revelation. "What do you mean, *you don't want it*? I don't understand." She shakes her head, baffled. "You brought Margo down!"

"This isn't about Margo." Delilah dismisses the notion with a bored roll of the eyes. "I couldn't care less about Margo Hart." Of course, she'd like to believe that Sofia's correct and Margo will be fired. Truthfully, she'd like to believe that Margo will be beaten silly with a splintery wooden stick and forced to wear a scarlet letter *P* for *Psycho*. It's difficult for Delilah to imagine Margo will be able to sweet-talk her way into keeping her job. That said, if anyone can do it, Margo can. Perhaps she'll find a way to con Agnes into letting her stick around, slithering by with a stern slap on the wrist. Not that it particularly matters one way or the other to Delilah. "Let's be real, Sofia. We both know Margo's certainly not the only cynical, deceitful, power-hungry pariah at *D.B.* Ha! Not by a long shot." She twists her face into a tired, disgusted scowl. "She has her Amelia Millers—her scared little minions and cohorts. Like any nasty weed, you can yank out her roots and toss her in the garbage, but, inevitably, a new weed, if not several more, will sprout back in her place. You know what I've realized, Sofia?"

Looking at her as if she has three heads and a full-grown beard, Sofia stammers, "Something tells me I couldn't begin to guess . . ."

"The Margo Harts of this world, sadly enough, are a dime a dozen. Our industry's crawling with them! Hell, the world's crawling with 'em! And you wanna know something else?"

Sofia just nods her head, staring at Delilah with her mouth slightly agape.

"I've lost all patience for tolerating their unnecessary negativity. As far as I'm concerned, there's simply no need. None at all."

"I couldn't agree with you more."

But something more significant than pitiable Margo weighs on Delilah's mind as she lightly tap-tap-taps her fingertips against the gleaming, classic Victorian tub, something that's been turning over in her mind for quite some time. It has to do with her future and what she really desires—what she wants most of all, *way* deep down inside, but has never possessed the bravery to act on. Perhaps in the past she was afraid to risk what she already had in order to gain something potentially greater. Perhaps she didn't really want it badly enough. Or maybe, she just had to sink to a certain level of desperation, the kind of desperation that makes one quake first with fear, and then with enlightenment, to find the courage required to face the truth and take the leap into the unknown, having the faith in herself to know she can succeed, if only she'll let herself try.

"Believe me, Sofia, I *know* this is gonna sound completely insane—and it probably *is*, I might add. I could very well need to be fastened into a tight white vest with lots of constricting little straps if you know what I'm saying. But, this isn't my dream come true, no matter how much I *wish* that it could be." Delilah shakes her head with growing assurance, sitting up a bit taller. "It's not. It's *not* what I want. And somehow, this whole weekend has proved it to me."

"But—"

"What's the point of lying to myself about *D.B.*?" She speaks over Sofia, jumping to her feet and beginning to pace back and forth in a short straight line before the tub. "Why should I try to *convince* myself that this is right? That it's enough when I know that it's not? Where will that get me?"

"I'm—"

"Nowhere," Delilah announces decisively, wagging her finger. "Nowhere good at least, *that's* for sure!" She stops and faces Sofia, pleading desperately, "Will you please tell me *WHAT IN THE WORLD I'M SO SCARED OF?*"

"I have no idea . . ." Sofia stares at her, completely and utterly baffled. "Will you please tell me what in the world you are talking about?"

Delilah has taken into account in the past how the new concepts she longs to incorporate at *Domestic Bliss* will radically alter it, ultimately rendering it a whole new television show. And therein lies the problem, for *D.B.* is an amazing success in its current state. It appeals to an unusually expansive target audience (a huge draw for advertisers) who loves and appreciates it just how it is. Odds are, they won't want to see their beloved how-to program change—not in any colossal ways at least. And Delilah can't blame them. She's no stranger to understanding people's natural aversion to change; she even owns a sassy T-shirt she picked up in a fashionable Beverly Hills boutique that reads CHANGE SHMANGE across the chest. Still, wanting to significantly alter a television program is one thing; feeling like you're cheating yourself, denying yourself because when it comes down to it you're frightened and weak, is another. "I'm talking about being tired of being told what I cannot do," Delilah explains to Sofia. "I'm talking about being sick of being forced to abandon ideas I love and am passionate about—ideas that might not be cookie-cutter mainstream," she concedes, "but are good and reflect who I am, and I *know* viewers will really enjoy. Why should I struggle to fit a confined, suffocating mold that no longer suits me? *Who knows?*" She gestures grandly with her hands. "Maybe it never did!" Letting her arms fall limply at her sides, she returns to Sofia, sitting back down on the edge of the tub. "I'm talking about *wanting more*, Sofia." And in that moment, it dawns on Delilah that her far-fetched, starry-eyed dream—the one that always made her feel silly to talk about—isn't really all that implausible after all. It's just a hell of a lot easier to believe that it is. Delilah draws in a deep breath. "I'm talking about *Heavenly High-Rise*."

"Heavenly what?"

"Heavenly High-Rise," she repeats with more conviction.

"Alright, now I'm lost," Sofia declares. "What's . . . What's *Heavenly High-Rise*?"

Delilah hesitates, staring across the room at an elegant flower arrangement that Sofia and Consuela made yesterday. She's very good about saving a portion of every paycheck, and thanks to some excellent investment tips from her father, she's managed to stash away enough cash to be able to get by for at least a year or two if need be—three if she sticks to a strict diet of Ramen noodles. And then there's the pending Theater Pants earnings, which Mr. T seems so positive will soon be landing in her bank account. Delilah figures these funds can be used as seed money for *Heavenly High-Rise*, providing her with a bit of added security, though she has little doubt that financing this new venture will prove to be a dilemma.

"Blink if you can hear me," Sofia prods impatiently. "What's *Heavenly High-Rise*?"

A slow, growing smile spreads across Delilah's face. "It's my new show."

"I'm shit-canned . . ." Sofia droops over, resting her elbows on her thighs, letting her eyelids sag shut. She begins rubbing her temples in a calming, circular motion. "No more to drink for me. Cut me off. Sounded like you said something about having a new show or something . . ."

"You're not shit-canned," Delilah assures her, "though that's a charming term. Pick it up at finishing school?"

Sofia cracks open her eyes, looking at her slyly. Straightening her spine, she cocks her head to the side, examining Delilah closer, observing, "Your sense of humor's coming back . . ." And then, as if rocked by a bolt of lightning, she blasts to her feet. "Wait wait wait wait wait . . . Go back!" she instructs. "What are you saying?! Are you telling me that you have a new job? That you're leaving *Domestic Bliss*? Why haven't I heard anything about this before?"

"Listen . . . Like I said, I'm *fully* aware of how crazy this sounds. Trust me, I'm as surprised as you are. It's not like I was planning this—I promise you." Delilah rises and goes to where Sofia stands, in a state of shock, by the double sink. "I've never mentioned this to you before, but I've been approached in the past by other networks with some compelling offers. Some of them have come knocking on my door more than once."

"And . . . this has something to do with *Heavenly High-Rise*?" Sofia asks, squint-eyed, wanting very much to understand.

"I hope so," Delilah answers truthfully. "We'll have to wait and see how the networks respond after I pitch it to them. Which brings me back to the fact that I'm probably in need of serious mental attention." She gazes up at the ceiling and exhales, blowing back a wisp of hair that was dangling near her eyes. "Not to toot my own horn, but the way I see it, as far as having the right connections and resources go, I'm in pretty good shape. I've been blessed to work with some of the most talented, highly regarded figures in television and the domestic arts. I could be wrong, but I don't suspect assembling a top-notch staff should be that much of a challenge."

"I wouldn't think so either," Sofia concurs, slowly but surely beginning to grasp that Delilah's entirely serious. "We have to rewind, though. Tell me more about *Heavenly High-Rise*. What is it?"

"Alright"—Delilah grins, shifting her body to face Sofia directly—"think of it as *D.B.*, only a lot less traditional and a lot more funky and hip and whimsical, and, most important, targeted toward today's modern city dweller." Her aqua-blue eyes sparkle back to life as she continues explaining. Growing more and more animated, she offers Sofia a similar, but more detailed, description of what she gave Jack during their "friendly" dinner of deceit.

Suddenly, Sofia gasps and places a hand over her heart. Her jaw all but hits the white granite floor.

"Well, I still haven't figured out most of the details," Delilah adds insecurely, discouraged by Sofia's reaction, "but that's, ya know, the *basic* idea of the show. It's not *that* shocking, *is it*?"

"Oh! No no, that's not it. I just . . . I just remembered something that Miss Beata predicted earlier tonight."

"What?"

Sofia presses her hands to her cheeks in sheer wonder. "I . . . can't believe it . . . I thought it was all some highfalutin' bullshit act and she was just making it up."

"Highfalutin?" Delilah cocks an eyebrow. "Tell me!" she pleads. *"What'd she say?"*

Sofia's eyes meet Delilah's. "That I'd soon experience a significant change in my professional work, and my new venture will turn out . . . *heavenly*!" She gasps again. *"Remember?!"*

Delilah's eyes grow large. "*Yes*, I do! *That's right* . . ." She considers it, wiggling a finger at Sofia. "Wow, that psychic's *good* . . ."

"D, think about it . . . ," Sofia urges, appearing to piece together an imaginary jigsaw puzzle in her mind. "If you're serious about this . . . If you're not messing around and you're honestly going do this—start your own show—then you're gonna need a marketing director. You're gonna need somebody who really knows their stuff, *someone good*. Someone who's familiar with this type of programming inside and out who can help build *Heavenly High-Rise* and make it a success." Taking a deep breath and straightening her dress, Sofia quotes her, "Not to toot my own horn, but I think I'm a qualified candidate for the job."

"Sofia . . ."

"What?" She shrugs. "You're gonna need someone to market your show. And I'm damn good at what I do," she reasons. "Why shouldn't it be me? I'd be honored to do the job." Glancing self-consciously away, she adds, "That is, assuming you'll have me."

"Assuming I'll have you?!" Delilah exclaims, bowled over. The very thought of it sends her soaring over the moon. "Hell yes, I'll take you! *Of course I will!*" But then, all of a sudden, she freezes in her tracks, a few feet away from the toilet. "But, wait . . . Wait, hold on a second . . ." Delilah crisscrosses her hands in front of her, gesturing to stop. "I couldn't ask you to do that, Sofia. *No way*. Not in a million years. I wouldn't dream of it. *D.B.*'s a dependable, established success. Who knows what the fate of *Heavenly High-Rise* will be? It's no secret that most new shows fail. No," she insists, having made up her mind. "It's far too great of a risk."

"Oh, I see . . ." Sofia folds her arms across her chest, sounding offended. "But it's not too much of a risk for *you*. How does that work again?"

"Well, it's a risk I'm willing to take because really, the way I see it, I don't have much of a choice. Not if I want to be happy," Delilah reasons.

"Well, I'm very lucky. Because I *do* have much of a choice." Sofia looks down, fidgeting awkwardly with her cuticles. "Delilah, you know I don't like talking about this stuff because it's tacky and impolite and it makes me totally uncomfortable, but"—she squeezes her eyes shut—"are you forgetting my last name and the trust fund that comes with it?" After a lengthy pause, she opens her eyes again, declaring without a trace of apology, "I have the luxury to be able to afford to take a professional risk if I want to."

Cathy Cries-a-Lot just stands there beaming, fighting back tears. "Yes, you certainly do, Sofia Trawler."

Sofia eyes her closely. "Soooo . . . then, I'm in?" she confirms, unsure.

Finally hit with that glorious rush of elation she'd been waiting for, Delilah nods, unable to speak, laughter tumbling out of her.

"Good, 'cause we were about to have our first big fight!" Sofia beams, giving her an enormous hug.

"You're too much!" Delilah squeaks, embracing her tighter.

"Besides," Sofia says and releases her, smiling, "I think it's *all* gonna turn out *heavenly.*"

"Oh, God help us! Maybe we should wait and see if Sam's ThighMaster turns up first before we do anything." Delilah grins, adding, "You really are too much!"

"No, *Margo's* too much." Sofia shakes her head, tensing. "I still can't get over it . . . How does someone manage to have so little regard for other people? How do they live with themselves without realizing what a vile way they've chosen to go about life?"

"Such a sad, sad waste!" sighs Delilah.

A Perfect Size 12

Sitting on the edge of the long, white pier, alone, her feet dangling lazily in the lukewarm lake, idly kicking back and forth every now and then, Delilah quietly reflects. She stares across Lake Minnonqua at a historic old lighthouse from the 1800s flashing rhythmically, its gentle blinking light soothing her on a subconscious level as she listens to the crickets spinning their night music and the occasional boom of a firecracker exploding somewhere off in the distance. Exhaling a long, cathartic sigh, she leans back on her elbows, ready for a serious vacation.

"*There* you are . . ." Jack walks down the pier, holding a tropical-looking beverage in each hand.

Holding her breath, Delilah closes her eyes.

"I've been searching all over for you," he says, drawing closer.

She doesn't bother mustering the energy to acknowledge him, or even move a muscle.

Pausing several feet behind her, Jack stands frozen in place, appearing to try to figure out what to say or do next.

Delilah prays with all her might that he'll just turn around and walk in the other direction. Remaining completely still, and silent, she waits for what feels like a very long time for him to leave. But instead, to her dismay, she feels Jack lower himself next to her on the edge of the dock. Stunned, she opens her eyes and looks at him, scooching over several inches to avoid physical contact.

Jack hands her an electric-red cocktail with a shiny American flag garnish and removes his shoes, dipping his feet in the water. He doesn't say a word.

Marveling at his nerve, Delilah sighs, annoyed, stealing a hurried glance at him out of the corner of her eye as she sets the glass down at her side. "I'm so tired . . . ," she finally mutters, staring at the old lighthouse across the lake. "Can we please not do this, Jack?"

"Not do what?" he asks softly.

"I saw you kissing Margo." She lays her cards on the table. "On the dance floor . . ."

Jack slowly nods his head, beginning to understand. "Sheesh, no wonder you want nothing to do with me."

"I realize it's none of my business," she assures him, "but when I saw you with *her*, of all people, it just . . . It took me by surprise, that's—"

"Delilah," Jack interrupts. "I swear to you, one minute we were dancing—at *Margo's* insistence—and the next minute she was a giant pair of lips all puckered up and coming at me." He shudders. "I . . . I felt like Lucy does when Snoopy licks her. And believe me, I didn't have to scream *BLECH! DOG KISSES!* for Margo to get that I'm not interested."

"You're not?" Delilah questions.

"Of course not." He smiles at her, his dimple denting his cheek. "But I can understand how you'd think otherwise after what you saw."

Delilah takes a sip of her drink. "What is this anyway?" she asks, examining it.

"That is an extra-special Fourth of July Trawlertini. Don't ask. It's one of Mr. T's creations."

"What's in it?"

"He won't say."

"I adore that man." She bites her bottom lip and clears her throat. "I'm sorry I was so mean to you, Jack."

"You don't need to be," he says gently.

"Oh, I was horrible."

"I'm sorry for adding to your confusion on a night like tonight when you've got much more important things to consider than me. I really am sorry, sunshine."

"You don't need to be."

A giant red, white, and blue firework suddenly bursts over Lake Minnonqua, followed by several more magnificent colorful explosions, capturing Delilah's and Jack's attention. They stop to watch, peering up at the brightly illuminated night sky. But the fireworks stop just as abruptly as they began.

"Huh. That's not it, is it?" Delilah asks, stumped.

"Nah, they're just getting warmed up. This is the Trawlers we're talking about. You'll know it when the real show begins."

She takes another sip of her drink. "I almost forgot about the fireworks."

"How could you forget about the fireworks? It's the Fourth of July. You call yourself an American?" Jack ever so softly nudges her side.

Delilah chuckles, gazing across the lake.

"The question is"—he looks at her thoughtfully—"how come I found you sitting out here alone on this pier rather than celebrating? Aren't you happy about how things worked out with Margo?"

"I'm thrilled about it." She absentmindedly removes the flag from her Trawlertini. "Absolutely."

"But?"

"How do you know there's a *but*?" Delilah eyes him, curiously.

"Just do." Jack shrugs. "I can feel it in my gut."

"*But* . . . ," she replies, twisting and untwisting the flag around its little red pole, "I have to quit my job."

An enormous purple, orange, and green firework explodes in the sky.

She gazes upward. "Ooooooh . . . Good one."

Only Jack didn't notice. He was too busy staring at Delilah.

"What? Why are you looking me at like that?" She lifts a hand to the corner of her mouth. "Do I have Trawlertini on my face?" Self-conscious, she kicks her feet in the water, back and forth, splishing around.

Jack just smiles, his big chocolate-brown eyes gazing at her knowingly. He points a finger in her direction. "You're gonna do it, aren't you?"

"Quit?" Delilah nods. "I have to, Jack. Even as executive producer, I'll never be able to do what I really desire with *Domestic Bliss*. There are certain things I can't change no matter how much I want to. The show's a huge success just how it is; it's what it's *supposed* to be. Who am I to change it?" She looks down at her flag, swirling it around between her finger and thumb. "If I don't resign now, I never will."

Seeming unable to lift his eyes from her, Jack shakes his head, amazed. "That's not what I meant."

"Oh." Delilah picks up her Trawlertini, taking a drink, confused. "Okay . . . Well, then what did you mean?"

His eyes penetrate hers. *"Heavenly High-Rise."*

Delilah stares at him, shocked, and also touched by his insight.

"Don't look so surprised. I heard what you said at dinner last night and the way your voice lifted just a *tiny* pitch when you said it. I saw the way your eyes sparkled when you talked about *Heavenly High-Rise.* Everything about you changed, Delilah."

A series of thundering shots rings out, indicating that the jaw-dropping display of fireworks, impeccably choreographed to Tchaikovsky's *1812 Overture* being piped in through loudspeakers, is about to begin. Guests scattered all over Cherry Pond immediately stop what they're doing and cast their attention up toward the spectacle in the sky, shouting and clapping.

"Now *this* is the real show," Jack declares.

They sit for a few minutes, side by side, with their heads tilted back, oohing and aahing—as Delilah believes one really ought to—at the dazzling bursts of color and light.

"Incredible!" she enthuses.

"Heavenly High-Rise?" says Jack, loud enough to be heard over the reverberating *bang* of the fireworks. "Yes, it will be."

Delilah turns to him, smiling radiantly, her cheeks growing a bit pink. Then, out of nowhere, she bursts out laughing, wholeheartedly. "Oh my gosh!!!! I can't believe I'm doing this, Jack! When I walk into Agnes's office on Tuesday morning to have our talk, we're not gonna be having the conversation I thought we were going to have. I'm about to give up a position that most sane people would kill for. Is there something wrong with me? Do you think I should be in an empty white room with padded walls?"

Jack looks at Delilah as though she's shining brighter than anything else in the sky. "Know what?"

"Hmm?"

"It's gonna be wonderful." He smiles warmly, his brown eyes twinkling.

Delilah smiles too. She looks at him sitting beside her on the pier, watching fireworks and drinking a special Fourth of July Trawlertini, and she's taken aback that she can feel so sincerely close to someone whom she's known for only three days.

"How do you know?" she asks.

"Because just listening to you talk about *H.H.* is inspiring. Audiences? They're gonna go wild for it! I smell an Emmy on the horizon."

Her smile widens and she giggles rather modestly, looking down at the water. "Wow . . . Thank you. I've never called it *H.H.* before. I like the sound of it."

"Talk about a whole new meaning to Independence Day." Jack grins at her unabashedly.

"No kidding." Delilah shakes her head, still absorbing this decision. "I just hope I'm not making a big mistake."

"You're not. But I understand what you're saying."

Standing up, Delilah stretches her back slightly, looking toward a sky filled with multiple golden shimmering bursts of light.

Following her lead, Jack rises as well, watching the luminous display.

"Do you love her?" Delilah keeps her eyes focused on the fireworks, too emotionally drained at this point to play coy or beat around the bush.

Jack's face contracts and he looks at her with a thoroughly confused expression. "After what she did to you? How could you even ask me that? I thought you understood. As far as I'm concerned, Margo's the devil's spawn."

"I'm not talking about Margo." Delilah remains focused on the sky.

"Then . . . who are you talking about?"

Drawing in a deep breath, Delilah says the name softly and as casually as she can: "Cee-Cee." She turns and faces Jack, her aqua-blue eyes searching his.

He slowly shakes his head. "I broke up with Cee-Cee a long time ago. It was never serious, although she'd like to think it was," he admits, lightly adding, "She'd also like to think she's a natural blonde." Then it dawns on him. "Who told you about Cee-Cee?"

"Margo."

He considers it for a moment. "*That's right* . . . The boat . . . That woman has no shame! I lied to her about Cee-Cee aboard *Lola* during her failed attempt at the ol' suntan lotion seduction strategy," he explains, rolling his eyes. "Pfff! One of the oldest tricks in the book. Next thing I knew, she was rubbing me all over like a Shake 'n Bake pork chop." Jack nervously shifts on his feet. "What can I say, Delilah? I'm an idiot. I was taken off guard, and I knew I wasn't interested in her, and I got flustered. I . . . I choked. I said the first, admittedly stupid and fictional, thing that sprang to mind. I'm not the smoothest person in the world, if you haven't noticed," he says and smiles. "Clumsy goof is more like it."

"Yeah . . . well . . . I happen to like clumsy goofs," Delilah quietly admits, staring at the old lighthouse.

Nervous and not quite sure what to say to each other, they both look up at the fireworks.

Standing together on the pier in silence, Delilah feels Jack's hand gently slip into hers. The dizzying sense of warmth that immediately envelops her almost takes her breath away, and they remain locked in this position for several long moments, relishing each other's touch. When at last Delilah turns and faces him, smiling up into his big brown eyes, he brushes his fingertips against her flushed cheeks. And then, holding her face in his hands, Jack slowly leans in, eyes closed, feeling the tingle and the rush as his lips ever so softly connect with hers, and they ease into a long, gentle, hungry kiss, their bodies melding into one.

When their lips eventually part, they gaze into each other's eyes, intoxicated and, quite frankly, amazed.

Jack presses his forehead against Delilah's and whispers, "You're so beautiful."

"You are," she whispers back.

Dozens of small, spectacularly hued fireworks explode like popcorn in the night sky.

Peering across the lake, Jack suddenly has a thought. "Hey, we never did get to take that moonlight swim."

Delilah realizes he's right. She smiles warmly, her aqua-blue eyes twinkling up at him. And after a moment, she gently releases his hand. Quietly slipping her elegant black dress up and over her head, she allows it to land wherever it may on the pier.

Jack steps out of his jeans and removes his shirt, his eyes remaining fixed on Delilah.

Standing in their unmentionables, on the edge of the Trawlers' long, white pier, they beam at each other without saying a word. Delilah grabs Jack's hand, and together they jump into Lake Minnonqua.

And there, in the Catskill Mountains, on the Fourth of July, beneath dazzling fireworks and the light of the moon, they surface, laughing.

The Beginning